THE ZAMINDAR'S GHOST

Celebrating
30 Years of Publishing
in India

THE ZAMINDAR'S GHOST

KHAYAAL PATEL

HarperCollins *Publishers* India

First published in India by HarperCollins *Publishers* 2023
4th Floor, Tower A, Building No. 10, DLF Cyber City,
DLF Phase II, Gurugram, Haryana – 122002
www.harpercollins.co.in

2 4 6 8 10 9 7 5 3 1

P-ISBN: 978-93-5699-302-0
E-ISBN: 978-93-5699-309-9

Typeset in 11.5/15.7 Arno Pro at
Manipal Technologies Limited, Manipal

Printed and bound at
Thomson Press (India) Ltd

This book is produced from independently certified FSC® paper
to ensure responsible forest management.

To the readers who look up at the stars and make wishes …
They'll come true.
I'm rooting for you.

Also, for Sanj & Rads,
Told you, I'd acknowledge you guys in the next book.
We miss you, Rads.

one

Tej Bahadur didn't believe in ghosts. There were no such things, he told himself, even though he had seen his first ghost at the age of ten. It was his mother's.

He had heard that ghosts always stayed behind when they had unfinished business in the land of the living. It was as if human proclivities passed onto their corporeal form: Hate. Revenge. Love. The list was endless.

Tej Bahadur stayed on in the sleepy town of Ooty years after his mother's passing.

'You are destined for great things,' she used to tell him. 'You have your father's blood running through your veins.'

Hah! He chuckled at the memory as he took another good, long swig of the local moonshine. It singed his innards as it made its way down, but he welcomed the old, familiar burn.

'Destined for great things,' he scoffed.

It would have been funny, had the joke not been on him. The job of a head constable in the sleepy town of Ooty in the 1930s didn't exactly entail social or financial advancement.

'Unlike the Zamindar, Digvijay Rana,' Tej Bahadur spat out in disdain. 'The Zamindar of Ooty!'

He took another swig of moonshine and wiped off the remnants around his lips with the sleeve of his once pristine uniform. His alcohol dependence had increased partly due to the onset of the numbing chill of winter and partly, even if only for a few hours, to forget his pitiful failure of an existence.

The sky was dark, nary a star to be seen, as the clouds loomed angrily overhead, threatening any moment to unleash their wrath. In his inebriated state, the head of the constabulary had inadvertently stumbled his way to Azad Manor, the grand archetypal residence of the Zamindar, prior to his death.

Tej Bahadur snorted as he took another sip of his drink; the imposing Azad Manor dwarfed the diminutive constable. He spat at the foot of the large bronze gates in disdain.

'The Zamindar and his charmed family,' he thought, 'responsible for countless deaths and squashed dreams, and yet, they donned a façade of respectability.'

There were two things every child in Ooty knew. The first was the Rana family motto: 'The Rana family's name is only as good as its reputation.'

'Such a fucking farce,' he thought, as he glared at the manor again. In the ubiquitous moonlight, the residence seemed almost sinister, darkness eating through each of its numerous windows, save for one.

The lone illuminated window had by it the one good thing that the Ranas brought to Ooty. A thin smile crept upon Tej's weathered face, as he warmed his eyes on the figure by the window. The shapely bosom in the silhouette was unmistakable. He could feel the heat building up in his loins; the view, and even its silhouette, was enough to warm the blood of any man.

For all purposes, Archana Rana was a widow. Arjun Rana, her husband, and the Zamindar's son, leading a small militia of the British East India Company, had ridden deep into the hills to quash a peasant uprising. He had left six years ago. Archana patiently waited for his return.

Tej Bahadur took another swig as he felt passion build between his legs. He needed some more liquid courage to continue 'keeping vigil' over Azad Manor.

The stillness of the night was shattered as lightning cracked over the manor for a brief second, illuminating it in all its grim glory.

It was then that Tej Bahadur noticed a pair of eyes that were fixed on him. They did not belong to the lady by the window.

When the lightning had struck, for a brief second, he had seen another figure staring at him from one of the unlit manor windows. The figure had glimmering eyes that radiated a kind of evil that words couldn't describe. There was something ominous about the sight and Tej could have sworn he saw a menacing grin spread across the face that accommodated that pair of eyes.

Tej's heart galloped within his chest. His hand that held the flask was covered in goosebumps. The constable found it difficult to breathe as the startling fact hit him with the force of a bullet: Archana Rana lived alone.

Tej Bahadur felt a chill on his nape.

It was then that the clouds burst out, releasing a torrential downpour over the sleepy little town.

The dread-filled nature of the manor reminded Tej Bahadur of the second thing every child in town knew.

The Zamindar's ghost haunted Azad Manor.

'It was just a trick of the light,' he mumbled to himself, but there was a crack in his voice. His hand trembled as he raised his arm for another swig from his flask, but quickly decided against it.

He told himself that his shivers were because of the cold, but he knew in his heart that he was lying. He could feel the unnatural drop in temperature, an eeriness in the space around him and then he felt a presence behind him, a second before he heard it.

'Bahadur,' a bloodcurdling whisper reached his ears and he felt someone's breath on his nape, but when he turned around, there was no one there.

'Just a trick of the light and wind,' he mumbled unconvincingly, as he made his way away from Azad Manor with an apparent haste in his step.

'Was Azad Manor truly haunted by the Zamindar's ghost?' he wondered aloud, once he was a good distance away from the manor.

'No,' he growled, as he downed the remaining moonshine in one long gulp; he enjoyed the burn it brought to his innards.

'Just a trick of the light and wind,' he repeated to reassure himself.

Tej Bahadur didn't believe in ghosts.

There were no such things.

Unfortunately, he was wrong.

two

'Perforated stomach, broken ribs, dislocated knees, sawed-off fingers and a sliced-off tongue, for starters,' said the feminine voice, but the anger in it was apparent. A Shih Tzu stood behind the lady, supplementing her threats with squeaky barks.

The children looked on in horror as she listed out the gory, graphic details of the fate that would befall them if they did not heed her words.

'I might …' she continued, 'decapitate you as well. And, that is before I let Tuffy loose upon you. You will be just as terrifying as the ghost that haunts Azad Manor. Mark my words, if I ever catch you stealing strawberries from my garden again, you will meet your maker.' She said this without a tinge of remorse. 'Do I have to repeat myself?' she asked, finally calming down.

She didn't.

The entire band of little rascals scurried away post-haste, many tripping over loose twigs as much as their own shoelaces.

They knew the old lady meant business.

Within a couple of seconds, her beloved garden was free of pests, specifically the two-legged kind.

All except one.

'You don't scare me, Mrs Mehra,' the boy said with a defiant glint in his eyes, which didn't hold the mischievous twinkle of youth the other children had; this boy's eyes only showed a contempt for authority.

Sharvani Mehra was disappointed.

'It's Miss Mehra,' she corrected him categorically.

'Mrs!' she thought to herself. 'Hmmph … the gall of the boy!'

She was still attractive for her age. Barely into her fifties, if it weren't for a few streaks of grey that adorned her hair, she could easily have passed off for being in her late thirties. She kept her hair tied in a perfect bun, not a strand out of place, impeccably accentuating her sensual face and hourglass figure. She hoped the boy was acting defiant to elicit some sort of response from her or maybe taking in a few extra minutes to mentally build a fantasy that Sharvani couldn't exactly approve, nor completely condone.

She was used to getting such responses from the opposite sex, even at her age. There was something inexplicably attractive about her, which she had come to, over time, welcome and embrace. But one look at the ruffian and it was clear the only fantasy that the prepubescent had about Sharvani involved a noose and her lifeless body hanging from its end.

'Didn't you hear me?' she repeated coldly.

In response, she was greeted with an overripe strawberry flung with deadly accuracy, catching her right in the middle of her forehead.

'ANGREZ BHARAT CHHODO … ANGREZ BHARAT CHHODO (British, quit India),' the boy began chanting with a mischievous glint in his eyes.

Sharvani sighed.

She was always made to endure such taunts because of her mixed heritage. A supposed English 'nobleman' had seduced her mother and charmed her off her feet, finally leaving her mother with only Sharvani and a deep sense of regret.

Sharvani had vowed to never let that happen to her; she would be the one twisting men around her fingers, and not the other way around.

When it came to men, Sharvani learnt it was always best to give them what they expected little by little, till they were hooked. That always had them eating out of her hand. And then, of course, without warning, she would take it all away.

If this ruffian expected her to play the part of the British, she would play it to the hilt.

She smiled and lifted up a finger signalling she would be back, and calmly made her way to her humble abode.

Both the boy and Tuffy looked on, visibly confused.

They didn't have to wait long.

The boy's confusion was replaced by sheer horror, when Sharvani came out of the house with an old but well-maintained Pattern 1853 Enfield musket, slung carelessly on her shoulder.

'For Queen and country,' she cried in an overtly English accent.

The hair on the back of the boy's nape rose, as he watched Sharvani place the rifle over her shoulder, taking careful aim.

'You wouldn't dare,' he whimpered. The last ounce of courage fought the tide of fear that was threatening to engulf him.

She put down her rifle, stunned by his words.

'Of course ...' she said with an apologetic ring, 'of course ... you're right ... I can't shoot you like this ... I might miss ...' as she put on her glasses that were held in place near her ample bosom, with a meshed, metal lanyard.

She took aim once again. 'Much better,' she said with a tinge of satisfaction.

The boy looked on, too petrified to move.

And then, she fired.

The sound of the powerful weapon cracked through the air, reverberating with a loud bang. Sharvani fell over from the force of the recoil, causing the glasses to be knocked off her face.

She looked at the boy.

He scampered through the bushes, running like someone had lit his trousers on fire.

Her aim had been perfect: exactly three feet above the boy's head, just about enough to dissuade him from any more one-man uprisings against the so-called British.

'Heavens, Miss Mehra,' cried another female voice from behind her. 'Is this the sort of activity a woman should be partaking in, especially at your age?'

Sharvani smiled, instantly placing the voice. 'You are only as old as you feel … now help me up! I think I pulled my back with that last shot.'

The young lady raced towards her, walking as fast as her clothing allowed. She wore a calf-length plain-cut dress, coupled with simple sandals; a plain hairband completed her ensemble.

'Ishita,' said Sharvani and smiled, 'how nice of you to stop by.'

Ishita looked at her. The younger woman's features were plain, yet beautiful. Without the slightest hint of make-up, she had a pure, raw femininity about her, which many would consider attractive. She was radiant and fresh like a ripe apple. Her thin figure and pale complexion betrayed her life as a homebody.

Tuffy excitedly scampered to Ishita, running circles around her, his furry tail wagging like a pendulum. She ruffled his fur lovingly, albeit absent-mindedly. Her attention was focused on Miss Mehra, who was still lying flat.

'Are you alright?' she asked, the concern in her voice genuine.

'Nothing a glass of sherry can't fix my dear,' Sharvani said with a smile, taking Ishita's hand.

'Miss Mehra,' she said exasperatedly, 'it's barely ten in the morning. This behaviour is unbecoming of a matron towards young orph—'

Ishita bit her tongue.

'They're still children,' Sharvani said, visibly cross.

Ishita replied, almost instantly, 'Yes … I'm sorry … it's just …'

'And ex-matron,' Sharvani corrected her coldly.

'What?'

'Ex-matron,' she repeated. 'I retired, remember …' Sharvani said with a grin, 'when I handed over the responsibilities to you … the new matron?'

Ishita heaved a sigh of relief. Sharvani's grin was a tell-tale sign that her anger had subsided. Ishita had learnt this the hard way, through countless years of tutelage under Miss Mehra.

Ishita was an orphan herself, and it was only because of her long-standing relationship with Sharvani, from caretaker, to teacher, to a mother figure, and now, eventually, a friend, that Sharvani decided to step down in favour of the younger Ishita as head of the Rana Orphanage, after it had reopened.

'I'm glad you are not angry …' Ishita exclaimed.

'Who says I'm not?' she asked, giving her younger counterpart the all-too-familiar death stare.

'Um … I …'

'Relax,' Sharvani said, as she unknotted her eyebrows, giving Ishita a slight smile. 'I'll stop being mad if you join me for a glass of sherry,' she said with a wink.

'But it's ten in the … oh what the hell,' Ishita said good-naturedly. 'One glass won't kill me,' she finished as she followed Sharvani and the dog into the house.

'What did I miss?' Ishita asked, taking a small sip. The weather outside the patio was perfect, and the cold, crisp air invigorated her. Perfect weather wasn't something one associated with the winters of Ooty. But today, the sun had come out after several days, and the greenery in Sharvani's garden looked fresh, touched by both rain and morning dew.

There was even a slight nip in the air that the town was now getting accustomed to and had even come to embrace.

It was the perfect weather for pakoras and piping hot tea.

Or sherry.

'So …?' Ishita asked again.

Sharvani looked on quizzically.

'When you were shooting this morning …'

'It was one shot my dear. Hardly what you would call a shooting.' Sharvani smiled, as she relished the familiar, chilled, fruity taste tingle her taste buds.

'It was one of your hooligans,' Sharvani finally answered her question.

'I think I know who you are talking about …' Ishita replied, 'little boy, wee height … button nose …'

'That's the one!'

'Vijay!' Ishita exclaimed. 'He's … he's always been a little bit of a rebel.'

'I think the correct word would be a rascal,' Sharvani said, taking a sip of her drink.

'Language, Miss Mehra.'

'I've told you a hundred times before, please call me Sharvani.'

Ishita grinned. 'Old habits die hard, Miss Mehra. I've been calling you that for as long as I remember … I can't up and change it at a moment's notice.' Ishita continued to smile as she took another small sip. 'I've been used to calling you Miss Mehra ever since I learnt how to speak English. I don't think you ever let up on your disciplinarian ... my mistake ... authoritarian attitude,' she said and winked.

Sharvani chuckled. 'It had to be done ... someone had to keep you little rascals in line and for whatever it was worth, I think I succeeded a little, but ...' she sighed deeply, 'given a chance, I would have done things differently, given you all a little more love, and a little less scolding, been a little more understanding and disciplined a little less with the belt.'

Ishita laughed, almost snorting out some of her sherry. 'Well ... a gun is a definite step up from spanking our bare bottoms. I remember clearly that was your favourite form of corporal punishment.'

'The boy needn't have been worried; that old relic is always only loaded with blanks. Truth be told, I don't even have any live ammunition.' Sharvani chuckled. 'I'm surprised it fired the way it did, but the old forms of punishment were always the best,' she said mischievously. 'Nothing better to remind a child of their mistakes than a stinging backside.'

'Miss Mehra,' Ishita said animatedly, 'you used to carry out the punishment even when the children were nine or ten.'

She chuckled. 'They used to stay in line more due to the embarrassment than the physical pain. But you are one to complain ... you were always the lamb of the group. It was always Arjun Rana who was the mischievous one ...'

Ishita laughed. 'He wasn't even part of the orphanage.'

Sharvani nodded.

'His father was the Zamindar, and the orphanage was in his name. The boy didn't have any friends to play with. I remember many a times he used to bring in Archana Sharma as well ... you know her ... the tea plantation owner's daughter ...'

Ishita nodded. 'Didn't that become the Rana Tea Plantation after her marriage to Arjun?'

Sharvani looked glum. 'Digvijay swindled Sharma out of his tea plantations, exploiting a father's love for his daughter.'

'Poor Archana.'

Sharvani nodded. 'It was so much easier when you all were kids, too distant from and untouched by the stark, ugly realities of life. Those days ...' Sharvani said melancholically, 'so, carefree ... they seem so, so long ago.'

A silence crept up between them, but soon enough a smile appeared on Ishita's face. It was very slight and very brief. Sharvani noticed it, but ignored it, for she knew it too well.

Ishita was never good at keeping secrets. She would spill it out sooner than later.

'Thank you ...' Ishita said out of the blue. There was a warm earnestness in her voice.

Sharvani looked at her, eyebrows raised.

'For everything. You have always been the closest thing to a mother for me. You are someone who took an abandoned child from the streets when no one would have her. You gave me food, shelter and the love and warmth that I wasn't destined to have.'

Sharvani smiled warmly. 'It's not ...'

But Ishita didn't let her finish. 'I've always tried, ever since I was young enough to understand, to emulate you in every way possible ... to try and be like you ... and I dare say, I've succeeded a little.'

'The children love you ...'

'You think?'

Sharvani nodded.

'I've always been worried, and scared of disappointing you ... I always felt I would fall short of your expectations. You were the only pillar that a scared little girl held onto in a storm, and I'm afraid of letting you down.'

Sharvani put her hand on her younger counterpart's shoulder. 'Don't be, for you have turned out to be a fine woman, one who is both loved and respected by all those who are lucky enough to know you. You spread happiness, Ishita. Don't let anyone tell you any different. And you truly care about the children.'

Ishita smiled. It was bittersweet. 'Really?'

'You are a person I've trusted with the future of countless young children. Hell ...' she said, downing her glass with a gulp, 'I'd trust you with my own life.'

Ishita smiled again. This time, her eyes sparkled.

'And besides ...' Sharvani said, 'you're not alone ... how is your aunt doing back in Bombay?'

'Oh,' Ishita said with a slight smile, 'she's doing fine. I just received a letter from her the other day; she misses me terribly.'

'Do you ever think of visiting her?' prodded Sharvani.

Ishita had downcast eyes, a frown appearing on her face, as if she was shouldering some invisible burden. 'I do at times, but I never follow through.'

Sharvani looked at her, visibly cross. 'Well I, for one, am disappointed.'

'Disappointed, Miss Mehra?' asked Ishita with visible agitation. 'Whatever for?'

'Well, ever since your aunt learnt of you, she sent for you to go stay with her. After you left the orphanage, you kept sending me letters, but never once did you come to visit. Eight years, Ishita ...' she said with mock exasperation, 'not a single visit from you for eight years, and all of a sudden you pop up back into our lives a year ago!'

'Well your replies to my letters helped ...' Ishita said with a smile.

Sharvani grinned. 'The one where I told you I was thinking of retiring and needed a replacement? I had written that six years ago.'

'Well ... that was a hint, if I ever saw one.'

Sharvani chuckled. 'Oh, come on, you must have been jumping with joy. Ever since you were a little girl, all you ever wanted to do was to be like ...'

'Sharvani Mehra in every way!' Ishita completed the sentence, trying to stifle a smile. 'Well you can take a girl out of Ooty, but you can't take Ooty out of her,' she said and let out a giggle. 'What can I say? It took me time to adjust to the idea that I wasn't alone and that I had family who cared for me. And although Bombay had its charms and bright lights, I'm afraid I'm an Ooty girl at heart. So, after a good eight years, I thought it was best for the hen to come home to roost.'

'And put this old foul-mouthed fowl out of a job, eh? Well if you don't want to visit your aunt, you can always ask her to come here?'

'I will,' she nodded.

'And Ishita ... don't ever say you don't have a family. These children here are your family. They care for you. I care for you,' Sharvani said sympathetically.

'Thank you ...' Ishita placed her hand over Sharvani's. 'Thank you for everything.' Ishita clumsily broke a biscuit with her other hand and Tuffy swiftly nibbled at the golden crumbs.

'You don't need to thank me,' Sharvani said with a smile. 'Now tell me, what is it you're hiding?' she asked, with a smirk on her face.

Ishita looked at her dumbfounded. 'How did you ...'

'I've raised you, as you can remember,' she winked. 'There's nothing that you can hide from me, including secretly feeding Tuffy, for that dog's gotten into a habit of sharing whatever it is that you're eating or drinking. I must, however, thank you for not sharing your sherry with him.'

Ishita grinned.

'But I know it's not that, so tell me ...' Sharvani said with a knowing smile, 'what is it that you came to tell me?'

'Arjun Rana is back. He's back from the dead.'

three

It was Sharvani's turn to be dumbstruck.

'What are you saying?' she exclaimed.

This needed another glass of sherry, she surmised.

Or two.

Or three.

'It's true ...' Ishita said beamingly. 'His return itself is an incredulous story, Miss Mehra, straight out of the crime-romance novels that you used to read.' Ishita bit her tongue, regretting the words as soon as they left her mouth.

'Those novels were in the recesses of my cupboard back then,' said Sharvani, cross at this information.

Ishita gave her a sheepish look. 'I wanted to try and be like you in every way possible,' she said with a wide grin.

Sharvani rolled her eyes. Those crime-romance novels, as her pupil so innocently described, were smutty, erotic dime novels smuggled in from the underbelly of London, gifted to her by one of her many lovers. She wondered about how much the students knew about their matron.

'Carry on,' Sharvani said flatly, attempting to return to the topic, something Ishita was only all too keen on doing.

'After Digvijay Rana's death ...' began Ishita animatedly, with the excitement of a child narrating a fairy tale.

'Arjun took up the mantle of Zamindar,' Sharvani completed lackadaisically, eager to speed up the process.

Ishita nodded. 'Being the new Zamindar ...' she continued with the same eagerness, unfazed by Sharvani's apparent boredom, 'he had a host of responsibilities to the people and the British East India Company. After he was sent on a heroic mission to quell an uprising of tribal peasants, along with a regiment of British soldiers, he disappeared for six long years,' Ishita said with the histrionic flourish of a campfire storyteller.

Sharvani looked on incredulously.

Would this lady ever get to the point?

'Many presumed him to be dead, but they were all proved wrong. He survived the war ... Because of his skill. Because of his courage. Because of his cunning ...'

Ishita stopped for effect, her eyes boring right into Sharvani's.

'... And most of all because he fell on his head whilst trying to get on his horse on the battlefield, and ended up with a case of acute amnesia.'

Sharvani burst out laughing.

Seeing her, Ishita followed suit.

'Really, Miss Mehra?' she said wiping off the tears from laughing so hard. 'This is most inappropriate.'

Sharvani chuckled, fighting off the last bouts of unexpected laughter. 'But they ... they found a body.'

'The English doctor assigned had never seen Arjun's face. Another body of similar height and build was retrieved from the battlefield, and that was confused to be the Zamindar's son.'

'Really Ishita? How can one just mistake the identity of a dead body?'

Ishita looked at her intently. 'With Arjun's one telltale sign—the body had patches of pale skin on the back and arms. Pale skin in patches on a brown body ...'

'Vitiligo,' gasped Sharvani. 'Of course,' she said, slapping her forehead. 'You rapscallions used to tease him by calling him a chessboard because of the discolouration.'

Ishita blushed. 'It made him look cute.'

'And then?'

Ishita shrugged. 'Our charmed boy was taken in by a farmer and his family, who after nursing him back to health, made him a stable boy for six long years. He seemed to have recovered his memory in only the last few weeks.'

'What happened to him?'

'I just told you.'

'Not him ... him,' Sharvani emphasized, 'the farmer?'

'The word out is Arjun will be rewarding him.'

Sharvani breathed a sigh of relief. 'Thank God! If his father were alive, he'd burn down the farmer's house with the farmer and his family in it. He couldn't stand his son mingling with commoners, even when he was a child.'

'But Arjun never listened and he isn't like that ...' Ishita protested.

Sharvani brushed off Ishita's protests. 'However Arjun is, it'll be interesting to see how the rest of the town will react to his return, especially Archana. The poor thing has been dancing with the demon in the bottle since her husband's disappearance, with only that British gardener to keep her company. I hope Arjun's return will free her from her pathetic meandering, before she drowns herself in more alcohol ... or the gardener's seeds,' she added as an afterthought.

'MISS MEHRA,' yelled Ishita angrily. 'That is no way to speak about the Zamindar's son and daughter-in-law. They were your students after all.'

'Calling a crow a peacock doesn't make it change its plumes; the truth stays the same no matter what I say,' she countered nonchalantly.

'But you nonetheless mustn't indulge in such idle gossip …' Ishita chided her.

'Oh, come on …' she said grinning, 'who doesn't love a good scandal? Besides, who wouldn't indulge? The gardener, Eric, is quite attractive in a rugged sort of way, wouldn't you say?'

Ishita thought of chiding her once again, but realized the amount of good it would do. She quietly resigned to her fate, which lay at the bottom of another glass of the fine sherry, before nodding in agreement.

'Well-built, rugged in an almost brutish sort of way …' Sharvani said, recollecting the gardener's persona. The two drinks had evidently relaxed her mood to open up on more private topics.

'Everything our poor, timid Arjun isn't, but it wasn't really his fault. Digvijay never let him get out of his shadow. His return, however, won't be taken well by Eric for sure; it'll be interesting to see which side Archana flips over to …'

'Eric won't nearly be half as upset as Alexander Stephan,' commented Ishita. Apparently, two glasses were her threshold as well.

'Yes,' Sharvani remarked. 'He has been after the Azad Manor property ever since he stepped into town.'

'But the Ranas have been refusing his offers to buy them out. I don't like that man; he gives me the creeps,' Ishita said, a scowl marring her otherwise pretty face.

'He has been persistent though, first with Digvijay, then Arjun, and now Archana. She would have been the easiest of the three to convince, I reckon, but with Arjun back, well, you know what they say about the best laid plans of mice and men …'

Ishita didn't respond. She merely gazed out at the picturesque hills. 'I wonder if there is anyone at all who would be happy to see our dear Arjun?'

Sharvani smiled and added, 'Well there are two people I know sitting right here.'

Ishita gave her a sheepish grin.

'I'm sure Anshul will also be glad to see his Mastah Arjun back,' Sharvani said, in a mock accent.

'Anshul Kaka!' Ishita cried excitedly.

'He's not hired help,' Sharvani scolded Ishita mockingly again, 'he's the butler.'

'He's been both a mother and a father to Arjun, ever since his mother passed away. His father was never around to see him grow up.'

Sharvani played with her glass, twirling her fingers around its rim, her eyes housing a forlorn expression which spoke volumes about what Ishita had said.

'So, will Rai Bahadur ...' she started, still playing with her glass.

'The head constable's father?'

Sharvani nodded.

'He has been Digvijay's closest confidant since forever.'

'I heard he spent more time with the Zamindar and his family than his own.'

Sharvani shrugged. 'He has been their aide-de-camp. It was he who suggested the alliance between Archana and Arjun. Not selling out to Alexander was also supposedly his idea.'

Ishita nodded, taking another sip. She frowned a little.

'Well, if you ask me, Arjun's return to Ooty couldn't have come at a worse possible time, with Archana's alleged affair, and these terrible, terrible rumours of the Zamindar's ghost walking around Azad Manor.'

'Knock, knock,' coughed a voice from behind Ishita. She turned around to see a familiar face.

He had aged a little, but the well-tailored suit beautifully fitted his slim body. His hairline had receded, but the gaps were expertly concealed with generous dollops of hair cream and meticulous combing. A perfectly shaped beard hid his soft jawline, and concealed the discolouration due to his disease. His small hands were tightly wrapped around an unusually large bouquet. It wasn't the nostalgia as much as his dreamy, baby blue eyes that made Ishita weak in the knees. They had the same effect back when she was small, and time had done little to change that.

The eyes were the same, and had remained just as dreamy today as they were nearly a decade ago.

'Arjun!' she exclaimed with an embarrassed grin, as the Zamindar's son stepped forward.

'How long has he been here?' Ishita whispered to Sharvani, her face turning tomato red.

'Not to worry, my dear. Just breathe,' replied Sharvani, pulling out another glass and filling it to the rim with sherry. 'Not nearly long enough,' she said with a sly smile. 'Just breathe.'

four

Rai Bahadur could have sworn he heard someone call him.

He could also have sworn that the manor was empty.

He felt his heartbeat quicken as he scurried across the large corridor adjacent to the stairs.

Azad Manor was once teeming with life until the Zamindar's wife committed suicide. Now, it remained an empty husk of its former self. Rai Bahadur knew the reason for her suicide, but he kept his mouth shut.

Even from Master Arjun.

For, like Lord Digvijay used to keep repeating whilst he was alive, 'The Rana family's name is only as good as its reputation.'

Digvijay Rana wasn't a fair man—that much was well known throughout Ooty. The number of lives he ruined to reach his position of power, however, wasn't common knowledge.

But Rai Bahadur knew.

He knew of every single misdeed done by the Zamindar, every life he had crushed and every body that he had buried.

It was his ruthlessness towards his fellow men and his animosity towards the local tribes in Ooty that prompted Major General William Sleeman to bestow the already affluent Digvijay Rana the title of Zamindar, giving him de facto control over Ooty.

And Rai Bahadur had stayed on with him. He watched from the sidelines as a wealthy landowner gradually turned into the most powerful man in Ooty. But as the Zamindar rose to power and prominence, material wealth did not matter to him as much as the Rana family's name and reputation.

For reasons unbeknownst to even Rai Bahadur, Digvijay Rana had taken to heart to uphold the time-honoured ancestral motto: *The Rana family's name is only as good as its reputation.*

And uphold the family reputation Digvijay Rana did, by inducing fear and being charitable, in equal measure. For both those reasons, the Rana name was still respected in Ooty.

And now there was the new maalkin, the lady of the house, Archana, wildly dragging the family name through the mud.

Every servant knew of her escapades with the gardener, Eric, but, for good measure, they all kept mum.

For they also knew the kind of power and influence the Rana name wielded in the community and, by marriage, Archana Sharma was now Archana Arjun Rana.

Even Rai Bahadur spared Arjun all the information, not from fear, but out of concern.

He didn't want to break poor Master Arjun's heart.

And he hoped better sense would prevail over the rest of the servants as well.

Apart from the thin rays of polluted light that slipped into the house—the sunshine blocked by thick, velvety curtains—the manor was engulfed in darkness. Only due to his familiarity with the space could Rai Bahadur recall the exact number of steps on the grandiose staircase. Majestic furniture and paintings adorned the walls, but they were carefully covered with cloth to preserve them from decrepitude.

The servants, their duties reduced to a bare minimum, had clocked in for the day. All except the gardener.

Rai Bahadur's blood boiled at the thought.

As he was walking around the manor, Rai Bahadur suddenly felt unsettled. He found it hard to pinpoint the exact reason for his anxiety. He had been in Azad Manor far too many times before, but never quite felt this uneasy.

The temperature was cooler than usual and the manor a little quieter, but other than that, there didn't seem to be any other difference. Rai Bahadur could feel a chill run down his spine starting from the nape and he sensed someone breathing on his ear, attempting to whisper, but when he turned around, there was nothing and nobody. The chills were getting stronger and he could feel his heart racing.

He gulped hard, took in multiple deep breaths and tried to slow down his racing heart and fight back the terror rising from the pit of his stomach, but it was futile.

'Rai Baahhhhaaduur ...' an overstretched voice, that sounded like rusted nails being dragged over a chalkboard, boomed all around him. It rose and fell, without apparent coherence.

But to Rai Bahadur, the words were as clear as day.

Without warning, even the slivers of sunlight began to disappear.

The light didn't dim slowly; it went like water draining away. The ceiling first turned black, and the darkness quickly percolated to the floor.

He heard the voice again.

'The will ...' it called out. It was a deep hollow voice. 'The will ...' it said, yet again.

The physical chill seeped through Rai Bahadur now. He could feel goosebumps all over his body. The temperature in the room seemed to fall several degrees in the blink of an eye. Rai Bahadur turned around and his heart almost gave up out of fright.

For in front of him stood his late master, Digvijay Singh Rana.

The Zamindar stood motionless, as still as a corpse. Hollow, empty sockets now replaced his eyes. His body was engulfed by an otherworldly bluish glow. His once regal clothes were tattered and torn, and his feet protected by his favourite thick shiny leather gardener's boots, which were coated in what seemed like a mixture of dry blood and mud. They were three feet above the ground, his body floating mid-air. The entire scene was bone-chillingly frightening.

'No. This can't be. You …' Rai Bahadur gulped, not willing to accept the sight in front of him.

'The will …' the Zamindar whispered again, his words coming out like white steam in the cold, darkened hall.

The Zamindar's complexion was paling before Rai Bahadur's eyes; dark blue veins appeared on his master's face like a gruesome cobweb of decay.

'Protect the family name …' he wailed, as he floated down the staircase. Rai Bahadur was rooted in place, frozen from fear, as the ghost of his dear, departed master reached closer to him.

'Bahaaaaduuuurrrrr …' the ghost moaned, as he gripped the old man's shoulder suddenly, cracked nails extending from bony fingers digging into Rai Bahadur, ice creeping into the old man's veins.

'Yes … yess …' he stammered, as he wriggled out of the Zamindar's grip. 'I'm here …' Rai Bahadur gulped and noticed that Digvijay's hand had withered. The bluish shine on his skin was beginning to crack, revealing grey dust beneath.

Panic engulfed Rai Bahadur's gut.

'Protect the Rana name,' the ghost whispered once more—his breath was putrid.

'Protect my legacy,' the ghost screeched as his throat split wide open and deep, black gashes appeared on his face and chest. 'Protect my legacy ...' the phantom howled, as the eyes that were hollow sockets turned black and his mouth stretched unusually wide in an eternal scream. The weathered flesh on his mouth tore apart, as it kept stretching inch by inch like dry rubber being pulled at its very seam.

Rai Bahadur screamed and rushed out towards the exit that led to the porch. Behind him, the Zamindar's ghost began to wither to dust; first his clothes, then his decomposing body started falling in clumps, dissipating into dust as soon as they touched the floor.

Rai Bahadur raced outside towards the main door, tripping over a footstool in the process. Never in his seventy-four-year journey of life had he run as fast as he did that day. He pulled at the rusty gates that swung open with a loud clang, and didn't stop until he felt his heart would give up.

Then he leaned against a tree for support, one hand tightly grasping his chest while the other was clapped to his mouth in sheer horror.

Had he actually seen that phantasm? He questioned himself and his sanity in that order, as his hand instinctively went over the points where the Zamindar's fingers had touched him.

His heart was galloping. It had experienced a lot in its long lifetime. Another strain, another shock of this magnitude, was sure to spell his doom—but even death seemed trivial at the moment, since his master had seemingly traversed it and returned. He had heard whispers many times late at night when Azad Manor had still been his residence, maybe even caught a glimpse of the supposed phantasm. But all those times he had dismissed it all as a dream, and a product of an overactive imagination, maybe.

But this time it was clear.

It was no dream. His own past eerie brushings and the rumours he heard, and so vehemently denied, were true, proved beyond a shadow of doubt.

Azad Manor was haunted by the ghost of Digvijay Singh Rana.

It was haunted by the Zamindar's ghost.

And it had chosen Rai Bahadur to protect his legacy.

five

Ishita looked as if she had seen a ghost.

An awkward tight grin plastered her face.

'As I was telling Ishita …' Sharvani cut in, 'Arjun JUST got here.'

Arjun let out a small chuckle as he handed Sharvani the bouquet and proceeded to give her a tight, warm, bear hug to the point where she could barely breathe.

'Wow,' she exclaimed, turning slightly red in the face, as she felt his grip tighten around her.

'It's good to see you, Miss Mehra. It's been so so long …' the exuberance and excitement in his voice was impossible to ignore. The sparkle in his eyes was like that of a child who had just been given a new toy.

Sharvani hesitated for a moment. She had been lifted off her feet for an instant, but she warmly embraced him back.

'It's good to see you too, beta.'

A slight smile still intact, a single, solitary tear ran down Ishita's cheek. It did her heart good to see those two united after so long. Tuffy had come and settled down next to her, giving out a long yawn. The morning exercise and subsequent biscuits primed him for his mid-morning siesta.

'Look at you …' Sharvani grinned, pulling back from the embrace to admire his face. 'You've returned unscathed from that terrible revolution business.'

Arjun chuckled. 'I don't remember most of it, and I'd like for it to stay that way,' he remarked.

'You remember Ishita though, don't you?' she asked, stepping aside.

'Of course, of course … of course,' he said, as he smiled and moved closer towards Ishita. Sharvani felt his words were a little too quick, and lacking sincerity, like a politician's.

He would have an affinity towards intrigue, no doubt. He had the blood of the Zamindar running through his veins after all. But she had known Arjun since childhood, and had practically raised him. He was a better man than his father. Nurture over nature perhaps, she wondered silently.

Ishita turned towards him; the wide grin plastered on his face grew wider.

Ishita nervously held out her hand, her face flustered.

'Hello … hello … Arj … my lord …'

His grin grew wider as he pulled her closer and embraced her in an even tighter hug than Sharvani's. The petite little woman was turning red, finding it hard to breathe.

'Of course, I do …' he said with a flourished grandeur, completing his answer to Sharvani's question.

'How have you been?' he asked, directing himself towards Ishita.

'I've been good, my lord.'

'Oh, come on …' he chuckled, ruffling his hair good-naturedly. 'I'll still be Arjun to you.'

She giggled nervously.

'Ishita Dhiman is the matron now,' Sharvani interjected. Although she knew Ishita to be introverted and reserved as a person, she had never seen her tongue-tied before. Maybe seeing her childhood friend after so many years had that effect. And he wasn't the friend that she used to chase hens with anymore; he was now the Zamindar of the town of Ooty.

'Oh … the matron?' he repeated, his curiosity piqued.

'Of the orphanage.'

'She's taken your place?'

'Nobody can take my place, Arjun, you know that,' Sharvani said with a mischievous glint in her eyes.

'Of course, of course,' he chuckled. 'How's the old place doing by the way?'

Both the women's faces fell. 'We have been managing ... the orphanage runs largely on donations and charity …' admitted Ishita.

'… of which your father was a sizeable contributor …' interrupted the elderly lady. 'After his death …' her voice trailed off.

'It's not easy to feed, clothe and teach a hundred mouths,' Ishita complained.

'I'll look into it,' Arjun smiled at Sharvani. Sharvani returned the smile.

This time, his smile seemed genuine, not that of a lord who tried to please everybody. 'Don't you worry!' he added.

There was a murmuring steadily growing in decibel outside Sharvani's gate. A crowd had gathered outside; they needed to see if the rumours were true.

There were hushed whispers and fingers pointing in their general direction. 'It's Arjun Rana,' a tsunami of voices said in differing tones and modulations, accumulating into an undecipherable static.

'It's the Zamindar's son.'

'The new Zamindar.'

Sharvani felt a wave of pride and dread envelop her, as she heard the people talking.

Pride, for they were referring to him and granting him the status of Zamindar, even though it was a position he had inherited through birth.

Dread, for the sycophancy brimming in their words.

'Please don't look at them,' he instructed calmly, still flashing his million-dollar smile. 'I don't want to draw so much attention.'

'Half the town must be here,' Ishita commented, her mouth agape.

'And a lot of them female,' Sharvani added with a wry smile.

Arjun Rana was undoubtedly an attractive man. He had a boyish charm about him, a sharp contrast to his father's rugged masculinity.

He dressed well, and had an air of confidence characteristic of those with a regal disposition.

Sharvani could see the dreamy, glazed-over look in many of the younger girls' eyes, as well as their mothers', and despite his words of not wanting attention, his actions proved otherwise.

He was at his flirtatious best, giving out smiles and winks to his adoring public.

'It seems that Archana is not the only Rana who like to play the field,' Sharvani whispered to Ishita.

Ishita merely nodded.

'I'm sorry ...' he said, the smile still plastered on his face. 'I was so overwhelmed at seeing my two favourite ladies from my childhood that I forgot why I actually came down here,' he said, as he reached into the breast pocket of his finely tailored jacket and handed an envelope to Sharvani.

'What's this?' she asked without opening the envelope.

He grinned. 'It's an invitation to my homecoming reception. Archana insisted, and besides, it would be a wonderful way to reconnect with all the people I lost touch with.'

'Well ...' she said with a broad smile, 'I'd be honoured to be there.'

'It'll be an honour to have you,' he remarked warmly, as he looked towards Ishita.

'Apologies Ishita, I hadn't counted on you being here, but why don't your lovely children and you come down as well? Maybe ask them to perform something: a little skit or a song and dance?' he said with a wink. 'Lots of wealthy, influential families are invited ... let's see if we can give some of those kids a good home and a loving family?'

'Yes ... yes ... of course, my lord,' she stuttered. 'Thank you.'

'Arjun, Ishita ...' he said with a hearty laugh. 'Please call me Arjun.'

'Of course, Arjun,' she smiled.

'See! That wasn't so hard, was it?'

'Hahaha ... you must tell me how you did that, Arjun. For the life of me, I haven't been able to get her to break her habit of calling me Miss Mehra,' Sharvani jested.

'I have my ways, Miss Mehra!'

She smiled.

'I'm guessing you must have hundreds like these,' she said, lifting up the invitation. 'Don't tell me you're hand delivering them all, when sending out Anshul or posting them could have worked just as well ... better even.'

He shrugged. 'I don't know? I just wanted this to be personal. I wanted to reconnect with people,' he said as he shot a flirty grin to a particularly pretty British girl in the crowd. 'I wanted to assure people of my existence.'

'Very well then, Arjun. We won't keep you long,' Sharvani said dismissively. 'It was good to see you. Take care of yourself from now on,' she smiled as she touched his cheek lovingly.

'Don't worry. I plan on being around for some time now. Now, ladies, if you'll excuse me …' he said, flashing his million-dollar smile, as he left through the fence and disappeared amidst the crowd.

'He's changed, hasn't he?' Ishita commented.

Sharvani shrugged. 'He seems happy and if the history of the Rana family is anything to go by, life doesn't allow that family, or anyone associated with them, to stay that way.'

six

The night was young.

Sharvani enjoyed the chilly breeze as it hit her in the face. People in her town were bundled up cozily in the warmth of their dwelling in the company of their loved ones.

But not Sharvani.

The cold night air invigorated her. The air was crisp, fresh—one of the perks of living in a hill station, as opposed to the city. It filled her up with a sense of exuberance and vitality that only a few other things were capable of.

The town of Ooty opened out in front of her.

She heaved a disappointed sigh while looking at the town.

It was her town. Picturesque little streets lined up perfectly, and the mist of the night fog enveloped them gently in a blanket.

She was born and brought up in Ooty, and all she could remember from her childhood were the clear skies, wide plantations and wonderful, quaint little cottages and town houses that dotted the landscape.

There was contentment in the air at the time, which seemed to be conspicuously missing now.

Maybe it was her nostalgia, she didn't know.

Ugly buildings had popped up where there used to be expansive meadows filled with grazing cows and beautiful flower blossoms—the hill station almost enjoyed an eternal spring. These buildings were erected at sporadic intervals and they seemed to eat the town from the inside like a cancer.

She didn't mind the progress. She didn't mind the urbanization. She specifically hated what some of these buildings stood for, and their creator, the nefarious Alexander Stephan.

Aneri Plume stood in front of her. Once an immaculate hotel, it had with time run into both disrepair and disrepute. It was the first blemish on the face of Ooty's integrity.

Way before the rumours of the Zamindar's spirit haunting Azad Manor, the British had already sent a ghost to plague the town in the form of Alexander Stephan.

He came into town only seven years ago, but now acted as if he had resided there since its inception. He wasn't affiliated with the East India Company. He was a small-time businessman, or so he said, who had come in to construct a lodging so that people from all over could come and enjoy Ooty's breathtaking natural beauty and partake in its warm hospitality.

And to that extent, Stephan had erected Aneri Plume: the first in a chain of hotels meant to commercialize the fresh air and scenic charm that Ooty held. The first in a string of hotels and guesthouses where travellers and holidaying families could rest their weary heads.

And she hated it.

It was a farce.

Aneri Plume was a brothel; nothing more, nothing less. A brothel with a veneer of respectability that the money and influence of her owner could now afford.

Sharvani personally had no qualms with sex outside marriage. Others in the community looked down upon it, but she was a little too forward-thinking for her time, and didn't have a problem in that regard. She had had a string of lovers, both married and otherwise, in her life.

She had chosen not to settle down; her work would not let her. And although she was responsible for a number of failed marriages, she found the act of indulging in the oldest profession in the world despicable.

Was she being hypocritical? Did she have double standards? Maybe. Maybe not.

She heard from those who were in the know that girls who were barely of legal age were being forced into the trade until they were no more than mere husks, lumps of flesh and blood without a soul, rather.

This profession had a way of breaking girls, both physically and emotionally—it wrecked them. To be pulled into the trade without proper consent turned young girls into women much earlier, denying them their innocence forever. Or even worse, it changed them and created in them a completely different personality altogether.

That is what Sharvani hated.

And that was precisely what the second estate loved. The nobility, businessmen, British diplomats and even Rajas would come down to Stephan's numerous establishments. Maybe it was the very act of depravity, stooping down to a certain level, or the secrecy of it all, that got their hearts racing and their blood roaring? She didn't know what it was that got their hearts pumping and the blood racing to a specific organ, but Stephan certainly did.

He also, through these establishments, very conveniently managed to form close-knit alliances with almost all of his clientele.

All except the one who would be his most regular, Zamindar Digvijay Rana. The Zamindar was a frequent visitor at Aneri Plume before his death.

Alexander Stephan had his heart set on the property since he stepped off the train in Ooty and laid his eyes on Azad Manor. It was no secret to anyone living there how badly he wanted to acquire Azad Manor and make it the pièce de résistance of his chain of hotels.

And to that extent, he catered to every whim and fancy of the Zamindar whilst he was alive, to the point where new girls were brought in only to be 'broken' into the business at the hands of the Zamindar.

Apparently, he liked them young.

But many in the town believed all of this to be mere gossip. Slander spread by Alexander Stephan himself in order to tarnish the reputation of the Zamindar because of the latter's constant rebuffs to Stephan's offers to purchase the Ranas' ancestral property.

But even with repeated rejections, Stephan persisted.

After the Zamindar's death, he put forth the same offer to his son Arjun, only to be refused with twice the anger and humiliation. After Arjun's alleged death on the battlefield, he put forth the offer to Archana.

She was by far the most inclined to hear and consider his offer. Living alone and with persistent rumours of the Zamindar's ghost haunting the manor, it would be no surprise to anyone would she have chosen to sell the property and settle down elsewhere.

But Arjun's arrival had thrown a monkey wrench in those plans.

Sharvani walked and stood in front of Aneri Plume, looking at the dilapidated building with equal parts wonder and repulsion. Stephan hadn't bothered investing in its maintenance and upkeep. The guests of the hotel were not as particular with the living conditions as much as they were with the 'amenities' it offered.

Sharvani had never been inside, nor did she want to visit, but she couldn't help wonder what the rooms were like. She looked at the building with an appraising eye this time: it was three storeys of decadence in the middle of the city, with crumbling bricks and uncemented bits of wood jutting out from the side of the building.

Clearly this was not the best example of British design and architecture. There were several open windows, each looking out onto the street, to let in the cool freshness of the night. There were some that were closed, its occupants engaged in matters of a more carnal nature. Sharvani could hear muffled moans from a window on the second floor.

She shook her head in disgust. A gold-plated plaque was nailed onto the side of the entrance.

ANERI PLUME

TRADITIONAL WARM BRITISH HOSPITALITY

FAMILY FRIENDLY

YOUR HOME AWAY FROM HOME

PROP. ALEXANDER STEPHAN

She grunted as she mouthed the words 'family friendly'.

What a joke.

In the stark clarity of the moonlight, Sharvani could make out how ugly and out of place the building looked with regard to its surroundings. It was an eyesore, a perfect example of modern British architecture encroaching upon the tranquility of India's serenity.

But urbanization was inevitable, she supposed.

If not now, maybe a few decades later.

The simple albeit heavy wooden door in front of her creaked open, and the portly figure of Alexander Stephan stood there, leaning up against the door frame.

'Saw you staring at the hotel for the past ten minutes,' he croaked. 'I was wondering if you wanted a room, though I'll be honest with you, not many ladies come in here,' he said with a wink. 'At least as guests … but if you're looking to blow off some steam …' he smiled lecherously, tapping on his overextended stomach.

'We can work something out. Room and breakfast will be complimentary, on the house.'

Sharvani felt a wave of nausea run through her body.

She felt repulsed.

With chubby, pockmarked cheeks, a bulbous nose, thick, unkempt eyebrows and beady eyes, Alexander Stephan had a face only a mother could truly love. A loose shirt and V-neck sweater tried their best to hide his obese body, but to little effect.

His teeth were rotten and yellowish brown from consistent cigar smoking. Even as he waddled closer to Sharvani with his stubby legs, he had a cigar clenched between his teeth.

'You're a rotten man,' she said to his face, as if she were describing the weather.

His eyes popped out of his head, unprepared for such an accusation. 'Excuse me?'

'These … these brothels of yours …' she said through gritted teeth, her frustration tipping over.

He grinned at her, then he blew a ring of smoke aimed at her face. She felt like retching as the rotten stink invaded her nostrils.

'They are nothing but luxury guest houses, my dear lady …' he corrected her. 'A refuge from the city life, a shelter where one may rest his head after his weary travels and indulge in good food, drink … and company.' It was apparent that he had chosen the last word with great care.

'And where do you procure this so-called company?'

'Why, madam?' he said in a show of exaggerated hurt. 'They are merely fine women who enjoy the company of well-to-do, influential citizens, often Englishmen, such as myself. I, for one, think it fosters a sense of inter-cultural exchange beneficial to both parties, who take advantage of each others' experiences and cultures.'

She looked at him visibly disinterested. 'I'm sure the ones who frequent your establishments are interested in culture.'

'Of course,' he said with an oily grin. 'After all, India is the land of the *Kama Sutra*.' He took off his bowler hat, licked his hands, coating them with generous dollops of saliva, and combed into place the few strands of stringy hair that made up his combover.

'And what do the girls think of this?'

He looked at her, unfazed. 'Why? I don't want to think about what it is that you are insinuating, but all I do is run a business. I merely provide people with shelter and some entertainment in exchange for a few rupees. I mean look at it: it's a means of improving bilateral relationships between two kinds of people, the whites and the Indians. And then there's you ...' he said, his eyes appraising her from head to toe. 'An unwanted mix of both, distrusted by the Indians and unwanted by the British,' he said sneeringly. His sneer quickly turned into a smile, accompanied with an expression that reflected his sense of accomplishment. 'Aneri Plume is opening up its sixth establishment in an equal number of years since its inception.'

The way he pronounced it, *Anayaree*, it grated against her ears. Aneri, meaning extraordinary in Hindi. And Plume, French, no less, had the same adverse effect.

Bold attempt, she would give him that, but the meaning would be lost to the populace by and large.

But it didn't matter; a rose is a rose as Shakespeare had once said.

'You still haven't acquired Azad Manor though,' she said with a sly smile. She knew the exact words that would hit him where it hurt.

Stephan's face reflected an unseen fury; his acne-scarred cheeks turned even redder, to the point that he looked like a tomato. The name itself got on his nerves, and Sharvani knew it.

'Azad Manor will be mine, one way or another. Doesn't matter what I have to do to get it,' he roared.

'Is that a threat?' Sharvani looked at him, visibly amused.

'It's a promise,' he growled.

Interesting, she thought. Through anger, one's true nature reveals itself, as it had done with Stephan.

He glared at her, breathing heavily. He quickly composed himself, realizing a little too late that he had inadvertently said more than he should have.

'Business is booming,' he said, calming himself. 'And as a good entrepreneur, I'll ensure that I give the Zamindar's son an offer he can't refuse.'

'Pimp …' she said under her breath.

'What?' he asked, his face turning red once again.

'Pimp,' she said clearly this time. 'I think the word you meant was pimp … that as a good *pimp* …' she paraphrased, 'you'll ensure that you give the Zamindar's son an offer he can't refuse.'

The veins on his neck popped out, cutting through the layers of fat, getting almost ready to burst.

'GET OUT … GET OUT …'

'Have a good night,' she said and smiled as she turned and moved away from the entrance of the establishment.

'No good harlot …' he mumbled out loud. 'Teapot calling the kettle black; don't think I haven't heard of your escapades,' he snarled out the words as he moved into Aneri Plume, slamming the door behind him.

'Harlot!' Hearing the word made Sharvani's blood boil.

'How dare he!'

She needed to have the last word, and she made up her mind to give the Britisher quite the earful. She turned around and moved back towards the lodge in a fit of pure, unadulterated rage.

Her head was bowed down, heavy with the words she would say; she would not insinuate or beat around the bush.

She wouldn't mince words this time around.

'Harlot.' The word ran in her head in his voice, playing on loop till she raced down the corner after him—

—and got the wind knocked out of her. She lay on her back for a moment, allowing her head to clear.

'Watch where you're going you blind baboon,' she roared, spitting fire. She had fallen and landed on her backside and her noggin suffered what she suspected was a mild bruise when she accidently banged into another person who was exiting the Plume in a hurry.

'I'm terribly sorry,' the other man said. He too was on the ground, due to the impact. He seemed to have also been walking with his head in the clouds. His voice seemed strangely familiar.

'ARJUN?' she asked surprised, as she inspected the bump on her head.

Her pupil was as visibly surprised to see her.

Her anger towards Stephan quickly diminished, giving way to rising embarrassment.

'I … I'm sorry. I'm afraid I wasn't quite looking at where I was going,' he blurted out, turning red in the face.

She grinned sheepishly. 'No, no … the fault was mine.'

There was awkwardness in the air. Both were at a loss for words.

'I … ah … will keep this to myself …'

Arjun raised his eyebrows, visibly confused by her statement.

'Your … umm … nocturnal stroll …' she emphasized, her eyes rolling over towards Aneri Plume.

'Oh ...' he grinned, finally understanding what she meant. 'You're mistaken,' he said, flashing his million-dollar smile.

'I was out scouting for accommodation,' he began.

She raised an eyebrow.

'Archana kicked you out so soon?' she jested.

He chuckled, but it was evident that the joke did not land well with him.

'For the guests, Miss Mehra.' It was apparent that Rana wanted the conversation to end as quickly as it had begun.

'Guests?'

He chuckled again, out of courtesy this time.

'For the reception ...'

'But the manor is large enough to accommodate them, isn't it?' she asked, visibly confused.

'Of course, it is,' he grinned and continued, 'but during my absence, Archana hadn't been the most fastidious,' he said, sounding worried. 'Barring a few rooms, almost everything in the mansion has been subject to neglect. She has been a little ... out of touch with the world, ever since my absence.'

'Oh!'

'Yes ... but not to worry,' he said, his face perking up once again. 'Nothing a few brooms and dust cloths can't fix.'

She nodded, but it was clear that she wasn't completely convinced.

'I have been out of touch as well, was fooled by the plaque on the door,' he said, pointing at the words FAMILY FRIENDLY emblazoned in bold letters. 'I didn't know the rooms here were let out on an hourly basis,' he said quietly. 'Oh dear ...' he said suddenly, 'I know what you must be thinking ...' An anxious look crept up on his face.

'Oh, don't worry. I didn't think anything of that sort,' she lied.

He smiled, but it was bittersweet, concealing a weight of some sort. She wanted to ask him about it, but decided against it at the last moment.

'Thank you. With the Rana family reputation being revered above all, I didn't want you thinking improper thoughts about my visit here. It seems like Archana isn't the only one out of touch with reality,' he said dejectedly.

His words rang true. Aneri Plume sprung to disrepute only after Arjun's absence. Regardless of what the town said about Digvijay Singh Rana and his shenanigans, his indirect rule over the town had kept the undesirable elements in check.

With his death and Arjun's subsequent disappearance, it was easy for Alexander Stephan to rise to prominence, infecting the town and its neighbouring provinces with his own brand of debauchery.

'You should do something about it. This is your town, Arjun,' Sharvani said, placing her hand on his shoulder.

'I just ... just don't know what to do,' he said with apathy while massaging his forehead.

'You must reclaim it,' she said sternly. 'It is your birthright ... You must take back all aspects of your life.'

Arjun was taken aback for a moment. He looked at her; what was she trying to imply?

But when he looked into her eyes, he could see the compassion and warmth shining through. She had been the venerable guiding light all throughout his childhood, and she was speaking the truth now.

'Yes,' he said with a renewed sense of purpose. 'I will do what it takes.'

Sharvani smiled.

'Well, first off, we can start by finding more suitable accommodation for your guests. Shall we?' she said with a smile, as she put out her arm. 'As I see it, I need a stroll and you need a guide.'

His face was beaming with happiness. 'Well, that'll be mighty helpful. I was away for only six years, but it feels as though I don't know my own town anymore,' he said with a sheepish grin as he interlocked his arm around hers.

'I'm sure there'll be something more suitable, away from such riffraff,' she said loud enough for the entire building to hear.

'I'm right next to you, Miss Mehra,' he chuckled.

'I know,' she grinned, turned around and sure enough from the window in the lobby, there was Alexander Stephan staring at both of them, rage filling his eyes, and evil brewing in his heart.

Sharvani smirked, staring at the exasperated Englishman right in the eye.

This wasn't as good as the last word she had hoped for, but it would do, she supposed, as she walked into the shimmering moonlight with her ex-student next to her.

The chill in the air worsened, becoming positively bitter. The biting cold began to pierce through her clothing, and Sharvani inevitably found herself snuggling closer to Arjun for warmth.

He didn't seem to mind and if he did, he didn't say anything.

The night, however, seemed to progressively become more beautiful. In what had become a rare sight, the stars had come out sparkling, lighting up the picturesque hill station in a kind of glow that could only be truly appreciated by poets.

Or lovers.

'So much has changed since I was gone!' Arjun commented, as he looked around the town. New buildings had cropped up, along with new stores, and an improved post office.

There was a sparkle in Arjun's eyes, Sharvani noted. Like that of a child who had just discovered a new toy. There was an overwhelming feeling of nostalgia coupled with the discovery of something completely new.

Arjun felt that way; he was discovering the town again and, in many ways, himself as well. Sharvani kept silent for a moment, allowing her ward to absorb the sights, to feel at home in a place that had changed a lot in his absence.

'Do you still remember everything?'

'Of course,' he said with a beaming smile. 'There's the post office, our tea plantation in the distance, behind that is the orphanage ... I remember it all.'

'Six years is a long time, Arjun ... way too long!'

Her words drained the colour out of his face.

'I hated it ... always working night and day, tilling the farmlands till my hands were red. There was always something missing, you know ...'

She nodded.

'There was always a feeling that I didn't belong there, but I suppose I must be grateful that they took care of me ... although I was treated like dirt. It pains me to know that I was working like a slave on land owned by my family,' he said exasperated. 'Rai Bahadur said the farmer and his family must have known about me, deriving some inane pleasure seeing the Zamindar's son till their lands for a piece of stale roti and watery dal.'

'Ishita says you are going to reward them?' Sharvani asked, trying to pacify him.

'I want to, but this anger ...' he let go of her arm.

'I just feel like ... like strangling him. All those years of my life lost ...'

'Don't ...' Sharvani said, placing her arm back into his. 'Let it go ...' she said soothingly. 'You cannot change the past, but you can rise above it ... be better that way, focus on what you have: your title, your land, your responsibility ... your wife.'

'Wife! Hah!' He grinned. 'I didn't really love her, Miss Mehra.'

'Oh!'

He nodded.

'It was a marriage of convenience. Father thought it was best that I marry Archana, as it would bode well for two of the most powerful families in Ooty to enter into an alliance through matrimony.'

'And take over the poor girl's father's plantations, no doubt,' Sharvani thought to herself.

'But over time, I came to admire her, maybe even love her, if such an emotion truly exists,' he confessed.

'I'm sure she feels the same.'

He chuckled; whether it signalled his acknowledgement or mortification, she did not know.

'She didn't take my disappearance well. We had only been married a few months before I was called off, but she found solace elsewhere.'

'Oh!' Sharvani exclaimed. She wondered if Arjun knew about his wife.

'She found her solace in alcohol … she has been dancing with the devil in the bottle every night. Maybe it helps her sleep, but I've seen her … she drowns herself in it,' he told her in a mellow tone.

She breathed a sigh of relief.

'It must have been a difficult time for you,' she added quickly.

'I didn't ask for this, you know?' he said, spreading his hand in an arc encircling the entire town. 'The name, the responsibility … any of it.'

'This isn't something you asked for, Arjun. It is something that has been bestowed upon you. You wield the power and influence to make or break the lives of these people and, frankly, I can think of no one better than you,' she said warmly.

She didn't make her feelings verbal, but she pitied him. Being the scion to the Zamindar was nothing less than a curse; his father had been a dictator. She only hoped the son would rise free of the shackles placed on him by his birthright.

'I wanted to become a writer, move to Calcutta; apparently, it is the city of scribes, I heard ...'

'Why didn't you?'

He smiled bitterly. 'After father's death, the entire running of affairs was thrust onto my shoulders, a burden that I was completely unready to handle. I was overwhelmed, Miss Mehra,' he blurted out.

She gave him a sympathetic nod.

Maybe it was the symphony of the night.

Maybe he just needed a sympathetic ear.

Arjun did need to verbally vent out his frustration.

And Sharvani let him.

'I was indirectly responsible for the welfare of the entire town. Everybody, from the lowliest tea gatherer to the head constable, owed my family, and you know what? Whether they admit it or not, they hated being in our pockets. I spent days listening to their problems, trying to be what people expected me to be and failed. I ended up being someone I was not.'

'I'm ... I'm sorry ... I didn't know.'

He chuckled. 'How could you have known? Within a year, I was packed up and was heading a bunch of British troops into battle against my own people. Why? Because they refused to bow down to the British ... that's why! Because that's what the Zamindar was supposed to do. It didn't matter if it was right or wrong. I was made to go up against my own people. Can you believe it?' he laughed. The laugh was forced, Sharvani noted.

Hollow, devoid of any real emotion.

She walked up to him again. 'It is what your father did, not you ... you cannot keep living in your father's shadow, Arjun. You must be your own man, and you are right: Ooty is your town. You will make the best happen ... all of Ooty is with you.'

He smiled at her. He needed someone to open up to.

Someone who wouldn't judge him, and unsurprisingly, her words filled him with warmth.

The whole of Ooty would be behind him.

'So would Archana …' he thought out loud.

Sharvani looked at him, unsure of what to say.

He grinned at her. 'How could I have been so blind? All this while, I was so self-absorbed, so thickheaded with my own problems that I didn't once stop to think what Archana was going through.'

Sharvani chuckled nervously. 'Yes, of course.'

He was certainly thickheaded, she thought to herself.

'But like you said, I'm not going to focus on the past; I will look to the future. Since the time of my unplanned exile, Archana found solace in the only escape available, the bottle. But regardless, she has chosen to stay with me and I will not let her down. I hope with my return I can change her habits, and maybe have a happier future together.'

'I wish you both nothing but happiness,' she said and smiled at him. Sharvani truly meant those words, without any ulterior motive or veiled sarcasm. Nothing rang truer in her heart than those words.

She was a teacher after all, and nothing gave a teacher's heart more joy than seeing their pupils' happiness.

'Focus on the happier times to come.'

'Of course,' he said, taking in a deep breath of the fresh, country air. 'Of course, I have always admired and respected her, you must understand that.'

Sharvani nodded.

'She has been no less than wonderful in many other aspects,' he began joyously. 'During my recovery, she was, in absentia, the head of the Rana family. She was all that was left of the Ranas, even if it was because she inherited the name through marriage. She had control over the estate, the manor and the fortune; yet she kept things exactly the way they were, giving the rats and cockroaches a gala time. Not a thing out of place, I tell you. The manor was exactly like I had left it,' he laughed.

'Mmm hmm,' she nodded with a little more sarcasm than required. Clearly, humour was not part of his charm.

'Yes ...' he said, as he relived some happier memories of his wife and him from the past. 'I will truly remain grateful for Archana's respect and fidelity.'

'Oh!' Sharvani exclaimed with raised eyebrows. She wanted to say something, but she held her tongue. Maybe it was in fact the time to look towards the future, towards a happier future, and forget and forgive past transgressions.

And what he didn't know wouldn't hurt him.

'Is J.D. Mistry still around?' he asked out of the blue. Sharvani shrugged her shoulders. 'I'm afraid I haven't heard that name before.'

He waved his hand, dismissing his own question nonchalantly.

'He's our family lawyer, Miss Mehra. Decidedly kooky fellow, but as a lawyer, he's as sharp as they come.'

'Funny time for you think about your lawyer.'

'Well, you are to blame for that.'

'Me?' she asked, visibly surprised.

'Of course. You've given me so much food for thought; so much could have gone wrong in these years I was away. I hadn't given my will a second thought, but after all these trying circumstances, I should officially put Archana in charge. She had just gained control of it because she was the last surviving member of the Rana family, but as you can see ...' he said, flashing his million-dollar smile again, 'I'm very much alive.'

Sharvani silently hoped that fate wasn't watching out, for this type of temptation would be too great to pass over.

'What if something happens to the both of you?'

'Well then I have a pretty teacher who can take care of things for me, can't she?' he said with a quick wink.

Sharvani blushed.

Flattery and generosity more than made up for the lack of a good sense of humour.

'Seriously though, have you both thought of um … continuing the Rana lineage?'

'What made you think I was joking about putting you in the will? As for the other question …' He bowed his head down. 'We tried a couple of times but …' He shook his head. 'Maybe God doesn't think we are ready yet; hopefully, he will be more merciful and bless us before I ride off to quell another uprising,' he chuckled. 'Maybe my last …'

'Hush … I hope your death comes after many, many long years, Arjun; you still have a lot to accomplish. I hope you become a nice, cranky old man like Rai Bahadur.'

Both of them were so engrossed in their conversation that they didn't realize when they passed the alternative hotel that Sharvani wanted to show Arjun for his reception guests, and continued moving forward. They were like two friends who were meeting after an eternity of separation, although one had a lot more stories to share than the other.

'Rai Bahadur,' he began laughing. 'That old relic … God bless him. If it wasn't for him, in all likelihood, I wouldn't be here today.'

'And yet he's been unceremoniously evicted from Azad Manor …' she said, a voice thick with sarcasm and her intent heavy with irony.

Arjun held his head down dejectedly. 'He was thrown out after I left with the troops.'

Sharvani knew this to be true. But she also knew that Rai Bahadur practically lived in Azad Manor when he was busy being his obsequious self, and lying between her sheets when he wasn't.

Rai Bahadur was seventy-four years old.

He had spent fifty-four of those years serving the Ranas, out of which forty-six were spent residing in Azad Manor, only to be categorically evicted after Arjun's disappearance.

The new maalkin apparently did not approve of his residence in the manor for reasons best known to her. Sharvani, however, heard the most colourful reasons through wagging tongues and the local grapevine. Rai Bahadur's own family meanwhile wanted to have nothing to do with him. So, Rai Bahadur was reduced to living out his days as a destitute in some ramshackle building whose name remained a mystery to Sharvani.

She didn't know.

Nor did she care.

But with Arjun's return, Rai Bahadur quickly tried to regain his original position of prominence and power, often coercing the hapless Arjun into following his 'words of wisdom'.

Since his return, Arjun Rana made no decision until he received Rai Bahadur's approval, but the geriatric still hadn't found a place back in Azad Manor.

'Archana didn't want him living there,' he explained, 'and she still doesn't.'

'Why?'

He shrugged his shoulders, implying his ignorance on that subject. Sharvani accepted the explanation; it wasn't the only thing he was being kept in the dark about.

'He lives in that squalid little building that passes itself off as a hotel.'

'Aneri Plume?' she gasped.

How the mighty had fallen, from never wanting to be associated with the 'untouchables', as he so conveniently called them, to sharing residence with them. It must have been a bitter pill for Rai Bahadur to swallow, indeed.

Rai Bahadur had worse sensibilities than the British when it came to caste, skin colour and creed. Sharvani had witnessed it firsthand several times during her association with him. But all of these rigid discernments were conveniently relaxed when it came to who he shared his bed with. At that point, the brown skin tone became 'exotic' rather than 'enraging'.

'Did you know?'

'No,' he replied earnestly, the words weighing heavily on his soul. 'I only came to know during my visit now.' His eyes teared up, thinking about and seeing a father-figure living in such squalor, and being unable to do anything about it because of his wife.

Truly, the man must have felt emasculated because of his wife. Sharvani shuddered to think what Arjun would do if he learnt he was a cuckold.

Maybe follow the footsteps of his father, she surmised.

'Rai Bahadur looked into my disappearance after my so-called death; he never gave up looking for me. When I regained my memory, word was already out that people were looking for me. My foster family ...' he said with a tinge of unmistakable anger, '... my foster family would hide me whenever they came around ... they knew my true identity. They must have,' his palm tightened itself into a fist.

'Let it go, Arjun ...' she implored him. 'Let it go.' She held his hand. She could feel the rage pulsating through him, and it reduced a little at first, before he let it all go with a deep sigh.

'If you insist, Miss Mehra,' he said with a smile.

'The servants talked, however ...' he began.

'About?'

'They said Rai Bahadur had gotten a little ... weird with age.'

'Hmmm ...'

'He would wake up in the middle of the night, screaming ... and on more than one occasion, he ... he has ...' his words stumbled.

'Go on ...'

'He claims to have seen my father!'

She looked at him, the shock apparent on her face.

'I know what the town already thinks of Azad Manor, and such rumours certainly don't help. Under those circumstances, I feel Archana did the right thing.'

Sharvani remained silent.

'You must understand, he used to scream that my father, I mean his ghost, haunted the house, vowing revenge on those who wronged him. Seeing an old friend of my father go delirious like that would have unnerved me; I shudder to think what Archana must have had to go through.'

'Do you ... do you believe him?'

He looked at her, his eyes piercing hers.

'Can you keep a secret?' he whispered.

She nodded.

'I can.'

The cold in the air got to Sharvani suddenly; a physical chill seeped through her.

'I feel his presence sometimes ...' he began, his voice thick with melancholy. 'There is an unnatural chill in the house, the lights go on and off inexplicably ... on some nights, much like this one, I wake up in a cold sweat, and if I look out of the window, I swear I can see him: his bloody, mutilated corpse, the deep gash on his neck, festering with maggots, his head precariously placed on his shoulders, ready to fall off at any moment.' Sharvani cringed as she heard him describe his visions.

'His head would look unstable on those bloodied shoulders, as if a strong gust of wind would be enough to take it off them; yet he looked on with his hollow, lifeless eyes, staring out from the recesses of the woods, looking over the familial mansion ...' he said with regret. 'I rush out to the spot, but there's nobody there. A spirit is only left behind in this world when it has some unfinished business, and my father, Miss Mehra …' She could sense in him a moment of rare vulnerability. 'My father … he wasn't the best of men.'

'What do you mean?'

He sighed deeply. 'He wronged a lot of people … he thought I didn't know, but I did … he committed such despicable acts …'

Sharvani listened on intently.

She wondered what he was going to say. What dark secret had the Zamindar been harbouring?

The stillness of the night was suddenly pierced by a bloodcurdling scream, which yanked Arjun Rana out of his talkative mood.

The chilling, shrill cry cut through the night like the wail of a banshee.

'That sounds like …'

'Ishita!' Arjun yelled, as he ran in the direction of the wail, with Sharvani following suit. The ominous scream only seemed to serve as a herald for darker times to come. Arjun and Sharvani had been so lost in their conversation that they had not noticed how the starry sky had given way to dark clouds. The clouds burst forth with an unnatural intensity. The rain stung Sharvani's face as she could barely follow the disappearing figure of Arjun in the deluge.

However, another bloodcurdling cry pointed her in the right direction. The screams were emanating from Ishita Dhiman's house. She raced towards the address, taking care to not slip and tumble down the roadside.

Arjun was already there, examining the small, wooden entrance to Ishita's abode.

He looked petrified.

Sharvani could see a streak of light coming out from the slightly ajar door.

Her heart raced.

Ishita never kept her door open.

She looked at Arjun, who had a glum expression, rubbing his thumb and forefinger together. They were stained with some sort of red liquid.

She gulped, as her mind processed the possibility.

'Is it?' she asked, unable to bring herself to complete the sentence.

He held onto the wooden gate; there were remnants of blood all over it, quickly being washed away by the torrential rain.

'I'm afraid so,' he replied. 'It's blood.'

seven

The previous swiftness in Arjun's steps was now replaced by a controlled caution; the situation had elevated itself to dangerous, in only a matter of seconds.

Neither of them could expect what would greet them inside Ishita Dhiman's modest dwelling.

Each step they took was a little more guarded than the last. Sharvani could feel the mud squish under her shoes.

Arjun let out a small yelp as the thunder crackled above him, and lightning blazed up the sky with streaks of white electricity. Other than that, the light escaping from Ishita's open door served as the only source of illumination, feebly fighting the darkness.

Arjun waited at the door, the apprehension apparent in his eyes.

Sharvani shook her head in apathy.

Could he really be Digvijay Rana's offspring?

That man wouldn't have thought twice before taking on a tiger with his bare hands, but his son was his polar opposite.

'Ishita,' she yelled.

There was a soft moan, a guttural sound of pain in response to her yell.

It was reason enough for Sharvani to act.

'Ishita,' she said assertively, as she pushed open the door entirely.

Her eyes widened with shock at the sight.

Ishita lay there with a deep gash on her forehead, and a bloodied kitchen knife in her limp hand.

'Miss … Miss Mehra …' she groaned with a slight smile.

'ISHITA,' yelled Arjun, as he entered the living room, right behind Sharvani. His face was as white as a sheet.

To Sharvani, it looked as if the Zamindar's son had seen a ghost.

'What … what're you doing here?' he mumbled.

'I … I live here, Arjun …' she uttered, visibly stunned by his question.

Sharvani glared at him. 'What is wrong with you, Arjun?' she chided.

'I'm sorry … I'm sorry, I wasn't quite thinking straight.'

'What happened?'

'The lights went out … someone attacked … someone attacked me…' she moaned, drifting in and out of consciousness. The shock and the blood loss was getting to her. 'I tried to defend …' she said, glancing at the knife clutched in her hand. Ishita tried moving it, but a sharp pain shot through her shoulder.

'My arm …' she moaned, teary eyed. 'I think it's broken.'

'There there, child,' Sharvani said, caressing her. 'You're safe now …'

'But the attacker …'

'He's gone …' Sharvani consoled her.

Ishita shook her head aggressively. 'He's … he's in the garden.'

Sharvani got goosebumps; her immediate reaction was to go after him, but Ishita feebly held her wrist.

'Please stay.'

Sharvani nodded her head lovingly, and then looked at the Zamindar's son, fire burning in her eyes.

'Arjun,' she said.

He nodded, with a steely look of determination on his face.

A word was enough for the wise.

He had proved to be a coward once already this night, and that was one too many times.

He dashed out of the house, grabbing a pot nearby, as a makeshift weapon.

'Rest, my child,' Sharvani whispered, once Arjun was out of earshot.

'Miss Mehra,' her pupil said with a strained smile.

It pained her heart to see Ishita like this. Who could have committed such a dastardly act? And why her?

Sharvani knew Ishita since she was a toddler; the girl wouldn't harm a fly.

'I know who did this ...' she whispered, struggling to remain conscious.

'Who?'

'It was the Zamindar's ghost,' she croaked. 'Digvijay Rana has come back from beyond the grave,' she whispered, before falling off the edge of consciousness.

The courage that Arjun Rana felt inside the house took flight as soon as he stepped out of the gate. He looked around: his clothes were drenched and a chill permeated through his skin and deep into his bones.

He dropped the pot and it landed with a soft squish on the muddy ground.

He wasn't like his father.

He wasn't made for these kinds of things; his sheltered upbringing made him nothing more than a liability in any fight.

The heavy rain made it difficult for him to see even ten metres ahead of him. He looked down dejectedly; he would go back and prove to them what they already knew.

That Arjun Rana, the Zamindar's son, was a coward. He felt the chilling rain hit his hair and trickle down his neck and onto his back. He shut his eyes trying hard to fight tears of frustration; he opened them as his skin tingled from the cold.

His eyes spied a murky footprint; faint at first, followed by another then another, as they eventually led into the dark, thick foliage next to the house which was now blanketed by the cover of the night.

He smiled.

Maybe he wouldn't be seen as a coward after all.

'The bastard escaped,' he said, rushing back into the house.

'You … you saw him?' exclaimed Sharvani, visibly surprised.

Arjun was taken aback. 'Yes … I mean no …'

Had Sharvani caught on to his fib, even before he had begun to sell his lie? Would he now be known as a coward and a liar? he wondered, fear rising from his gut.

'I saw someone going into the woods …' he lied quickly. 'There were footprints in the soft mud outside …'

'Footprints?'

'Yes,' he sighed. Maybe his lie wouldn't be caught after all.

'What kind of footprints?'

'They were embedded deep in the mud, the type left behind by heavy gardener's boots.'

'Like the ones your father wore?'

Arjun kept silent.

'Well, now that you mention it …' he nodded his head.

Sharvani acknowledged it with a slight grunt.

'Arjun, please fetch Dr Khuranna …' her tone more of a command than a request.

'Is she ...'

'She's fine. The shock has gotten to her. The wound and the shoulder should heal soon enough. That's all.'

He nodded absentmindedly.

'The doctor,' she asked again, curtly this time.

'Yes ... yes, of course,' he said, as he moved out of the house in a rush.

'The coming of the Zamindar ...' Sharvani grumbled under her breath, as she caressed the unconscious Ishita, whose head lay cradled in her lap.

'The coming of the Zamindar always brings in grim tidings.'

eight

'BLAZE KILLS FAMILY OF FOUR NEAR NARAGIRI,' screamed the headlines. The news was minor, considering the revolts and protests cropping up all over the country against the British, but the words rang out at Sharvani.

They seemed to jump off the ink on the newspaper and grab her by the throat. She felt goosebumps as her eyes darted across the written word.

A farming family of four lost their lives to a blazing fire that occurred near the town of Naragiri. The family perished along with their house and farmland, as the fire ate through the property and its inhabitants. Authorities say that the family was locked inside the house, and were supposedly alive before being burnt to death. Pranav Anandan (44), his wife Mahesha (38) and their two children were amongst the casualties. Authorities express confusion on why the farmer and his family didn't flee the property. The fire, whose origin is still unknown, began at roughly …

Sharvani put down the paper.

She breathed deeply. 'It's just a coincidence … just a coincidence … it can be any family,' she said to herself.

Yes, that was it. She explained to her nagging conscience that she wasn't sure this was the same family that had taken in Arjun.

And Arjun was a better man than his father.

He would never stoop to such a brutal act of revenge.

She looked at the sky; the sun was shining and the birds were chirping. Ooty was bathed in a radiant glow, with warm sunshine cutting through the dampness of last night. The sun shone bright like an omen of good things to come.

There was a feeling of freshness, like the morning dew, as she took in a deep breath and filled her lungs with the cool, crisp air and pushed the morbid thoughts to the back of her mind.

Sharvani smiled to herself, after what seemed like an eternity.

She relished the piping hot tea, as she slowly sipped on the cup.

Personally though, she would have preferred something a bit stronger.

A fact she would have normally insisted upon.

But today wasn't her day, she reminded herself, as she looked at Ishita Dhiman.

Her one-time pupil sat there, quietly taking in the warm morning sunshine, whilst sipping on the freshly brewed tea. Tuffy scampered down to her, and sat quietly, patiently awaiting his treats, while licking Ishita's hand with copious amounts of sloppy saliva.

Ishita giggled at the action. Her head was bandaged; the blood and iodine over the deep gash had dried, but still served as remnants of the horrific attack she just survived. Her eye was bruised, and ruptured blood vessels gave her the proverbial black eye. Her arm was bandaged as well.

Even after all this, it was good to see her smile, Sharvani thought. Ishita poured Tuffy a little bit of tea on a saucer and placed some crushed biscuits next to him.

'No fractures,' Dr Khuranna had said.

But the sprain was painful enough to warrant a bandage, rendering her partially handicapped.

Yet, there was a tranquil serenity on Ishita's face.

And that was what truly made Sharvani smile.

There was a creak of her garden's gate and Sharvani's smile broadened.

A stout old man, his head full of hair all turned snow-white with age, walked in jovially. A thick white beard bristled over his face. Even though age was not on his side, he seemed to be in the pink of health.

A portly stomach and lively jump in his step served as a testament to this fact.

'And how are we feeling today?' he asked no one in particular, with a beaming grin.

His voice was high-pitched, almost jovial, like every sentence he was saying was a celebration of sorts.

'Well, not half as good as you, definitely,' said Sharvani as she wondered how much 'happy' medicine the doctor was administering to himself on a daily basis.

Lord knew she needed it more than him.

He walked over to Ishita and grinned at her. 'Very nice … very nice …' he said, as Sharvani courteously handed him a cup of tea.

Ishita chuckled awkwardly, visibly uncomfortable by the doctor's proximity.

'The wounds are healing up nicely,' he said, examining the gash on her forehead as he took a deep drink from the cup, visibly unfazed by the temperature of the liquid.

Ishita was pleasantly surprised when she heard the good doctor's words and saw his broad smile, but her spirit was quickly dampened when she realized that it was his default tone and expression.

'And your hand ... any better?'

'Well ... I think I can move it a little better now.'

'Splendid ... splendid,' Khuranna replied, disregarding her words completely. 'Let's keep it on for a few days now, shall we?'

Ishita shrugged and nodded.

There wasn't much she could do by way of protest.

'Tej tells me that they have already apprehended a suspect,' he said as he gave Ishita a refill of her prescribed painkillers, and handed her his empty cup of tea.

'Oh!' Sharvani exclaimed.

'Yes ... Eric Matheson, the Ranas' gardener,' he said. 'Never really liked that man ... he always seemed like a troublemaker to me,' he continued, still smiling. 'In fact, Tej asked me to tell you to come down to maybe identify the culprit, but I was very clear ...' he said assertively, '... that Ishita is in no condition to do anything like that ...'

'I'll go,' Ishita said stoically.

Sharvani looked at her with another smile on her face. The dogged determination of her young protégé hadn't ceased to impress her back in the day and it wasn't about to stop now.

'Oh!' exclaimed Khuranna, visibly surprised. 'Um ... I don't think ... err... that is to say ...'

'I mean my legs still function perfectly,' Ishita chimed in. This time, there was a grin on her face. 'And like you said yourself, my wounds seem to be healing up nicely.'

'Um ... yes that's ...'

'Splendid,' she said as she handed the cup back to Dr Ankush Khuranna. '... besides, sitting around all day ... it's not my cup of tea.' And without another word, she was out of the gate with Sharvani following suit, leaving behind a bewildered Dr Khuranna alone with a head full of questions and an empty cup of tea.

Eric Matheson had a sardonic grin on his face as he walked out of the police station a free man.

He turned around and spat in disdain at Tej Bahadur's feet, before entering the waiting Austin Carlton.

Tej narrowed his eyes, silently cursing every possible form of anguish on the gardener who had just been released from custody.

Sharvani looked on worried.

Eric had seen the duo approaching. He winked lecherously at Ishita, licking his lips suggestively, before being pushed into the car by Arjun Rana. Rai Bahadur was also present, the rage evident in his eyes.

Ishita's eyes were downcast, in a mixture of both shame and fear.

To Sharvani, suddenly the sun didn't seem so bright anymore.

'What happened?' Sharvani barked, walking towards Tej.

'We let him go,' he replied, seemingly uninterested in the conversation.

'What?' roared Sharvani spitting fire. 'Why?'

'Because we have no bloody proof,' Tej yelled back at her.

The frustration that was boiling inside of him spilled out onto Sharvani.

'He attacked her!'

'GIVE ME PROOF.'

'THE FOOTPRINTS … CHECK THEM.'

'THEY MATCHED,' he roared louder, 'but just because the Zamindar's son saw the footprints of a gardener's shoes, we can't go around arresting everyone for it.'

'You don't need to arrest everyone, only Eric. He is the only one who wears such heavy boots for gardening; the rest of us work bare feet …'

'Even the Zamindar wore those shoes,' mumbled Ishita softly, 'right before he killed himself …' she added with a shudder.

'We questioned Eric; he had a watertight alibi and he made bail. We follow laws here, Miss Mehra … innocent until proven guilty. That's how it works, otherwise I would have locked you up years ago.'

Both Ishita and Arjun rushed towards Sharvani and Tej, to hold them back, for if the yelling contest continued the way it was going, it wouldn't be long before they were at each other's throats.

'Miss Mehra,' gasped Arjun, his little sprint putting him out of breath. 'I paid his bail.'

Sharvani stood there, stunned for a moment.

'What? Why?'

Arjun's confession knocked the wind out of her sails.

'Anshul Kaka vouches for him,' Arjun said calmly. 'He saw Archana and Eric in the greenhouse at the time of the attack.'

'And you trust him?' asked Tej.

'I trust Anshul,' Arjun said matter-of-factly. 'He has been with me ever since I was born. I trust him with my life. Besides, it's not just him,' he sighed. 'Even Archana vouched for Eric.'

'Who does their gardening at night?' scoffed Tej.

Arjun narrowed his eyes at him. 'I don't think I care much for your tone, constable, and I have no obligations to answer your question, but for the sake of your investigation, I will comply. There is a specific type of plant …' he began, looking at Rai Bahadur, who was visibly upset with Arjun partaking in the discussion. 'The *Mirabilis jalapa* … I don't think you would have heard of it?'

'No, I have not …' admitted Tej, as the other two women listened on with rapt attention.

'It's also known as the four o'clock flower, if I'm correct.' He looked at Rai Bahadur again, who gave his acknowledgement with a flick of his hand. 'It only blooms and opens at that particular hour, and it is not unusual to tend to it at night. Azad Manor is the only estate to have such a flower in the entire region. Father had the seeds imported all the way from Brazil,' he said with a hint of pride.

'Arjun ...' barked Rai Bahadur, a permanent scowl plastered on his face. 'Jawaharlal Nehru isn't known to be an especially patient man,' he grunted, as he got into the motor vehicle, slamming the door loudly.

'What a horrible, horrible man,' blurted out Ishita but then she looked at Tej and Arjun, realizing the folly of her words a little too late.

Tej did not flinch.

Arjun chuckled, making light of the situation, 'His bark is worse than his bite, believe me you ...'

Ishita smiled.

'Come, let me have a look at you,' he instructed.

She walked closer to him. A frown appeared on his face when he saw the full extent of her injuries. The blood on her forehead had caked into the bandage, and despite Khuranna's best efforts, he knew it would leave a scar.

'I promise ...' he said earnestly, 'I promise you that the person responsible will be behind those bars, and be punished to the full extent of the law.'

'Thank you,' she whispered back.

Sharvani smiled. Maybe the return of the Zamindar could bring fortuitous tidings after all.

'Tej ...' he said, whilst putting his hand on his shoulder, 'Eric may be a lot of things, but trust me you, he was not responsible for the attack on Ishita. I entrust you to find the one responsible.'

Tej rolled his eyes. 'It's my job ... now that I have your permission, I'll do it to the best of my capabilities.'

'Good man ... good man,' Arjun grunted, oblivious to the sarcasm in the constable's voice. 'Well, I have to leave,' he said, pointing at the motor vehicle. 'Duty calls.'

'Take care, Ishita,' he flashed his pearly whites, which still made women go weak in the knees, and turned towards the car.

Sharvani followed him quietly. 'Arjun, wait!'

He stopped.

'Yes, Miss Mehra?' he asked, visibly concerned.

'Last night,' she began, when she was sure that she was out of earshot, 'you were going to tell me something ... before ... before the incident.'

He looked at her; there was a restrained sadness in his eyes. He was quiet for a second, as if mentally debating on whether to bring Sharvani into confidence. She wondered whether he would trust her with the secrets he was so closely guarding in his chest.

'It was nothing,' he replied, after some deliberation. 'My father wasn't a particularly good man. He committed a lot of atrocities against this town and its people ... talking to you brought about a lot of unpleasant memories, especially those after his suicide. I just hope that I can atone for his sins, and prove to the people that I'm not the man my father was ... that I'm better than him. I hope I can redeem the Rana name and reputation.'

Sharvani put a comforting hand on his shoulder. She picked up on his nervous tics; he was definitely lying.

Apparently, he didn't trust her enough.

'You are already a much better man than your father ever was,' she said earnestly. 'No disrespect to Digvijay, but you are the only Rana to care for someone other than himself.'

'Thank you,' he smiled, and his eyes moistened a little. 'I needed to hear that,' he whispered before entering the car.

'Incidentally,' asked Sharvani, massaging her brow, as if she had just recalled something that was gnawing at her from the back of her mind, like the proverbial itch that hadn't been scratched, 'What was the name of the farmer who took you in?'

'Oh,' Arjun replied, visibly distraught by her question. 'That … that is a funny question,' he said, followed by an uncomfortable chuckle.

'Humour me,' Sharvani replied, straightfaced. 'What was his name?'

Arjun looked at her. He recognized her death stare. He had encountered it one too many times in his youth to know that he would not be able to squirm his way out of this.

'His name was Pranav Anandan,' he replied stoically.

'Was?' Sharvani asked, with raised eyebrows.

'Is … Miss Mehra, is Pranav Anandan,' he said, his face breaking out into the wide, charming grin that was known to melt hearts. 'You know what I mean … after all, English is a funny language.'

Sharvani nodded, although truth be told, she was very unsure of what he meant.

'Anyway, I hope to see you at the reception …' he said, as he waved and got into the car.

Sharvani looked on as the motorcar took off, unleashing cacophony and a steady stream of noxious fumes and dust into the air.

Both Tej and Ishita were in an animated discussion by the time Sharvani joined them.

'It cannot be,' Ishita mumbled.

'I know for a fact that it is true,' he countered matter-of-factly.

'What cannot be true?' Sharvani asked, joining in.

'Nothing that concerns you,' growled Tej grumpily.

Ishita ignored him. 'Tej thinks that there is a spy in Ooty.'

'A spy?' exclaimed Sharvani. 'What nonsense!'

Tej raised his hands in frustration.

'It is called a secret for a reason, Ishita,' he grumbled.

'*Arey kaisi secret* (Come on, how is this a secret)?' chimed in Ishita cheerfully. 'Plus, it's Miss Mehra after all. She can keep a secret, can't you?' she winked.

'Yes, of course she can,' he replied, the spite thick in his voice as he stormed into the police station.

'What was that about?' Ishita asked, visibly confused.

'Tej's usual mood swings,' Sharvani replied, and in an attempt to divert the conversation continued, 'What were you saying about the spy?'

'Oh yes,' she cried excitedly.

Good old Ishita, smiled Sharvani. She never could keep a secret.

'Tej suspects there is a spy from the Indian Revolutionaries, who wants to disrupt the British control over the land.'

'Ishita, how is that even connected?'

'Tej believes the attack was done by the spy.'

'And pray tell me …' Sharvani replied, massaging her forehead, 'Why would he do that?'

Ishita looked confused. 'Well, Tej didn't tell me that part.'

'What else did he say?' Sharvani sighed.

Ishita's face lit up again. 'That the spy had been sent in by the Revolutionaries, to uproot the Zamindar's hold on the area, because of his close ties with the British East India Company. Intriguing, isn't it?'

'Hmm … yes … most intriguing.'

'I must get going, Miss Mehra. I must pick the vegetables for the soup tonight,' she said, as she looked at the sky. 'I think it will rain tonight. There's already a chill in the air.'

'Yes,' Sharvani said. 'Hurry along, child, I'll be with you momentarily.'

Ishita smiled. 'Thank you, once again, for letting me stay with you. After the attack, I feel safer staying around someone I trust, and I know you'll protect me … With your antique rifle loaded with blanks,' she chuckled good-naturedly.

Sharvani smiled back. She looked at the sky once again, compartmentalizing all the information she had just heard.

The sun was being swallowed up by dark clouds, bringing about a sense of gloom, like an omen of worse things to come.

nine

Rai Bahadur paced around his little room in Aneri Plume.

Four walls and a small window, along with a dusty bed and a dirty toilet, were a far, far cry from the luxuries he was used to when he was the Zamindar's aide.

'Curse that Arjun Rana and his wife!'

He had already worn the floor thin with his continuous pacing; a single candle was the only source of light in the tiny room, holding back the darkness.

Ever since Archana had him thrown out of Azad Manor, he was forced to rent a room at the Aneri Plume, much to the delight of Alexander Stephan.

'I bet you regret advising the Zamindar against selling Azad Manor.' Alexander's face flashed before Rai Bahadur's eyes, and the words rang in his ears.

'But I like you, Rai Bahadur,' he had said with a snicker, 'I'll give you the deluxe room, the best in the entire hotel.'

Alexander had the grin of a fox when he had taken Rai Bahadur's advance payment with wide-open palms.

'Deluxe room my foot!' Rai Bahadur spat at the ground. He was given the worst room in the hotel at three times the regular rate, he had learnt later from Manohar Mishra, the caretaker.

He was duped, that much was certain, but he knew Alexander Stephan was a jackal who would pick on the bones of a wounded animal.

And Rai Bahadur was just that.

After the Zamindar's suicide and Arjun Rana's subsequent disappearance, Archana Rana had come into power.

She categorically expelled him from the manor there on; all his visits were limited, and he was treated like a pariah in the house of the family he spent his entire life serving.

And then, just recently, he had laid eyes on the Zamindar's ghost in the manor. He could have learnt more … so much more, had Archana allowed him to stay. During his tenure, every enemy that Digvijay Rana made was by extension an enemy of Rai Bahadur. He trampled over countless lives when he was by his master's side, and committed deeds that people would have not forgotten easily.

Or forgiven.

He was reduced to living in such squalor because of that bitch, Archana Rana.

Even her spineless husband wouldn't take a stand. How that charismatic, assertive Digvijay Rana fathered such a wimp was beyond his understanding.

The walls in his room were thin; he could hear the moans of a woman of the night from the room adjacent to him.

He could even hear the squeaking of the cheap mattress and its termite-infested wooden stand.

'Another whore, no doubt,' he grunted under his breath. 'This is a more appropriate place for the mistress of Azad Manor to squat in, with her questionable morals.'

He had kept the secret from Arjun long enough, he had decided.

He would tell him the terrible truth that Digvijay Rana wanted so badly hidden.

At that very moment, there was a knock on his door. He grudgingly went and opened it, only to be taken aback.

Rai Bahadur felt his breathing quicken, as his senile heart pumped wildly to keep up with the growing terror in his chest.

'I ... I ... destroyed you ... you should have died,' Rai Bahadur grunted, as he stepped back. 'What do you want now?' he stammered.

Silence was the only answer he got.

'Stay back ... stay back, I'm warning you,' he gasped as the figure walked in and the door closed in front of him. The candle, which was the one solitary source of light, now unveiled the terror that stepped out from the darkness.

His heart was racing; he could feel his skin crawl and the hair on his neck stood up in fright as the visitor moved closer towards him.

There was a slight altercation, but the sound was drowned out by the overenthusiastic moans of the whore next door.

All it took was a few minutes.

The man and his escort for the night in the room adjacent to Rai Bahadur's were spent, and stopped in that span of time, as did Rai Bahadur's heart.

ten

Tej wordlessly stood next to his father's body.

The old man's face was frozen in a grotesque expression of terror. His eyes were bulging out, and his tongue lolled out of his mouth, lifelessly.

The body was strewn across the chair, hanging like a discarded ragdoll. The first signs of rigor mortis had begun to set in.

Tej stared at the body apathetically. Strangely, he didn't feel anything.

Not an overwhelming anger like he had expected.

Nor a sense of relief, like he had hoped.

He felt nothing.

A fly swooped in and landed on Rai Bahadur's glassy, open eye, rubbing its germ-infested feet together. Tej looked at it, considered shooing it away for a moment, but decided against it at the last second.

He instead turned his attention to Dr Khuranna. 'What's your prognosis, Doctor?' he asked dryly.

For a change, Khuranna's expression turned dark.

The doctor had a grim look of bewilderment plastered on his face. 'His heart stopped,' he said quietly. 'Plain and simple.'

'Old age, huh?' Tej asked.

The doctor shook his head. 'No, this man died of fright,' he said, pointing at the telltale signs—the goosebumps on his aged, craggy skin were still visible.

'Something scared this man to death.'

Tej was confused. As far as he knew, his father hadn't known fear his entire life.

Even at this ripe old age, it would have taken no less than a ghost to scare him out of his wits.

'A ghost?' Tej thought. 'Could it be?'

'Are you absolutely certain?' he asked the doctor again.

Khuranna adjusted his spectacles, visibly insulted by the head constable's remarks. 'I'm a doctor, sir,' he replied coldly. 'And your father was scared to death.'

A screech came from the open door. The plump figure of Mrs Manohar Mishra had her hand over her mouth.

'It's the ghost ... the Zamindar's ghost,' she shrieked.

Tej slapped his forehead. 'Take her away ... please,' he said, frustration dripping off his every word.

'The Zamindar's ghost is out for revenge ...' her voice echoed in his ears, even as the sub-constable escorted her away from the room.

'Don't pay her any heed,' said Dr Khuranna as he walked up next to the perplexed head constable, 'his death was of natural causes, but for the life of me, I cannot imagine what could have caused this man's heart to stop from sheer terror.'

'Well ...' shrugged Tej, 'if Rai Bahadur's body cannot testify, the floor will,' he said. The wooden floor was poorly constructed, sturdy enough to withstand and endure for a few years, but that was it. The floor was dusty, sparsely furnished with an old, moth-eaten rug, and had on it a number of muddy boot prints.

'The muddy boots again …' Tej grunted under his breath.

The trail of prints began from the entrance of Aneri Plume, and stopped right at the chair where Rai Bahadur lay slumped, dead as a doornail.

There was no sign of a break-in; the door and windows were untampered. A trail of muddy footprints, exactly like the ones at Ishita Dhiman's garden, now led up to his father's corpse, without any exiting trail.

The trail passed through the reception, surmised Tej.

Being the head constable, these kinds of investigative practices were practically second nature to Tej. Manohar Mishra, the caretaker, would definitely have some idea, Tej Bahadur was sure of it. Mishra would undoubtedly have an idea about the identity of the entity in the muddy boots.

'I have absolutely no idea,' Manohar Mishra roared. 'I didn't see anyone coming in, or leaving for that matter.' His carefully arranged combover was going haywire as he yelled those words, and his plump face, obtained by a routine of unhealthy eating and a sedentary lifestyle, turned red.

'So, you saw no one?' asked Tej, narrowing his eyes.

'This establishment respects its guests' right to privacy, and I see no reason to divulge who came and who left.'

'This is an investigation into the death of Rai Bahadur,' roared Tej, his voice mirroring his level of frustration.

'He lived alone, and he would visit Azad Manor from time to time since Arjun's return.'

'And …?'

'The last time he came back from the manor, he was blabbering something about how the manor is haunted, how Digvijay Rana has returned from the grave and has asked him to protect his legacy,' he said disdainfully, with a menacing chuckle. 'If you ask me, the old fool was slowly descending into madness.'

A part of Tej, long buried and forgotten, felt an anger rise in his gut as Mishra uttered those words, but he didn't let it overwhelm him.

There was a lot of truth in what Mishra said.

And the truth was always bitter.

'Anything else …?'

Mishra shrugged. 'He would order food sometimes; earlier it was premium dishes, what the whites prefer … chicken and the like, but off late it has only been dal and rice, the fare given to the servants. He would lock his room at night and nobody came to visit him. Ever …' he said, with a sneer. 'Not even his own son.'

The taunt was made in bad taste, but Tej chose to ignore it. His duty as a constable came first.

'And the muddy footprints?' he asked.

'I don't know what else to tell you …' Mishra shrugged. 'I saw nobody come in or leave, especially wearing muddy boots, or coming to visit Rai Bahadur.'

Tej grunted passively. 'In that case, sir, you were either drunk, sleeping or are outright lying, because I cannot believe someone might have walked right past you.'

Mishra glared at him. 'Your father wasn't particularly well-liked, even here; he made a lot of enemies … didn't the old doctor say he died of fright? If I didn't see anyone come in and leave …' Mishra stayed quiet for a second, allowing the meaning of the words to seep into Tej. 'Ironic that the ghost of the person he toadied after the most, the Zamindar, may be the cause of his death. I swear on my dead mother, sir, nobody came in through here … I was here the entire night, and not one living soul came through. As for the dead, I cannot see …' Mishra glared at Tej.

There was a burning anger in Mishra's eyes, seen in men who had secrets in their hearts or honesty on their lips. Tej didn't know which category Manohar Mishra belonged to.

'Tej …' Khuranna called out. 'I'm closing this case as "on account of death from natural causes".'

Tej heard the words, but he didn't want to believe them.

There was more to his father's death, but whether its causes were grounded in the real world or the supernatural were unclear.

'Do you wish to spend some time with him before we take him away?' the doctor checked.

Tej shook his head. 'Load the body,' he instructed his subordinates.

'Let's burn this bastard today,' he mumbled impassively.

eleven

Rai Bahadur wasn't a good man.

While he staunchly followed and believed in outdated principles like loyalty, which he generously dispensed towards the Rana family, those practices didn't necessarily extend to the rest of his life.

Like his own family.

The dark gloom in the sky that extended from the past two days had culminated into an unwelcome rain, permeating through clothing, and leaving a chill in the bones.

The turnout for the funeral surprised Sharvani; it was a known fact that Rai Bahadur wasn't well-liked, but the turnout was far less than what she expected.

Unsurprisingly, Arjun Rana was present.

Along with his loyal manservant Anshul Baghri behind him, unflinchingly holding an umbrella over his master's head.

Unsurprisingly again, Mrs Archana Arjun Rana was conspicuously missing.

The only other person present there was Rai Bahadur's son. Tej Bahadur. In official capacity.

The only thing more frigid than the air was Tej's demeanour towards the turnout.

She watched in silence, as Arjun Rana completed the last rites, a ritual which Tej categorically refused to perform.

All she could see throughout was the blaze in Tej's eyes, as he watched the fire eat up the funeral pyre and the rain slowly, yet surely, quench those flames.

'I'm sorry for your loss,' Sharvani came up to Tej and said. They were both staring at the fire, mesmerized by its hypnotic trance, as it ate away whatever remained of Rai Bahadur.

'You weren't sorry twenty years ago; why are you sorry now?' he said spitefully.

Sharvani remained silent.

The gentle pitter-patter of the rain gnawed away at the last of the dying flames.

'There was no love lost ...' he spoke, after what seemed like an eternity. 'Rai Bahadur wasn't a good man ... he was a womanizer, who gave my mother nothing but grief and me, in that order.'

'Tej ...' she said, her voice brimming with concern.

He didn't let her continue.

'He devoted his entire life to the servitude of the Rana family, neglecting my mother and me in the process.'

Sharvani could make out the hate in his voice; years of frustration had turned to anger and that anger, unchecked for so many years, had paved the way for hate.

'My mother died alone and heartbroken, while my father lay warm in the bosom of another woman,' he said, glaring at Sharvani. Sharvani didn't notice the rain; Tej's piercing gaze and frigid tone were enough to turn the blood in her veins to ice. He didn't need any more words, he had insinuated enough through his behaviour.

Sharvani gulped. A multitude of memories that she had long buried, was beginning to resurface, culminate in a tsunami of emotions, and engulf her in shame, guilt, sadness and regret.

'Tej ... your father ...' she said again, in an attempt to calm him down.

'Rai Bahadur only emptied his seed in my mother ... that's as much right he has to call me his son. The rest of the time, he was busy heating up the nights with some bitch,' he said, once again staring right at Sharvani, his words spitting venom and his eyes brimming with hate.

'I know about the two of you,' he said, through gritted teeth, 'and as far as I'm concerned, you're just as responsible for destroying my family as the Ranas are.'

Sharvani slowly stepped back.

There was a madness in Tej's eyes, one she had seen before, and knew all too well.

'Hello ... what's going on here?'

They both stopped dead in their tracks.

Arjun Rana stood there in his bespoke tailored white suit, with his trademark million-dollar smile plastered on his face.

'Tej was just reliving ... his memories with his father,' interjected Sharvani.

Tej clammed up.

'Oh,' Arjun began, 'sorry about your father, old boy ...' he said, extending his hand towards Tej. 'He was a good man.'

Tej looked at Arjun, then the overstretched hand and then back at Arjun. It was clear that Tej was debating whether or not to accept his condolences, at least to keep up appearances.

The more tactful side won in the end, and he grudgingly shook Arjun's hand for a second, and mumbled some incoherent words about gratitude.

And then there was silence.

There was a palpable tension in the air, none of them wanting to be present in that particular situation.

Arjun was the first to break off. 'Well, I have to rush off ...' he exclaimed, like he suddenly remembered he had a train to catch.

Sharvani raised her eyebrows.

'The reception is still on for tonight, and Archana really wants me to oversee the decorations of the manor,' he said, offering an explanation to Sharvani, even though she hadn't asked for one. 'And believe me, Tej, after I heard about your father's unfortunate passing, this was the last thing on my mind. In fact, I even thought of cancelling it,' he said animatedly, a deep frown plastered on his face.

'Of course you did,' grunted Tej, visibly unconvinced.

'But then we had already sent out the invites, and people are on their way from Bombay and Delhi ... some are coming from as far as Rajasthan, and you know appearance and decorum must be kept ...'

'Of course they must,' Tej grunted lackadaisically.

'After all, keeping one's word is part of the Zamindar's decorum, and that is what, in part, builds a reputation,' he said and grinned. 'And like father used to keep saying ...'

'The Rana family's name is only as good as its reputation,' droned on both Sharvani and Tej apathetically. Sharvani bit her lip to keep from smiling at the irony of the situation. And with those words, a cheerful smile and a wave, Arjun departed, leaving Sharvani and Tej in the exact situation as the one before he joined them.

'Rana family reputation,' scoffed Tej. 'What a joke! What kind of self-entitled prick wears a fucking suit to a fucking funeral?'

'The kind your father ran after, like a lapdog ...'

Tej chuckled.

Sharvani joined him.

'What do you think happened?' she asked quickly.

Tej remained silent.

'Don't be so pigheaded, Tej ...' she pleaded. 'If you harbour animosity against me for what happened, stay mad and remain that way. Your father wasn't necessarily a good man, but he was a brave one. All this business of him being scared to death smells like a week-old dead fish, and your conceited arrogance and misdirected anger are just what the killer is counting on, to slip through your fingers.'

'Digvijay Rana ... the Zamindar's ghost, killed my father,' he grunted, after much deliberation. 'Even after death that man hasn't ceased to be the bane of Ooty and its inhabitants. I don't want to believe it myself, but it appears that we have little else to go by. Like Holmes said, once you eliminate the impossible, whatever remains, no matter how improbable, must be the truth.'

Sharvani narrowed her eyes. 'And the muddy footprints?'

Tej shrugged. 'Mishra eventually admitted to falling asleep. His wife came forward and said she found him slumped over the counter at some point in the night.'

'Mishra's wife?' exclaimed Sharvani. 'That old cow? Figures why Mishra would prefer to sleep over the counter than with her.'

Tej narrowed his eyes, glaring at her. The unintended allusion brought about memories, which Sharvani knew didn't paint her in the most flattering light.

She couldn't explain the situation to him then, for he was too young, and she wouldn't explain the situation to him now, for he wouldn't listen.

'I still can't believe someone's mere presence could drive a man to his death,' she exclaimed quickly, trying to change the topic. 'Poison, maybe?'

Tej shook his head. 'There are no signs of foul play.'

'Dr Khuranna did a full post-mortem. He declared Rai Bahadur to have died of fright,' he commented. 'Nothing could faze that iron-hearted bastard, not the tears of his wife nor the pleadings of his son. That man was vicious. It's funny how his one-time master, the one whom he had served his entire life, came back from beyond the grave to bring about his demise.'

'Seriously, Tej … don't tell me that you believe in that nonsense.'

Tej grinned sardonically. 'You know how people like to talk in Ooty? Rumours spread like wildfire; by now, the entire town will be talking about how the Zamindar's ghost killed Rai Bahadur.'

'You know what I think?' she asked softly.

Tej grunted.

She took it as a sign of his acknowledgement.

'Someplace, beneath all the repressed anger, and all the bad memories, at least you have made peace with your father. He will be happy.'

Tej snorted. 'I wanted to say that I came here only in my official capacity. That I was here because the deceased was a victim in a police case, but I'd be lying.'

Sharvani smiled at the revelation.

'I wanted to watch the bastard burn. I'm laughing inside …' he grunted. 'All those years of neglect, of being treated like I was a mistake … the rains haven't even let the fire do its job properly … even the natural world doesn't want such scum to be purified.'

Sharvani felt a little part of herself die inside when she heard those words. Neglect towards a child had festered into such an abomination of hate, and she could not help but feel partly responsible.

And she hated herself for it.

'But …' said Tej calmly. 'You know the only thing that would make me happier?'

Sharvani smiled. Maybe there was hope for Tej after all.

'What's that?'

'Can you keep a secret?'

'Been doing that all my life,' she said, with a tinge of remorse.

Tej smiled.

'So, what would make you happier?'

'Seeing you burn there along with him,' he said, without remorse.

twelve

Azad Manor was decked up like a blushing bride-to-be. The lights adorning every wall of the manor made it seem like Diwali had come early that year.

Sharvani was pleasantly surprised to see the building this way. She had decided to walk to the manor that night.

For the first time in forty years, there was a traffic jam in the picturesque little town of Ooty.

Sharvani smiled as she sauntered down the streets in the moonlight, welcoming the cool night breeze. The third estate were out in their balconies, witnessing rows and rows of carriages, tongas and the revolutionary horseless carriage, which many in the second estate called the *automobile*. The line was waiting in a seemingly endless, completely still queue, but most of the eyes, both within the transport and outside it, were glued to the sparkling diamond that was Azad Manor.

The lights adorning the manor could be seen for miles. Sharvani made good time, bypassing all the blocked lanes filled with automobiles, the unique modes of transportation that supposedly cut travel time in half on roads, but were also the reason for traffic snarls.

'At least it hasn't rained,' she thought to herself.

And then the drizzling started.

She smiled. She was in the mood to tempt fate.

'At least it can't get any worse.'

She passed the rows of guests at the entrance of the manor, each one exiting their mode of transportation and then moving into the manor. Only one horse-drawn carriage, black as the night, stood stationary, a little distance away from the doors of the manor.

Its driver, Eric Matheson, had a blacker heart, she thought. Her mood instantly turned sour when she looked at Eric, who shot her a dirty glare before turning his attention back to the horses.

She averted her eyes instinctively, lest she be unable to control her anger at the man. He looked ill at ease in his awkwardly fitted suit, worn no doubt on the instructions of the owner of the manor.

She looked at the crowd inside the manor. One glance and she wished she were anywhere but there.

The hall was decorated tastefully, just short of becoming gaudy. It was chock-a-block with British diplomats, emissaries, Indian landowners and Maharajas or their representatives.

She had known many of them intimately during the course of her life, and had hoped to never cross paths with them again.

But life, as it were, had other plans.

For half of the people there, plastic grins and superficial pleasantries were the norm of the night. Sharvani did her best to blend in, and put on her best plastic smile, which complemented her hourglass figure, perfectly accentuated by a dress that she had last worn twenty years ago.

The first hour passed in a blur and a flurry of specious, fallacious pleasantries, handshakes and kisses; the only thing that kept her going was the copious amount of alcohol that seemed to be flowing freely.

She had always been one who was able to hold her liquor, consistently surpassing her male lovers when it came to alcohol tolerance and capacity. She learnt through the years what her threshold was, and fortunately for her, alcohol seemed to sharpen her senses rather than dull them, so she didn't mind indulging in the habit.

And the affinity towards alcohol, especially when it was free, extended itself to other guests as well.

Including one guest, much younger than what was to be considered the proper drinking age.

Vijay was lost amongst the throng of guests. His small, sinewy figure made it easy for him to zip through the guests. He looked smart in a blazer and shorts which, judging from their condition, must have been hand-me-downs. His hands were wrapped around a glass filled with an amber liquid, which she guessed wasn't apple juice.

Vijay took a small sip and his face looked like he had bitten into a sharp lemon, but he persisted nonetheless, taking another gulp. Before the third sip, however, the glass was out of his hand and his ears turned red, as he let out a stifled, startled yelp.

'I thought it was juice,' he stammered, as Sharvani pulled his ear even tighter. She downed his drink in one quick sip.

She felt the all too familiar burn go down her body.

'Juice, is it?'

He shook his head in disagreement.

'Then why did you take another sip?'

'Just making sure it wasn't juice.' She pulled his ear tighter as she dragged him through the crowd.

'There you are,' cried a visibly relieved Ishita Dhiman, as she pushed through the crowd. The matron seemed completely out of place at the reception. She was still dressed in her usual drab garb, with her head bandaged and arm in a sling.

'Where did you disappear off to?' she admonished the boy before hugging him tightly. 'Run along now ... find your friends. Your performance will be on shortly.'

He smiled warmly at Ishita, before sticking his tongue out at Sharvani, and scurrying through the crowd of black tails and gowns.

'So, you listened to Arjun?'

Ishita smiled and nodded. 'The children will perform a very popular English song.'

Sharvani shrugged. 'That must have taken some doing.'

'Well ...' Ishita replied good-naturedly, 'who can refuse the Zamindar?'

Sharvani smiled, acknowledging the truth in that statement.

'It's a full house today ...' Ishita commented. 'I hope some of them decide to give the children a good home, or at least a generous donation to the orphanage; it is literally on its last legs.'

Sharvani looked over her pupil's shoulders. Vijay hadn't gone to his friends like Ishita had instructed him to, but had made a beeline for the bar and flicked another glass of whiskey, which he was using to wash down the pastries he was gorging on.

'I don't think anybody would want to adopt that little troublemaker ...'

'MISS MEHRA!' Ishita said sternly, loud enough for the people next to her to hear. 'I'm ... I'm sorry,' she added quickly. 'You cannot begin to imagine what the boy has been through.'

'He is different, isn't he?'

Ishita nodded. 'He has had a hard time adjusting. He was transferred here from the Venkatesh Care Home and Orphanage in Nilgiri.'

'Oh ...' Sharvani exclaimed. 'The one that was engulfed in that terrible fire a few years ago?'

'The very same,' Ishita said sadly. 'Nobody but him survived; he was barely two years old. He was transferred as per protocol, to the closest orphanage.'

'Digvijay Rana Orphanage.'

She nodded. 'He just needs some love and guidance ... he will come around.'

'FUCK YOU and FUCK YOUR REPUTATION.' The shrill cry broke through the jovial murmurs and conversations running through the crowded hall.

And just like that, the crowd went silent.

So silent that Sharvani could have heard a pin drop.

All eyes were on the man who wouldn't stop yelling.

Alexander Stephan.

'YOUR FATHER WAS THE BIGGEST MENACE IN OOTY ... WHAT HE COULDN'T GET, HE WOULD SNATCH ... AND YOU. A BASTARD SON JUST FURTHERING THAT LINEAGE ...' Stephan roared, his face turning beet red with anger.

'Kindly leave, sir; you are upsetting my guests and ruining their evening. I don't encourage such a tone or such wrongful accusations about my father or the family name,' Arjun replied calmly. 'You must thank your lucky stars that I'm in a good mood today, but rest assured, your words will have consequences. I will make sure of it.' His tone hadn't changed, but the words had a sinister tinge in them.

They sounded like a threat.

'Besides, why must I be bothered by someone whose main source of income comes from abusing young girls and forcing them into the flesh trade?' Arjun continued with an uncharacteristic confidence.

'HOW ... DARE ... YOU?' Stephan's words were deliberately slow. His tone had calmed down, but his rage was just as apparent.

'You come here with your despicable offers and expect me to accept it and roll over?'

'Your father …' Stephan said through gritted teeth. 'He was the one who picked out and broke in half of the girls in the business.'

'GET … OUT!' Arjun growled. The anger in his voice was restrained, but the veins in his neck were beginning to pop out.

Stephan sneered. 'This party was getting a little too stale for my taste anyway,' he grunted as he turned around and walked away in a huff.

Only to bump straight into Anshul Baghri and fall backwards. The butler had his hands full. A tray full of filled champagne glasses flew through the air, as Stephan nursed his bruised backside and ego.

The silent crowd now burst out into an uproarious laughter.

'I'm … I'm so terribly sorry, sir,' Anshul mumbled, as he walked over to help the Englishman up.

'Leave him, Anshul,' Arjun commanded. 'I'm sure the gentleman is capable of handling himself well, even if he's had a little too much of my free liquor,' he smirked.

The crowd laughed again.

Arjun looked at Sharvani. 'It's good to know that I'm not the only clumsy person in Ooty,' he said with a wink.

People laughed again, not completely understanding the inside joke. The chuckles and guffaws seemed forced, but they laughed anyway.

Nobody wanted to risk getting onto the new Zamindar's bad side.

His father's reputation and the power the title wielded preceded him.

'Such sycophants,' Sharvani whispered, looking at Ishita, but her ward was already out of earshot. She was already on her knees, helping the portly Englishman back on his feet.

Sharvani sighed, nonverbally expressing her displeasure.

Sometimes, Ishita was just too nice.

'Get your hands off me, you pathetic failure,' he said, as he violently let go of her hand, only *after* he had used it to support himself back up.

'I believe you were on your way out, Mr Stephan,' Arjun said in an ice-cold tone, as he stepped in to defend his friend. 'And look on the bright side: you'll avoid the rush hour back home,' Sharvani added.

'Nothing to look alarmed about, folks,' Arjun said, addressing the crowd. 'Our little friend here has just had a drop too much to drink ... please continue to enjoy this wonderful evening ... we will be serving a surprise for dessert: fresh strawberry cream cake, just like you have in merry ol' England.'

The crowd cheered, raising their glasses, and then went back to their mingling. The unfortunate little incident was all but forgotten.

'I'm sorry you had to hear that, Ishita,' Arjun calmly said, as he placed a hand over her shoulder.

She was frowning.

'All I was trying to do was help him ...' she stuttered.

Sharvani assessed the damage: bits of glass were on the floor, and a cigarette lay among it. She picked it up nonchalantly.

Maspero Gold.

She smiled. It was her favourite brand.

'I thought that man only smoked cigars,' she said, as she brought the cigarette to her lips.

'He might be scaling back a bit due to his failing business,' Arjun jested, as he pulled out a lighter and helped Sharvani with a light.

Neither Sharvani nor Ishita laughed. They didn't need to prove anything to Arjun Rana, nor would they incur his wrath.

Ishita smiled from the corner of her mouth. 'Chivalry isn't dead,' she remarked, but a fraction of a second later, her expression turned grim.

'MISS MEHRA ...' she chided. 'That's a deplorable habit.'

Sharvani smiled at her. 'Well, the Britishers say differently ... they say smoking relieves stress and promotes a sense of well-being,' she chuckled. 'And I recall you hated the smell of it, even when you were younger.'

'That's right …' guffawed Arjun. 'You would run like your skirt was on fire to escape Miss Mehra's smoky breath.'

'Well, if anything …' Ishita retorted, 'you must thank Miss Mehra's breath for not getting me into this filthy habit. It's quite a part of the lifestyle in Bombay.'

'Pardon me, madam…' Anshul walked up to them. 'The little masters and misses are getting a tad bit restless.'

Ishita acknowledged his words, apologized and assured him she would resolve the issue.

'It's way past their bedtime …' Ishita explained. 'They are not used to staying up so late … it gets them … cranky,' she said softly, as she quickly turned to Arjun. 'Apologies, my lord; I'll admonish them immediately.'

'Nonsense, Ishita …' he grinned wide. 'If anything, I must apologize. I invited the children and you over to perform as my guests, and yet you're here, waiting.'

'Why haven't they performed?' asked Sharvani.

'Archana hasn't come down yet. I have to give a homecoming speech as well. It's nearly finished … just a few touches are remaining. I was hoping to give it after the children's performance.'

'Well, ask her to come down then,' Sharvani said matter-of-factly.

'I did …' he said shrugging his shoulders. 'Thrice,' he raised an equal number of fingers for added effect.

'Maybe if Ishita could come up and help convince her …' he suggested, scratching his head as if he had a sudden brainstorm.

Sharvani smiled. Arjun's eyes had the same mischievous glint as they did when he was boy.

Ishita would join, but she would need some coercing.

Her first reaction would be 'no', surmised Sharvani.

'No, my lord …' Ishita said on cue. Sharvani smiled; there was nothing about this girl she didn't know.

'Arjun.'

'No, Arjun,' Ishita corrected herself quickly. '…I'm sure she will come down soon enough.'

'Oh, come on … she was your best friend in school. Plus, you can tell her about the plight of the children, their bedtime and crankiness, and I'm betting that would be more persuasive than my patience.'

Sharvani smiled again.

It was playing out exactly like it had countless times before, in their childhood.

Arjun would propose a plan.

Ishita would be hesitant.

And finally, Archana would coerce her into doing it.

The three were inseparable.

'I don't think it is truly right for me to disturb our hostess like this,' Ishita thought out loud.

Archana wasn't there for coercion this time around, thought Sharvani. So, she would have to step in.

'Well, if I recall correctly, it wasn't too long ago that you used to sling mud, quite literally, at the other children with your hostess … you were so close to her that there were times when you used to follow her like a shadow, sleeping and cuddling up next to her on the nights I told you ghost stories …' she chuckled.

'Miss Mehra …' Ishita said with a slight smile, turning red in the face.

'You used to be scared stiff … her parents didn't approve of their daughter mingling with such commoners, apparently, but Archana was adamant … spending nights at the orphanage, making sure you weren't scared.'

Ishita gave a bittersweet smile, as her teacher's words reminded her of the happier times she spent at the orphanage. 'A lot has changed since then, Miss Mehra; we are now aware of our positions and stations in life.' The words were filled with hurt, Sharvani knew that, but the reason was still a mystery to her.

But Arjun would have none of it. Without warning, he grabbed Ishita's hand and pulled her up the stairs.

'Etiquette be damned; all three of us were, are, and will remain close friends.'

'That's no reason to forget our statuses ...' Ishita tried to protest, but her words fell on deaf ears, as Arjun led her up towards Archana's room.

'Then you should start calling me Chessboard again,' he retorted playfully.

Ishita couldn't help but stifle a giggle.

The old lady smiled to herself as she saw her two favourite students saunter up the stairs. They were always fond of each other as students. Sharvani even once felt that they would end up together, but the universe, obviously, had other plans.

Life with all its idiosyncrasies and societal constraints like class, position and power had separated two pure souls.

But they were both happier for it.

Still, Sharvani couldn't help but think of the outcome, had they taken the road less traversed.

'Well, aren't you looking particularly stunning?' a voice called out to Sharvani from the crowd.

The slightly inebriated Dr Khuranna stumbled into view; the alcohol had made his bulbous nose turn even redder. His bowtie was undone and his scant hair ruffled, but his everlasting smile was broader than ever.

'Well, you certainly have had a good evening,' she answered him with a deadpan expression on her face.

'Well …' he said, as he rambled on, coming in closer to her, a little too close for comfort. 'We can make it a good night as well.' In an attempt to flirt, he winked lecherously.

His breath reeked of alcohol and chicken kebabs.

Sharvani would have considered the proposal had she been ten drinks down or ten years younger; it had been a while since she had indulged in activities of a more sexual nature.

But, as it stood, she wasn't interested.

'Excuse me, Doctor …' she said dryly, 'but I think I spot a lone glass of whiskey which needs my attention,' and turned to walk away.

Khuranna grabbed her hand violently. 'You think you can just brush me off like that?' There was anger in his voice, a knee-jerk reaction to the blow to his ego.

Rejection, as she had come to learn, was not something men took well.

A man's ego was just as fragile as a woman's heart. She had learnt to protect hers and stroke the male ego perfectly in her wonder years.

But today, she wasn't feeling particularly charitable.

'I'm a doctor,' Khuranna grunted. 'Granted, I may not be as powerful or influential as the other men you have been with,' his speech was slurred. 'I may not be a diplomat, an army general … hic … an … an emissary or a fucking Zamindar, for that matter, but I can … I can make you happy.' His eyes were red, perhaps from the alcohol or anger towards her—she did not know.

And she didn't care.

'Let go,' she cried as she felt his grip tighten around her wrist.

'I love you, Sharvani Mehra,' he pleaded. 'I have always loved you.' There was a quiet desperation in his voice, one that drowned out the murmur of the crowd.

But even that didn't elicit any emotion within Sharvani.

Except pity.

She had let go of love ages ago; it was an emotion which was dead inside of her, and would require more than a pathetic, aging doctor to stir.

'I've watched you from afar ...' he half rambled and half slurred. 'Even when you were busy with your countless affairs with the British, with Rai Bahadur, with some lord who came to Ooty for a visit, and countless others ... even Digvijay Rana ...'

'How dare you?' she gasped.

Sharvani was shocked.

Not at these accusations, for she knew very well that they were true.

But at his intimate knowledge of such things.

'What is it that I don't have?' he mumbled. 'Why won't you love me?'

'You don't have power,' she replied coldly.

'Everything okay here?' Tej spoke up assertively. He had manoeuvred through the crowd, silently, like a snake in the grass, and observed the turn of events for longer than required.

For the first time that night, Sharvani was glad to see a known face.

'Yes ...' Dr Khuranna stuttered. 'I was just educating Miss Mehra on the finer points of British wine.'

'And he was just leaving ...' she added dryly.

'Yes ... yes ... I was,' Khuranna said, dejectedly. 'Have a good evening,' he mumbled incoherently as he disappeared into the crowd. After a long, long time, there was finally a frown on his jovial face.

His frown made Sharvani smile.

'Does everyone's life you enter culminate in disappointment?' asked Tej dryly.

Sharvani wanted to thank him for the timely intervention, but his words made her reconsider.

'Tej, why are you here?'

'Last I checked, you weren't the host.'

'Still ...'

'I have learnt through reliable sources that the Revolutionaries'
spy ...'

She rolled her eyes. 'Not this again ...' she sighed.

'Besides, I'm the head constable. A lot of important people are
present here and, if I'm honest, I'm not entirely pleased about keeping
such a grand party at a manor that is allegedly haunted and certainly
harbouring a murder suspect.'

'Because of the gardener's boots?' she asked.

'Because of the gardener's boots.'

She rolled her eyes.

'To be honest, we don't have another suspect and, besides, if it
weren't for me, who would have bailed you out of that particularly
sticky situation?'

She nodded in acknowledgement.

'Never got around to thank you for that.'

'No, you didn't.'

Apparently, that was all the thanks he was going to get.

'While your theory on the manor being haunted is ... interesting, I
wonder why the Ranas chose to keep Eric around, at least for tonight?
I noticed him waiting outside, by the reins of some carriage.'

'I inquired about that; he is the chauffeur for Ishita and the children.'

Sharvani was surprised to hear that, but she didn't let it show.
'Pretty dodgy, relying on a prime suspect in an assault and murder case
to take the children home.'

'*Only* suspect,' he corrected her, 'but it's just a way for his master to
publicly show his trust in him.'

'The gardener,' Sharvani scoffed. 'I still wonder what his motive
was ... In all the crime novels that I have read, it is always the butler

who did it. I wonder why Arjun agreed to such a thing? Choosing him of all people, to safeguard the children.'

'Archana,' he replied blankly.

'And why would Archana?'

'Well …' he shrugged and said as he pointed at the stairs. 'You can ask her that yourself.'

Archana Rana was dressed in a dazzling, golden gown. She looked ethereal from afar.

Her make-up was perfect, and her walk slightly wobbly. Ishita stood behind her, her one good arm fastened safely over Archana's shoulders, as she helped her childhood friend down the stairs.

Archana was drunk.

It was crystal clear to Sharvani, but not so much to the rest of the guests. She wasn't able to walk in a straight line, and would have probably tripped down the stairs if it weren't for Ishita's meticulous guidance.

Sharvani excused herself from Tej, and moved over closer to the bottom of the stairs, near her erstwhile students.

'Get your hand off me …' she could hear Archana's slurred speech. 'My good-for-nothing husband was incapable of bringing me down, so he had to send lowly, common scum, and a cripple that too? You always had eyes on Arjun, didn't you? Ever since we were little, you little gold-digging bitch! But guess what?' Archana slurred, a trickle of drool running down her lip. 'The best girl won; Arjun is mine …' she hissed. 'Arjun and all that he owns, is all mine!'

Her speech was slurred but it seemed that she was thinking out loud, the alcohol numbing her ability to be politically correct. But her voice was down, and not many could hear her words.

Except the ones closest to her.

Sharvani could see a tear trickle from Ishita's eye. It wasn't the words that hurt as much as the person who spoke them. There was a time when Archana wouldn't think twice before giving her life for her friend, and to hear this from her childhood friend shattered poor Ishita's heart. Archana immediately shrugged off her friend's support when she reached downstairs, like Ishita was no more than yesterday's dandruff.

Archana immediately slid into the role of a charming hostess, smiling, posing and kissing cheeks, as she greeted her guests. She had seen her old teacher and conveniently ignored her.

'Are you okay?' Sharvani asked Ishita.

Ishita nodded, wiping off her tears. 'She's just a little overwhelmed by Arjun's sudden reappearance, I guess? She didn't mean those words.'

Both of them knew Ishita was lying.

Sharvani shot a hateful glance at Archana, who was busy mingling with her guests. She was flocked by a group of males, all of them surrounding her like bees attracted to honey. She was clearly enjoying the attention dolloped on her, giggling and laughing at the secrets whispered in her ear as they surrounded her, copping a feel and touching her inappropriately on the pretext of being 'friendly'.

But it didn't look like the mistress of Azad Manor seemed to mind. Conversely, she seemed to be enjoying the covert touches.

'Doesn't look like she's missing Arjun much …' remarked Sharvani coldly. 'Where is he though?'

Ishita's didn't reply. Her eyes were transfixed on Archana and her bevy of admirers.

'Ishita …' Sharvani said, louder this time.

'Huh?'

'Arjun?'

'Yes?'

'Where is he?'

'In his study …' she replied quickly, turning her gaze back onto Archana. 'He said he wanted to put in the final touches to his homecoming speech.'

'Hmmm ...' Sharvani turned her gaze towards the study.

'If you'll excuse me,' Ishita said hurriedly, 'I must prepare the children for their little programme.'

'Of course,' Sharvani said with a smile. 'Do you need help?'

'I'd appreciate it.'

The festivities of the evening were now on in full swing.

The children started singing. The songs were traditional English ballads, keeping in mind the sensibilities of the guests.

Ishita Dhiman was proud of her wards, as Sharvani Mehra was proud of hers. Truly, Ishita had blossomed into her own woman. She had worked tirelessly with them—it had taken several hours to refine and perfect their pronunciations and hit the high and low notes of the song just right.

And she had succeeded.

The children didn't miss a beat, and the song played out just as well as Flanagan and Allen, if not better.

'I'm surprised you managed to get them to perform so well,' Sharvani said with a broad grin across her face.

'Just some love and understanding, Miss Mehra; that's all it takes.'

'And not bare-bottom spanking?' Sharvani asked, with mock surprise.

Ishita chuckled.

'Well ... that depends really ... on ...' but she never got to complete her sentence, as the manor was suddenly bathed in darkness.

All the bright lights were killed instantaneously, engulfing the entire manor in pitch darkness.

There was a confused murmur among the crowd, followed by a shrill, unearthly scream.

The lights came back on just in time for the entire crowd to see the body of Arjun Rana being flung off the first-floor railing, and come crashing down on the buffet table.

The cacophony of glass shattering was interspersed with the shrill screams of terror.

One sound, fleeting as it was, completely stood out from the racket: the sound of Rana's neck snapping, as it hit the table.

Silence engulfed the room for a second.

It seemed like an hour.

And then, Archana Rana screamed.

Her screeching cry pulled the other guests out of their trance.

'The curse of the Zamindar's ghost,' someone from the crowd yelled. The children became hysterical; their young minds had never been subjected to horror like the one they had just witnessed. Ishita reacted instantly, moving into damage-control mode, consoling the children, and trying to shield them from the gruesome sight, but it was a second too late. The macabre sight of Arjun's body thrown through the air would be forever etched onto their impressionable little minds.

Sharvani and Tej reacted as well. But only in a way they were accustomed to; they fought against the crowd and rushed up the stairs.

If Arjun Rana was flung off the stairs with such ferocity, it wasn't without the machination of an outside force.

Tej had his baton ready as they entered the dimly lit study where Arjun Rana was, not minutes ago. There were papers on his desk: Arjun Rana's homecoming speech, his unfinished symphony, so to speak. Other than that, there were no signs of a struggle.

Just the ominous muddy boot prints that led towards the expansive French windows.

Tej rushed to the windows, and looked through the glass panels at the muddy prints that led outside the study, into the balcony. He pushed the door handles, which rattled, refusing to budge.

'Strange,' he thought. The doors were locked.

From inside.

He looked behind him. Sharvani was already present, surveying the scene.

And she was equally flabbergasted.

The trail of footprints seemed to originate out of thin air, and end past the parapet beyond the windows.

Tej rattled the locked windows again, and then looked at Sharvani. She nodded.

The time for tact had passed.

With one strong push, the lock gave way, and Tej was outside.

It started raining, and the trail of muddy footprints began to fade, washed away by the tears of the sky.

Tej moved to the balcony and looked down. There was only the carriage and its dubious driver, Eric Matheson, sitting at the reins.

'The trail ends here,' Tej cried.

Sharvani rushed out and headed downstairs, pushing and shoving guests aside like they were no more than cattle. Outside, what had begun as a light drizzle, slowly progressed and turned into a storm. Sharvani felt like a hundred hungry hornets were stinging her as the droplets hit her face and body.

'Only an idiot would be out here,' she muttered and a second later, she was proved right.

Alexander Stephan stood there, his back against the wall, and his hands clutched around the lapels of his coat, a thick cigar burning between his teeth.

'Why are you still here?' she asked him coldly, as she looked over his shoulder, towards the carriage. It was still in the same place as it was when she entered the manor, with the driver rooted in place as well.

In the ubiquitous light of the moon, coupled with the manor's decoration, there was no mistaking it. It was Eric Matheson at the helm of the carriage.

She turned her attention back to Stephan.

'What do you mean "why"?' he asked, visibly insulted.

'Why are you here?' she asked again, through gritted teeth. Stephan knew better than to argue.

'It was a nice night to enjoy the view, and I wanted to ...'

'Quit the bullshit, Stephan,' she retorted, exasperated. 'This is the worst night to be caught outside ... but you stay right where you are,' she warned him, as she ran through the rain pointing a mean finger at him. 'I'm not done with you yet.'

There were a hundred thoughts running through her head. 'How had the footprints come to be and how did they disappear?'

She was visibly out of breath when she reached the carriage.

'Top of the evening to ya, Miss Mehra,' Eric cried with a plastic smile. 'What brings you out here, this luverly evening?'

'Quit it, Matheson,' she huffed. 'I know your game.'

He looked at her, visibly confused. 'Why miss ... whatever is it that you're going on about?'

Sharvani ignored him for the moment. She would deal with his bullshit later.

She looked up; the carriage was parked exactly under the balcony outside Arjun Rana's study.

She looked around; there was a trail of footprints.

It was slight, almost undetectable. She reckoned that she caught on only because she knew what to look for. Anybody else would have missed it, and the heavy rain wasn't helping much. A few more minutes, and the footprints would've been gone forever.

She cursed her luck. The footprints disappeared into the surrounding foliage, in the very same direction where Digvijay Rana had wandered off years ago, and slit his own throat.

She looked around furiously. First at Matheson, who still looked genuinely befuddled, and then back at the trail. Her head ached, as she focused her eyes intently.

There was a faint trail of footprints leading *away* from the carriage, but nothing coming back.

'Did you see anyone go this way?' she asked him quickly.

'No … not a solitary soul,' he began. 'I've been alone in this chilly rain all night, without a drink to give me company or warmth ... I …'

'Shut it,' she hissed. 'Answer only what you've been asked.'

He nodded sheepishly.

'Did you move from your seat at all?'

'No, miss …' he said, shaking his head vigorously. 'Cross my heart and hope to die … I have not moved a single muscle; my bladder's bout to give way. It is, but I still haven't moved at all …'

'Eric …' she said with a loving smile.

'Yes miss?' he smiled back.

'What the fuck did I just say about only answering what you've been asked?' she screeched.

Eric stayed silent, startled by her hysterical outbreak.

'Don't you move …' she warned him as she moved away from the carriage, towards the manor.

'But I need to pee …' he complained.

'Pee your pants, you sod bastard. No one will know in the rain,' she roared.

The ambience inside the manor had plunged from jovial to hysterical in a matter of minutes.

One minute ended the life of Arjun Rana, the Zamindar of Ooty.

And that one minute would, in turn, change the fate of Ooty.

Tej Bahadur sent word through one of the servants. The rest of Ooty's meagre police force would be joining him shortly. The manor was now a hub of activity, with an incessant buzzing filling the air, from each of the terrified dignitaries present there.

Tej stood at the door, allowing Sharvani in, but none of the others present at the manor, out.

'Stephan and Matheson are outside,' she said, trying to catch her breath.

'Stephan?' exclaimed Tej. 'But I thought he was …'

'Me too … I'll explain later.'

Tej opened the door and peeked outside. His backup had arrived.

He felt his chest swell with pride, and a satisfied smile crept up on his face.

Even with the deluge, his subordinates had taken less than ten minutes to arrive at the scene. More importantly, they rounded up both Stephan and Matheson and from the looks on their faces, both the Britishers were less than pleased about the situation. He allowed some of the constables inside before closing the door behind them.

The police immediately began rounding up the guests, despite their heavy protests.

'Archana would have a fit if she saw how we were treating her guests,' Sharvani remarked sharply.

'Good thing she's fainted then,' Tej replied dryly, as he stood in the way of another middle-ranking diplomat, who was trying to leave. One stern look and a raised baton was enough to convince the Britisher to turn tail.

'Fainted?' she exclaimed. 'When?'

He shrugged. 'Just moments after her husband was flung off the first floor of his house. The servants are tending to her.'

'What do you think?'

'Khuranna had a look at the body. He said the impact from the fall broke his neck. He's of the opinion that Rana was alive when he went off the railing, but this is only his preliminary assessment. He isn't in the … best of conditions to judge.'

She nodded. 'So I've noticed.'

'What do you really think?' she asked again.

He shrugged. 'You saw what I saw: the footprints appear out of nowhere and disappear …' he waited for her to finish his sentence.

'They disappeared into the foliage. True, they originate at Rana's desk and move to the windows outside Rana's study and then next to the carriage outside the manor, but then they move towards the foliage in the dark and then…' she trailed off.

'And then … ?'

'… nothing comes back.'

'You're sure about that?'

She nodded. 'By the time you get there, the rain would have wiped clear all remnants of the prints.'

Tej groaned, but didn't say anything.

'It's Eric then,' he muttered after a moment.

'He claims to have not moved the entire night, seen nothing, and the footprints, well, they go away from the carriage, but not back towards it.'

'Eric is the only one with enough strength to have thrown the body with such force that it travelled such a distance. That or something …' he didn't complete the sentence.

'You don't really think … ?'

'The footprints originate from thin air, only to disappear into the forest where the Zamindar killed himself. That doesn't bode well.'

She could make out from his tone that he was considering the supernatural element that surrounded Arjun Rana's death. And if she was honest to herself, so was she.

'The doors were locked from inside, Miss Mehra … *inside*,' he repeated, emphasizing the word. 'There was no struggle, nothing. I can only think of Eric, because if not him, nobody in this town would have the strength to throw a full-grown man with such force and velocity. Nobody other than …'

'The Zamindar's ghost,' Sharvani mumbled.

thirteen

I t was going to be a long night.

Sharvani knew this the moment Arjun Rana's body was flung off from the balcony.

The remainder of the night had been a logistical nightmare.

More than a hundred and fifty of India's and Britain's elite were herded through the different rooms of the mansion by a severely understaffed police force.

Threats of transfer, death and more than a thousand variations of 'Do you know who I am and what I can do?' later, there was some semblance of order.

Tej Bahadur insisted that this was the work of the Revolutionaries' spy, despite Sharvani's repeated logical protests that spoke to the contrary.

All the guests were ushered into different rooms, and a sub-constable each was made responsible for taking statements and the subsequent interrogations.

Sharvani knew this to be no more than an exercise in futility, but she didn't want to ruffle Tej's feathers.

She could see the glint in his eyes, and the feeling of power, as he ordered dignitaries and landowners to be pushed around like cattle.

Apparently, the apple didn't fall far from the tree.

She stayed mum throughout; he allowed her to sit in on the interrogations as a personal favour to her, although they both knew it would be Sharvani doing him the favour by picking up on subtleties that he could miss, or look closely for the overlooked.

She hadn't bothered sticking around in one of the umpteen rooms where statements of the other guests were being recorded.

She was where she was supposed to be: in an empty, forgotten room, in some obscure corner of the manor, surrounded by dusty furniture, a wooden table, a single light bulb and Eric Matheson.

Only the statements of two people interested her at this point.

Eric Matheson was the first.

The gardener had a scowl on his face. His muscles were bulging under his ill-fitted shirt, and his veins popped. He was grunting like a wild animal.

'Why am I here?' he growled.

'Your master, Arjun, is dead,' Tej said calmly.

'God rest his soul then,' he grunted in response, but his demeanour, expression and tone all suggested otherwise.

'We have a few questions for you,' Tej continued.

'Bugger off,' he grumbled, spitting on the floor.

'Excuse me?'

'Arjun Rana died in the manor ... *inside*, and I was *outside* the manor. I can guess that such a concept might be difficult for you to grasp, but inside and outside are two different places,' he snarled, a smirk appearing on his face.

He grinned at Sharvani.

She remained stoic.

Tej followed suit.

The seconds passed like hours, until Matheson spoke again.

'Why am I here again?' he roared. 'There were more than a hundred guests inside the manor. I was outside, and yet here I am being interrogated.'

'You're not a guest,' Tej replied unperturbed. He chose to keep out the part about the other guests being interrogated in the other rooms, much to Sharvani's relief.

'What do you know about the Revolutionaries' spy?'

Eric stared at him, visibly confused.

Sharvani massaged her forehead in apathy. Tej wasn't willing to listen to reason. He was always doing what he thought was right.

Until he would be irrevocably proven wrong.

Just like his father.

'What spy man? What in bollocks are ye yapping about?' Eric growled. 'You have me singled out for no fault of my own. But I know … you're only doing it because I'm white, aren't you? And not blue-blooded, ain't that right?'

He had chosen to play the racism card, that too in reverse. Sharvani raised her eyebrows; she was impressed.

'No …' Tej grunted back. 'It has nothing to do with your heritage or class, but the fact that you are implicated in two separate cases: the assault on Ishita Dhiman, and the alleged murder of Arjun Digvijay Rana, which kind of leans towards you being singled out.'

Well done, thought Sharvani. She didn't expect Tej to give such a response. Evidently, this was a night of surprises.

'Hah,' scoffed Eric. 'You and I both know that the only reason I'm here is because of your shoddy police work and because you need a soft target to blame,' he said with a disdainful chuckle.

'Soft target?' Tej mumbled sardonically. 'I knew you would be trouble ever since you stepped foot into this town. I ran a little background check on you; you have multiple criminal charges pending against you ...' Tej said, nary an emotion in his voice.

'Assault, extortion, robbery, blackmail ...' Tej continued, counting the misdemeanours on his fingers. 'It wouldn't be too far a stretch to add murder to this list ...'

'All lies ... slander to spoil my reputation,' Eric groaned. The veins on his neck were bulging, and there was rage in his voice, like that of a caged animal who was under control, but only for the moment. 'None of them, not a single one's been proven ...'

'That may be true ...' replied Tej calmly, 'but that was only because some witnesses changed their statements at the last minute ...'

'While others may have conveniently developed amnesia,' Sharvani remarked snidely.

'The cases pending against you are from all over ... Delhi, Bombay, Calcutta ...' Tej went on, 'you've been around, haven't you?'

'None of the past matters ...' Eric spat out. 'The Ranas have been good to me, they've! My employers knew of my alleged chalky past, and yet they chose to give me a chance to stand on my feet. They trusted me, and they still do ...' he said earnestly.

Sharvani wasn't sure if Matheson was putting on an act, because if he were, he was surely doing a good job. Perhaps he could try his hand at theatre, for he'd be good at it.

'The only reason that I'm wrongly placed here is my bad luck. In the Ishita Dhiman case, my employers vouched for me; it was proven that I wasn't in the location in question. So, I fail to see what else is required of me. The only way I can be of some good here is if you leave the good teacher and me alone for about twenty minutes,' he said, as he smiled lecherously. 'Or, on second thought, make it thirty, and lock the door behind you.'

Sharvani looked at him with disgust.

Tej sighed. 'Forget the other time, let's talk about tonight.'

'Yes, let's …' grunted Eric, 'because so far, we have been yapping about the weather, haven't we?'

'How can you prove that you did not put on those boots before climbing into the study, and throwing Arjun Rana off the railing? Only a few men present here have that kind of strength.'

Hearing his words, Eric laughed uproariously. 'Are you fucking daft, man? The footprints show the movement going clearly into another side, towards the forest, *away* from where I was seated. It can't have possibly been me.'

'And yet you conveniently saw nothing …'

'There was nothing to see … I swear it. Those prints appeared out of thin air… like magic, or a … ghost.'

Tej began massaging his forehead furiously; as much as he wanted to, he couldn't deny Eric's explanation. 'But you wear those boots, and the prints match …'

Eric shrugged. 'Being a gardener, sometimes, as strange as it may sound, I have to wear gardener's boots,' he grunted. 'And about my physique …' he said, staring angrily at Tej, the contempt growing in his eyes. 'Well, I won't even dignify that with a response.'

Tej sighed. 'Help us help you … tell us the truth.'

Eric looked at him, heaving out a deep sigh as well. 'Look, Rai Bahadur was good to me …' he began.

Sharvani moved in closer, listening to him intently.

Why bring this up now, she wondered. What was Eric Matheson's game?

'Your father, God rest his soul, used to talk about the manor being haunted. You can ask the other servants if you don't believe me.'

One look at Tej, and it was clear to Sharvani that he did believe the gardener.

'He was worried that Digvijay Rana put a curse on this house and that his ghost still roamed around. Rai Bahadur died of fright, didn't he?'

Tej didn't respond, but through his demeanour, Sharvani could make out he was buying into the British gardener's words.

'I'm telling you, consider the other aspects of the case with care. Your father's words, his mysterious death, the lights going off suddenly, and now Arjun's death.'

'That's absurd,' Tej cried.

'Is it really?' asked Eric, staring at Tej. 'But that's not all … the most telltale giveaway,' Eric said with a sinister tinge in his voice which previously wasn't there, 'are the muddy footprints.'

'What?'

'Think about it for a moment, sir,' he said pleadingly, his voice now a bit more timid than usual.

He was neatly trying to sell them the idea of the Zamindar's ghost, but Sharvani wasn't buying it.

'Before me, there was no gardener in the Rana household.'

Tej nodded, acknowledging Eric's point. There was no gardener for Azad Manor, prior to Matheson.

'That's because the Zamindar would tend to all his plants himself. The servants all talk about it, as does Miss Rana, when she's feeling a wee more … talkative, but trust me, sir, all the words I speak are naught if not true, else lightning strike me down at this very spot.'

'Go on …' said Tej, twirling his moustache.

'It was a night very much like this, a few years before Master Arjun's disappearance …'

'From Arjun, to Master Arjun now? Interesting,' Sharvani thought.

'There was a scandal, sir.'

'What scandal?'

'Be the death of me if I know, sir. In fact, nobody does, not the servants, nor Miss Rana or Master Arjun. Your father kept it all hushed.'

Tej nodded.

'There was a scandal, sir, believe me you, and it took all of the Zamindar's power and influence to cover the matter, but the family was never the same again. Master Arjun's mother also put a gun in her mouth, and blew her brains out, in this very room, if I'm not mistaken.'

'The Revolutionaries' spy!' Tej blurted out, almost involuntarily.

Eric picked up on Tej's words, along with the surprise on the constable's face and the empathy in his voice. Eric smiled slyly, almost imperceptibly enough to have been missed by anyone.

But Sharvani Mehra wasn't anyone.

'Of course, sir,' Eric said, slamming his hands on the table, in way of applause. 'That's true, sir …' Eric said, trying to portray innocence, which actually made him sound more like a madman.

'Maybe, the spy had some information that he wanted to sell to the British … maybe that's why the Zamindar, you know …' he trailed off ominously. Tej smiled, his chest swelling up with pride. 'I'm always right,' he said, as Sharvani rolled her eyes.

'But why would the Revolutionaries' spy have anything to do with toppling Digvijay Rana?' Tej wondered out loud. 'I know …' Tej paused momentarily. 'From a …' there was a pause again, as if he were contemplating his next words.

Or to even say them at all.

'From a reliable source …' he continued, 'I have that Digvijay Rana supported the rebels; he provided them with food and guns …' he said, leaving the words hanging in the air.

Sharvani instantly picked up on Tej's tics: the slight change in his demeanour, the pause while he thought of the right words to say, the twitch in his eye, and the anger in his voice as he finally said the words.

Without doubt, it was information he overheard from his late father.

'Let's leave the spy, imaginary or real, aside for a moment, shall we?' Sharvani rolled her eyes.

The silence in the room was palpable, and the tension so thick, it could have been cut cleanly with a knife.

'I'm not ... I'm not entirely sure I should tell you this, sir, for you might think me mad ...' Eric stammered, his voice was low and almost akin to a whisper, 'but I fear, I ... I can't keep it in my chest any longer ...' he mumbled.

'Out with it, man,' Tej grunted, his voice as sharp as the crack of a whip.

Eric looked around, his eyes darting from left to right, even though only Sharvani and Tej were present in the small room.

The hulking Englishman's voice went even softer as he spoke, prompting Tej to lean in closer, but Sharvani stood rooted in place.

'Sir, there have been strange happenings in the manor,' Eric gulped hard.

'Strange?' repeated Tej, unsure of what he heard the first time around.

Eric nodded. 'There are times when we feel a presence ...'

'We?' Sharvani asked, raising a single eyebrow.

Eric grimaced, his face housing an ugly scowl. 'I mean the servants ...'

'Carry on,' Tej said with a flick of his wrist, dismissing Sharvani's question and Eric's answer.

'There's been strange creaking sounds and moans across the manor, sir. At first we dismissed it; it could have well been the wind howling through an open window, but we all learnt very quickly that this was, in fact, something far more sinister ...'

Eric paused momentarily.

'It is the work of something supernatural; there have been doors creaking open and closed even though there's nobody and no wind.

There are times where an unnatural chilled breeze blows through the manor, tainting all that it touches with its frigid kiss, but there is something evil about it, sir …'

'This is all well and good if you need fluff to fill out a Victorian ghost story, but you still haven't given us anything concrete,' Sharvani commented dryly.

Eric glared at her, before turning his attention back to the head constable. 'This happened not two days ago, sir,' he mumbled. 'Cross my heart and hope to die, if a single word of untruth comes out my lips.'

It was unknown whether Eric had a green thumb, but he certainly had a flair for the dramatic.

And Tej was visibly spellbound, twirling his moustache as he considered the burly gardener's words.

'After the death of the missus, one rainy night, unbeknownst to all, the Zamindar went to the woods after tending to the plants, wearing his gardener's boots no less, and went and slit his own throat. It was days before they found his body, rotten and half eaten by the critters in the forest. Eat his corpse, they did. Maggots ate out his eyeballs and laid eggs in the sockets, sir. Wild pigs ate his hands and legs whole … it was horrible and since then, sir, the Zamindar's ghost has been roaming the hallowed halls of Azad Manor, vowing revenge on all those who were responsible for his predicament.'

'So you're saying, the ghost of Digvijay Rana is exacting revenge from beyond the grave? Is that what you're implying?' Sharvani commented.

Tej's eyes darted towards her for a fleeting second, before looking back to Eric.

'I would have dismissed it too, sir,' he said, lowering his voice back to an innocent mumble, 'had it not been for the sight I saw with my own two eyes nary two nights ago ... I was busy in my garden, tending to the flowers, pulling out weeds and the like ...'

'At night?' Sharvani asked, with thinly disguised contempt.

Eric ignored her. 'The master and the missus are very accommodating to my work timings, as long as the garden doesn't suffer ...' he added hastily. 'And I do my best work at night: fewer people and distractions to deal with. I'm sure our respected head constable would agree with the same.'

Tej nodded reluctantly, more as a means to get Matheson to continue, rather than actual agreement.

'So there I was, minding my business alone with only the symphony of the night in tow as my company. I was busy cutting the thorns off the roses, you see, so that the master may be able to give them to the missus as a present,' he said and smiled.

Sharvani stifled a groan, as she rolled her eyes in disgust. Again.

'And clumsy ol' me, I managed to prick my thumb on one of them, and believe me you, sir, those things may be small, but they are as sharp as a wolf's fang.'

'The point, Eric?' Sharvani asked, the annoyance in her voice becoming apparent to all.

'I was busy tending to my bruised thumb, and that was when I first laid eyes on him ...' Eric's eyes widened in fear as he spoke those words.

'Who?' Tej blurted.

Eric gulped hard, and his eyes glazed over as he talked into the distance. 'The ghost; the Zamindar's ghost,' he mumbled.

There was genuine terror in his voice, as he said the words, and Sharvani silently applauded the gardener's acting skills for a fleeting moment.

Even though a very primal instinct was gnawing at her deeply, convinced he was telling the truth.

'The Zamindar's ghost?' Tej cried out. 'Are you certain?'

'As sure as I'm seeing you sir,' Eric mumbled. 'The late Digvijay Rana was standing in the distance, his body illuminated by the silver light of the moon. Now I'll admit it, I was scared, sir ... I was, but my loyalty to the Ranas won in the end,' he added, looking at the constable, his eyes begging for sympathy.

Tej Bahadur grunted dismissively.

'I walked closer to him, I did. Sir, I said, sir, is you all right? I called out to him, but there was no answer. The clouds had given way by then, and I was already feeling a chill run down my spine; was it the chill of the rain or fear from the proximity to the spectre, I know not and trust me you, I have since been wondering which one it was. As I walked closer, I felt my heart stop for a moment ... the Zamindar, Digvijay Rana, was floating in front of me, wearing the same soggy clothes that he was wearing at the time of his death, his feet wrapped in his favourite muddy gardener's boots. The master's eyes were hollow, empty sockets with maggots festering in them, his throat had an ugly open gash, with worms squirming in the open wound.'

Eric stopped for a moment, beads of sweat trickling down his forehead. There was a crack in his voice and genuine terror in his eyes, a fact that wasn't overlooked by the attentive Sharvani.

The brawny gardener was genuinely overcome by fear as he recalled the incident, and took a deep breath before continuing to narrate his tale.

'The ghost opened his mouth and let out an unholy wail. My blood froze in my veins, it did ...'

'Did he say anything?' Tej Bahadur asked.

Eric nodded. 'After that ungodly moan, his jaw stretched open, wide enough to fit a man's head and screeched, "Protect him, protect my legacy."'

'Arjun?' Sharvani whispered under her breath, her attention invariably drawn to the gardener's testimony.

'What then?'

'I was rooted in place sir, I was. My body was too petrified to move, unable to look away from the apparition floating in front of me, as he wailed again; another shrill, piercing cry cut through the air and the Zamindar's head toppled from his body, and rolled through the wet mud, stopping right at me feet.' Eric looked down, as the memory seemed to trigger an involuntary shudder from deep within him.

Sharvani looked at him, studying him more intricately this time.

It wasn't possible, all of his subtle movements—the blinking of his eye, the sweat on his forehead—they indicated he was telling the truth.

'How is this possible?' she wondered. Eric seemed to tick all the telltale signs; his story had details which an uncouth brute like Eric couldn't possibly fabricate, his breathing, his voice and a host of other tics.

But most importantly, Sharvani's instincts told her he was telling the truth.

'His eyes were closed, deathly still,' Eric continued, pulling Sharvani out of her thoughts. 'I could feel my heart pound in my chest, sir, as I looked at the disembodied head lying at me feet. The rest of his body began crumbling to dust, and the unholy remnants were being washed away by the rain. Only the head remained …' Eric said with a gulp. Sharvani could see the genuine terror in his eyes, and hear the crack and shudder in his voice.

She knew from experience that there were certain things that couldn't be faked.

'The eyes opened, sir, and inside there was only hollow, withered flesh; the eggs laid by maggots were beginning to hatch. I felt my heart stop for a second, as the grotesque, blackened lips widened into a sinister smile.'

'Go on …' Tej mumbled, holding onto the gardener's each and every word.

'I was startled, sir,' Eric said meekly. Tej nodded.

'I stumbled back, lost my footing, slipped on the wet mud, and landed on my back. I could see the head staring right at me, laughing evilly. The cackle was the most unholy sound on God's green earth, and I felt, I swear on God, that my soul shuddered hearing it. PROTECT MY LEGACY OR PERISH, it screeched. PROTECT MY LEGACY OR PERISH ... it kept repeating in a shrill voice between its cackles.'

'And what did you do then?' Sharvani asked, her intent to feign disinterest visibly apparent.

'I ran ma'am. I did, like any good soul who has the fear of God in his heart, and the blessing of the lord in his limbs. I ran and ran until the hideous cackle was drowned out by the sound of the pouring rain, and it remained no more than a painful distant memory. I never brought this up before, not even to the master, for fear of disturbing him, and tainting his respected father's memory, but now that you asked me and the poor sir is no more, I feel it's my duty to shed some light on this rather unfortunate turn of events, but like I said, sir, this is the truth and I will not hesitate to swear on it in a court of law, if need be,' Eric concluded timidly.

Tej stood silent for a moment. 'Well, if that's the case, we know Rai Bahadur covered up the scandal, but what was Arjun's fault? Why would a father murder his own son? Or even the spy murder Arjun for that matter?'

Sharvani sighed loudly, and shook her head in frustration, an act that didn't go unnoticed by Tej, nor did its implications.

Eric glared at Sharvani with a hateful scowl, before turning to Tej, his wide eyes out of place in his rugged, thug-like appearance. 'Believe me, sir,' he said softly. 'There is something supernatural at work.'

Tej had a choice.

To choose to further the line of investigation using Sharvani's approach grounded in reality, or pursue the more supernatural aspects of the case. He thought about it for a moment.

And then made his choice.

Tej straightened up. 'Are you telling me how to do my job? Going on about this nonsense about ghosts and spirits? Do not think you can throw mud in the eyes of the law with your two-bit cock and bull story.'

'I DIDN'T DO IT,' Eric roared, slamming his fists on the table so hard, it nearly broke into two.

Evidently, Eric was a man of limited patience. To see his entire account of the matter being so utterly disregarded pushed him to the end of his rope.

'If you didn't do it ...' Tej commented, 'do you have anyone who saw you at the purported time? Anyone who will vouch for you?'

'I have nothing to prove,' he said, raising his hands. 'I was waiting for the young lads and lasses to drop them back to the orphanage all safe like, and hundreds of guests passed by me all evening, as I waited patiently, never moving off the carriage, not even to attend to nature's call.'

'Yet not one of them saw you at the crucial stage,' he clarified.

Eric snarled at him, his eyes filled with hate, and then pointed both his hands directly at Sharvani.

'ASK HER,' he yelled, 'She saw me seconds after his death,' he yelled again.

'Say something,' he roared. 'You've been sitting there like a ghost, listening to all of this for over an hour, and you have not said a word about finding me by the carriage. Your attestation will save me ... you know I didn't kill him ...' his voice started cracking, and tears welled up in his eyes.

'I beg of you ... please say something.'

Sharvani sighed. 'Are you having an affair with Archana Rana?'

Both of them looked at her flabbergasted. Tej felt his jaw drop.

Eric stared at her, his tears seemingly dried up, with rage taking their place. His eyes reddened, and the veins on his forehead threatened to pop and burst at any moment.

She shrugged nonchalantly. 'Well, you did ask me to say something.'

fourteen

'FUCKING BITCH!' The roars shattered the still of the night. 'I'LL FUCKING RIP HER THROAT OUT,' Eric Matheson yelled, as he was forcibly led out by the police.

'My god …' Ishita said, as she put her hand over her mouth. 'Such language.'

Sharvani chuckled. 'Well, English has a reputation of being a colourful language,' she said as she handed Ishita a piece of strawberry buttercream cake. Sharvani herself nibbled on it, but found it a little too sweet for her liking; she preferred the Indian desserts. They had a balance, seldom found elsewhere.

'You need to keep your strength up,' she insisted, before Ishita had a chance to utter her refusal. 'I've had the rest of it packed up for the children.'

'But the guests?'

'I'm sure they're content with the bitter taste in their mouths.'

'Do you need me to stay back?' Ishita asked earnestly.

Sharvani shook her head.

'Take care of yourself … and the kids … in that order.'

Ishita smiled. 'Thank you, Miss Mehra.'

'Goodnight, Ishita,' she smiled back warmly.

She sighed as she watched her protégé climb into the carriage and ride off into the night with the children. Anshul Baghri was at the helm of the carriage. It pained Sharvani's heart to know that the children had witnessed what they did.

But she needed to get to the bottom of things.

Arjun Rana was, amongst other things, her student.

One she had vowed to protect, ever since he first stepped into the old halls of the Digvijay Rana Orphanage.

From the hundreds of guests invited that night, Sharvani was clear from the start that she was interested in the testimonies of just two.

One of whom she had already heard, and he consequently won a free night's stay at the local police station, breakfast included.

She wondered if the second would be so lucky.

'It's 2.30 a.m.,' Tej grumbled, as he stifled a yawn and rubbed his eyes vigorously in a bid to stave off sleep for a little longer.

'The constables have noted the names and addresses of the other guests. Those whose statements we have not yet recorded have been called in to the police station first thing tomorrow morning. Nobody is allowed to leave town without permission.' He looked at Sharvani, as if awaiting her approval.

She nodded. 'Well … we might have time for one more interrogation.'

His eyes widened. 'Madam, with all due respect, it's the middle of the night.'

'If we're awake,' she replied nonchalantly, 'I see no reason why a self-obsessed, egoistical Brit bastard should be sleeping soundly!'

Not fifteen minutes after their conversation, Alexander Stephan was dragged into the police station in his pyjamas.

The stout Englishman was kicking and screaming profanities left, right and centre. He was decidedly not happy being there.

'You brown-skinned bastards,' he spluttered, as two hefty constables seated him on a wooden chair, which had rusted nails jutting out in strategic positions. Sharvani had picked the chair specifically for that reason; Stephan got up with a yelp as his posterior felt the burn of the nails eating into his skin, his cotton pyjamas providing scant protection against the sharp sting of the nails.

'SIT DOWN,' Tej growled.

Alexander complied. He had never seen such ferocity from the head constable. The Britisher sat down carefully, grumbling, as he wiped the sleep off his eyes.

'Why am I here? I am a respected businessman with a reputation to maintain …'

Sharvani rolled her eyes. They always had such trite explanations.

'Really? Really, Mr Stephan?' Tej asked, narrowing his eyes at the Englishman. 'Do you really not have an idea as to why you are here?'

Stephan glared at him. 'Humour me … why am I here?'

'Because …' this time, Sharvani spoke; her voice was as cold as ice, as she walked out of the shadows, '… Arjun Rana has been murdered.'

'You,' he sputtered, staring at Sharvani, his eyes nearly bulging out of their sockets. 'What … what … what is she doing here?' he grumbled.

'Sharvani Mehra is here in an official capacity to assist in this investigation,' Tej replied, ignoring Stephan's outburst.

'On whose order?'

'Mine!' Tej looked cross. There was a scowl plastered on his face. He had to make it clear who was the boss, asking the questions.

Stephan grunted. He folded his arms and looked away from the duo, his brow knitted in an expression of pure anger. He was determined to make this as difficult for them as possible.

'I'm innocent,' he replied flatly.

'Well, I wouldn't say that,' Sharvani said indifferently. 'But with regards to your involvement in Arjun's murder ... well that remains to be seen now, doesn't it?'

'How dare you accuse me?' he growled.

'No one's accusing you of anything ...' Tej interjected, looking to defuse the situation. 'Not yet, at least.'

Stephan stared at Sharvani for a moment. She didn't break the gaze; she could see the beads of sweat trickle down his greasy, wrinkled forehead and onto his brow.

He would crack.

He had to.

But one part of her disagreed; was it her prejudice that was guiding her accusations? She couldn't get that out of her head.

There was a twitch at the side of his mouth. It slowly grew into a crooked smile, and he then burst out laughing.

The laugh was triumphant, evil almost.

Sharvani raised her eyebrows.

'For fuck's sake, you can't be serious!' he said, wiping off the tears that followed.

'Oh, I assure you, Mr Stephan,' Tej glared at him, 'when it comes to murder, we are very, very serious.'

'You want my alibi?' he questioned. 'There's my alibi,' he said, pointing a mean finger towards Sharvani.

She didn't react.

'She saw me ... merely moments after Rana's accident.'

'I'd hardly call being flung from the stairs and falling twenty feet into the main hall, an accident.'

He shrugged.

The Englishman couldn't even pretend to care.

'He tripped, who knows? Rana was fond of the coloured liquids, just like his wife and his father before him. They say liquor consumption is detrimental to one's health and, in Rana's case, I would say fatally so,' he said with a sardonic chuckle.

His lack of empathy reminded her why she hated him so.

'If that's all the questioning you have …' he said, as he rose from his chair.

'SIT BACK DOWN!' grunted Tej.

Stephan glared at him.

'Oye …' Stephan barked, disregarding Tej's command and snapping his fingers. 'Are you deaf? I told you *she saw me*, not minutes after his unfortunate and untimely fall. It couldn't have possibly been me.' He was sticking to his statements staunchly.

Tej gave a quick glance to Sharvani who nodded her acknowledgement.

Stephan was telling the truth, at least this part. Sharvani had rushed out merely minutes after Rana's body had been flung off the railing.

And Stephan was in the courtyard, busy enjoying his cigar.

No, she thought. There was something he was hiding. Prejudice be damned.

She needed to figure out another line of questioning.

'You were amongst the last persons to have seen him alive!'

'HAH,' he scoffed. 'It was his homecoming party; he was being passed around like jam to be spread on bread. More than a hundred people were amongst the last to have seen him alive. Hell …' he growled, 'you would have seen him even after I left the manor.'

'That may be true …' she replied calmly, 'but you were, in fact, the last person to have accosted him.'

'It was merely a quarrel, which I admit, got a bit out of hand,' he replied nonchalantly.

'You issued him a death threat … in front of more than a hundred witnesses; I'm willing to say that that qualifies as more than a quarrel, wouldn't you say?' Sharvani asked. 'I mean, you benefit immensely from his death, don't you?'

Stephan spluttered, 'This is an outrage!' His face turned red, to the point where it seemed he might up and explode out of anger.

'You want the truth?' he roared.

'What else, Mr Stephan?'

'Fine …' he growled. 'I'll give you the truth,' he said, as he removed a cigar stub from his pyjama set's breast pocket.

'Do you mind?' he asked.

Tej grunted and showed his approval with a flick of his fingers.

'Rana was drunk. He had had a drop too much; I could smell the whiskey off him, from over a mile away. I asked something and it rubbed him the wrong way.' As the nicotine coursed through his lungs, Stephan's voice mellowed down, and his demeanour became sufficiently calmer after his outburst.

'It was a very verbal quarrel, like you rightly said, Mr Stephan,' Sharvani said, restating the facts. 'That too, publicly, and in front of some very wealthy people, some of whom were your investors and many other potential …'

Stephan grunted in response.

'Pardon me for being so curious, but I cannot help but wonder, what could have been so important that you argued with him on his homecoming reception, in front of so many people?'

Stephan threw his hands up in frustration. 'If you must know, it was over the sale of the manor. Are you happy now?'

'Azad Manor?'

He nodded. 'After Arjun's disappearance, I tried my luck with his widow over wanting to sell the property. She was staunchly against it at first, but was increasingly becoming more predisposed to listening to my offer after Arjun's return. I merely told him of that little development, and he exploded at me for no reason at all. I was offering him a good price, way beyond the going market rate …' he said, as he rubbed out the cigar butt against the table. 'I wasn't trying to cheat him or anything … after all, I'm a …'

'Yes … legitimate businessman ... so we've heard,' Sharvani said, rolling her eyes. Her words held a little more sarcasm than was deemed necessary.

'He asked you to leave, didn't he?' Tej questioned.

Stephan replied in the affirmative.

'What were you doing lingering outside the manor then?' Tej asked.

Stephan gave both of them an oily grin, like he had already acquitted himself in this case, as though they had forgotten to ask him the one question that would implicate him.

Even Sharvani felt that, and a nagging feeling was eating her up from inside.

'Running out of questions, are you?' he asked with a sly smile.

'I ask them … and you answer,' Tej said stoically. 'This is how interrogation works.'

'I WAS ANGRY,' Stephan confessed. 'The weather was pleasant, and I enjoyed the cool breeze, so I decided to afford myself a little treat that calms me down whenever I'm angry or stressed.'

'And what is that?'

He merely smiled in response as he pulled out another cigar from his pocket and lit it.

'I'd offer you one, but I'm afraid it's a little too rich for your untrained palates.'

'You said you smoke those only when you're angry or stressed?' Sharvani asked.

He nodded as he blew out a ring of smoke.

'You have smoked continuously here. What should I make of that?'

'Whatever you wish,' he replied nonchalantly. 'Clearly you are overutilizing your imagination as with other aspects of this case as well.'

'Double Coronas. Is that all you smoke?'

'Yes.'

'Are you sure?'

'I said "yes".' There was finality in his voice. 'Why do you ask?'

She shrugged. 'No reason, and like you said, we're running out of questions.'

He smiled triumphantly, visibly satisfied by her answer. 'Oh wait ...' he added suddenly, slapping the side of his head absentmindedly. 'I also carry the cheaper Maspero Gold ...'

'Why?'

He shrugged. 'In my line of work, you meet all kinds of people: from paupers to princes; not everyone shares my affinity towards cigars, so I keep the cigarettes to share at times like those.'

She nodded, visibly distrusting his answer.

'Did anyone see you between the time you left and the moment I saw you ... ?'

'You mean in the fifteen minutes or so?'

'Yes,' she nodded. 'Give or take.'

'Of course,' he said. 'Eric did.'

This time, Tej's eyes nearly popped out of their sockets.

'Eric ... Eric Matheson? The Rana family's gardener?'

'Yes,' Stephan replied coolly, blowing out another ring of smoke.

'Are you certain?'

'As certain as I am that I'm seeing you.'

'And what was he doing?'

'Sitting at the reins of the carriage, waiting to take those little orphaned bastards back to their asylum, I suppose?'

Sharvani felt her heartbeat quicken, rage rushing through her veins.

The audacity of this man.

It took all of her self-restraint and more to keep her from strangling him then and there, but she would wait. It would be infinitely more satisfying seeing him hang from the end of a noose, tried by a court of law.

'ARE YOU ONE HUNDRED PER CENT SURE?' Tej yelled out each word slowly and deliberately.

'YES, I'M A HUNDRED PER CENT SURE,' Stephan yelled, mimicking Tej's tone.

'HE WAS BY THE CARRIAGE. Where did you want him to be?' Stephan mumbled. 'All these pressure tactics and baseless accusations just prove that you know nothing ... nothing at all.'

Sharvani rubbed her forehead. She could feel a migraine coming on. Stephan had them; he had slipped through their hands ... for now.

'Your loud voice and accusatory tone cannot cover up for the third-rate police work, head constable. And in case I wasn't very clear, let me spell it out for you: Eric never moved between the time I exited the manor and this crazy old lady found me. I saw the gardener and the gardener saw me ... it's as simple as that.'

'For your knowledge,' Sharvani commented, 'Eric admitted to no such thing.'

Stephan was silent, but remained unfazed. 'His testimony is his to make,' he said, unruffled. 'I will maintain what I said: Eric was in my sight the whole time. Now if there's anything else ...'

Tej sighed. 'Leave.'

'Good night,' Stephan growled, as he got up from the chair in a huff, glared at Sharvani, and left the room, slamming the door on his way out.

'How did you know?' Tej asked her, without moving his sight from the door.

'About?'

'The people at the reception being his investors?'

'I didn't ...' she smiled, 'it was a calculated guess at best ... the industry he is in, and the way he is moving is a little too fast, and one doesn't get that way without having people with deep pockets behind them.'

Tej sighed heavily again. 'I hoped his version would shed some light on things, and make things easier.'

The door slammed again.

Archana Rana barged in, breathing fire, with a piece of paper tightly wrapped around her fist. Her make-up had begun to run, with kajal streaking down her cheeks from her bloodshot eyes, making her look like a preternatural entity, a far cry from the ethereal beauty that was the mistress of Azad Manor.

It didn't take long for Sharvani to guess what the paper could have been.

'There is no end to this night, is there now?' Sharvani muttered under her breath.

'How dare you?' she roared. 'How fucking dare you?' She dashed straight towards Tej and caught the appointed upholder of the law by the collar.

'You have ruined the night.'

Sharvani looked at her dumbstruck. The girl's husband had been murdered, and here she was accusing the constable of ruining her night.

Where and how had she gone so, so wrong, Sharvani wondered.

'Madam, with all due respect, I was conducting an investigation,' he said, as he slid her hands off him. 'We have reason to believe your

husband was murdered, and that there could be a threat to your life …
There could be a spy, from the Revolutionaries.'

'SHUT UP …' she hissed. 'Shut up.' She slammed the paper she
had been holding down on the desk.

Tej Bahadur knew what it was even before seeing it. J.D. Mistry's
seal served as a testament to the authenticity of the document.

He had seen it several times before in the course of the past few
days. It was anticipatory bail for her gardener, Eric Matheson. Tej
couldn't help but wonder if the senile old Mistry had a bundle of these
laying around, just filling in the date and stamp whenever required.

'You won't need this,' he mumbled. There was a look of defeat in
his eyes.

Archana looked at him, an expression of shock slowly creeping up
on her face.

'Stephan has testified in his favour. Alexander Stephan is Eric's alibi
at the time of the murder.'

A sly smile crept up on the side of Archana's face, but she was quick
to cover it.

'Maybe that talking fungus isn't as bad as I thought, but that still
doesn't excuse you from the fact that you threw my staff in jail without
probable cause.'

'Mrs Rana,' Tej began assertively.

'It's miss now,' she said nonchalantly.

Her words took the wind out of his sails. 'Eric Matheson attempted
to violently assault Miss Mehra when we interrogated him earlier. It
was imperative that we restrain him. He is in the cell for that reason
only; nobody has implicated him in any crime whatsoever.'

Archana chuckled. 'Nothing out of the ordinary about that. I always
wanted to violently assault Miss Mehra ever since I was eight. Kudos
to Eric for acting on his instincts,' she said, giving Sharvani an icy grin.

Sharvani smiled courteously in response. 'The feeling wasn't mutual, my dear,' she replied, 'not until now,' she whispered under her breath.

Archana turned her attention back to Tej. 'And you ... wasn't it enough that my husband had such a fatal accident in public? You just had to go and badger my guests, treating them like common criminals, before indiscriminately jailing one of my most trusted staff?'

'Murder,' Sharvani said coldly.

'Excuse me?'

'We will treat this as a murder case until proven otherwise. He was my student, and I won't rest easy till I find the killer.'

Archana laughed again. This time, it sounded like a shallow laugh. 'He was my husband, Miss Mehra, and as difficult as it is for me to believe this, I must accept the truth. He had an unfortunate accident.'

'You don't seem too upset about it?' Tej asked, the suspicion heavy in his voice.

Her eyes bulged out of her sockets. 'Unbelievable! You dare to suspect me ... ME?' she said dismissively. 'Of all the people?'

'Answer the question, Archana,' Sharvani instructed calmly. 'Do it for me.'

Archana looked at her, rolled her eyes, and shrugged her shoulders. 'What do you want me to say? I wept enough during the time he disappeared, thinking him dead, and now to know he has truly passed on from this world, makes me feel numb ... it's like a bad prophecy waiting to be fulfilled. You dread it happening, but when it does, you feel strangely calm, euphoric even, like you finally got a sense of closure. Maybe it all just caught up to him, I don't know?'

'What caught up to him?

'Nothing,' she shrugged. 'Just a figure of speech.'

She was lying. Sharvani was sure of it.

'Now, if you don't mind, it's been a long night. I don't want Eric to spend another minute in this vermin-infested place.'

'You seem to worry about him a lot,' Sharvani remarked. Tej was thinking of mentioning this himself, but he was made to know his place early on in the conversation.

'I care for all my staff,' she replied coldly.

The door was ajar.

'RELEASE MATHESON,' Tej yelled.

He realized there was no reason to prolong this any longer than required.

'Wait a second,' Sharvani interjected. 'The bail must be for him as a suspect in this case, and the other case of assault.'

Archana scowled, 'Alleged assault.'

Sharvani smiled. 'But he definitely attempted to assault me, and that too in front of a police constable.'

Tej nodded.

Archana's eyes looked like they would pop out of her head. 'You provoked him.'

'I did no such thing,' Sharvani replied apathetically, 'but considering the circumstances, I would feel much safer at home tonight if Eric was behind bars.'

Tej stifled a smile. 'She has a point Mrs ... Miss Rana ...' he quickly corrected himself.

Archana glared at Sharvani, the icy, daggered stare stabbing the teacher.

'HMMPH, so be it. Let him stay in jail ... builds character,' Archana grunted, as she turned around and began to walk away.

'One last thing, Archana,' her teacher said softly.

Tej could feel his heart gallop. He knew the question she was about to ask.

'Are you having an affair with the gardener?' she asked softly, in a tone that seemed like she was talking about the weather.

Tej steeled himself mentally and physically for an outburst, not much different from the one shown by the jailed gardener, but he was in for a surprise.

Archana turned around, a sardonic grin on her face.

'Why am I not surprised, Miss Mehra? Only somebody like you would think of something so downright petty and disgusting! You think all of us are like you?' Her words were laced with venom. Even Tej could not help but feel a tinge of animosity towards the elderly matron, as a lifetime of harboured ill will came raging to the forefront of his mind.

'That will be all, Archana, have a good night,' Sharvani said, smiling politely.

'You too, Miss Mehra. I would have invited you to spend the night at Azad Manor, but the house is now a mess, and quite frankly, I'm not sure you would be comfortable.'

'And why is that?'

'I don't think the ghost of your ex-lover would let you sleep in peace, and I don't mean the good kind of staying awake,' she said with a quick wink, and with that she was off.

'You see now, Miss Mehra,' said an exasperated Tej, 'you see now that the manor is haunted, and if not by the Zamindar's ghost, I'd bet it will be by his son's.'

'Don't talk nonsense, Tej,' she said, stifling a yawn. 'Go home, and get some sleep. I want you and two constables at Azad Manor first thing tomorrow morning.'

He looked at her utterly dumbfounded. 'Whatever for? I have to visit the surrounding talukas for my weekly visits tomorrow.'

'Do that the day after then ...' She brushed him off. 'Be there tomorrow morning.'

'You mean in three hours?' he sighed, resigning to his fate. 'If you were to ask me, I think this little affair is all due to the Revolutionaries' spy,' he said, twirling his moustache.

Sharvani rolled her eyes. 'Rubbish, Tej,' she said dismissively. Tej nodded, but deep down, his gut told him otherwise, and his instincts were never wrong.

'What then?' he asked. 'Maybe, there *are* ghosts in that manor. These murders are not natural.'

'Rubbish,' she said. 'There are no such things as ghosts,' she said, as she walked out of the room, but in her mind, she wondered whether she truly believed what she said.

fifteen

'Even the birds are sleeping, sir,' bemoaned one of the constables.

'Hush Sanjeev ...' Tej Bahadur chided him, as he stifled a yawn. His eyes were bloodshot. His mind and body were begging him to go curl up into a ball and sleep for a week. The last forty-eight hours had been exhausting, placing an unbearable strain on him physically, mentally and emotionally.

But Sharvani wouldn't let go.

And as long as she persevered, Tej would follow suit, come hell or high water.

Although, secretly, he cursed her for having a seemingly infinite amount of energy, which she regularly tapped into, he wondered how she did it.

It was 6.30 in the morning.

He looked up at the dull slate of the sky. A chilly breeze ghosted its way across the open land.

138

He heard a slight rumbling noise and felt a few pebbles launch out from the grey fog above, falling prey to the forces of gravity. He stepped out of the way just in time, as a pair of heavy boots rained down from the ether, and landed on the ground with a soft thud.

'Miss Mehra,' he grunted through gritted teeth, trying to make his anger apparent.

'Sorry,' came a voice from nowhere. 'I told you to pay attention.'

Tej growled.

When Sharvani told him to be ready at dawn, he hadn't the faintest idea that it was to recreate the crime scene at Azad Manor.

Unauthorized.

If Archana Rana found out, he would lose his job and be dishonourably kicked out of the police force, but Sharvani was undeterred; she told him in no clear terms that she would be going ahead with it.

With or without his support.

'You said you wanted to recreate the crime scene,' he whispered, 'then what are we doing out here?'

'Oh, I know Arjun was murdered, Tej,' she said good-naturedly, as she made a quick hop from the parapet outside the window and onto the sloping roof. 'Question is, how?'

'Err …' Sanjeev, the constable spoke again, 'sir, shouldn't you be the one up there … um … doing that?'

'I'm … er … afflicted with … acrophobia,' he said, and took a long gulp on seeing the elderly woman balance precariously over the ledge, as she made her way to the ladder.

It was easy for him to wish for her to fall: the wind was strong, and the building, old. It was rotten in places, and her position was perilous, at best.

He wouldn't mind gloating over her dead body; she was the lady he blamed for ruining his life, but somehow, he couldn't.

It was difficult not to want to see her suffer, such was the human psyche, but that matter was trivial compared to the others at hand. His personal vendetta would have to wait till another day.

He was entrusted with a duty: to protect and enforce the law in the town of Ooty.

And he learnt the importance of duty and honour early on. Eight years after his mother's death, he enlisted in the British Indian Army. When he was ten years old, burning up with fever, he had seen his dead mother. His father was nowhere to be found, away on his increasingly frequent trips. His mother's ghost asked Tej to make a life for himself, to help protect those who were weak. He lay awake many a night wondering whether he had actually seen his mother, or whether it was a hallucination brought about by the high fever, perhaps unlocking some aspect of his memory that was previously suppressed? But whatever it was, it gave him the purpose that was missing in his life.

In the army, he was a part of the troops that opened fire in the Jallianwala Bagh Massacre.

And it was there that he understood the importance of honour and duty. When the jawans stood in front of the line of fire to protect women and children, he knew what he was doing was wrong.

Not one life was lost that day because of Tej Bahadur's bullets, but neither was a single one saved due to his actions. Disillusioned, he returned to his hometown, Ooty, taking up the position of head constable. And now, someone or something was killing people in the town he was assigned to protect. People died under his watch in Amritsar, and he would be damned if he let any more lives fall under suspicious circumstances in Ooty.

Sleep and personal grudges were indulgences he would gladly forego for the moment, to stop the menace wreaking havoc in Ooty, irrespective of whether it was mortal or supernatural. Death be damned, he wouldn't stop until he apprehended the killer and put them behind bars and, to that extent, a temporary alliance with the lady who snatched his father from him was a small price to pay.

'Are you all right?' he asked her as she descended down the ladder. His words were more due to courtesy than genuine concern, a fact not lost upon Sharvani.

'I'm okay. It was just a short descent, Tej … granted it was twenty metres above the ground.'

He nodded.

'Did the shoes leave behind any prints?' she asked matter-of-factly.

He shook his head. He hadn't checked, but as they walked over, the shoes had indeed not left any discernible prints in the wet mud. The light drizzle of the morning would have easily wiped away any and all traces of the same.

'Hmmm … if Eric wore the shoes and made the jump, there would have been an imprint, and since the boots themselves didn't leave a print, he could have thrown them off the roof, jumped down and walked towards the foliage before coming back, with another pair of shoes or even bare feet. Any and or,' she shrugged, 'doesn't quite make a difference.'

'But there are testimonies from guests who saw both Eric and Stephan at varying times. It would have been impossible for them to have disappeared for such a long period of time.'

'He could have hidden the shoes …' she thought out loud.

'Or it could have been the Zamindar's ghost,' Sanjeev gulped.

Sharvani rolled her eyes, while Tej considered the possibility. 'You know Miss Mehra …' he said, twirling his moustache. 'He does have …'

'There is no ghost, Tej …' she cut him off abruptly.

'This little exercise didn't reveal much to prove otherwise,' Tej grunted, the animosity growing in his voice. It was apparent that he wasn't used to having his opinion questioned.

Sharvani accepted the fact. She had hoped that this little excursion would shed some more light on how the killer managed to escape.

'I bet the prints will match the ones found in Ishita's house, and the ones at Aneri Plume,' she commented.

'And what will that prove?' Tej asked.

'That the ghost of the Zamindar has returned from the grave, and that he is out to take revenge,' Sanjeev said and visibly shuddered.

Sharvani massaged her forehead in apathy. 'Go home, Sanjeev … get some sleep.'

The constable smiled and warmly welcomed the idea, while Tej frowned. He was hoping that those words would be directed at him and not his subordinate. He looked on enviously, as Sanjeev made his way straight for the gate.

'The added evidence changes nothing,' Sharvani commented, driving the point home. 'Even if it wasn't for the anticipatory bail, Stephan's testimony exonerates Eric.'

'Maybe they are both covering for each other?' he suggested.

'Maybe,' she agreed, 'but to what end?'

'Matheson's testimony was sufficiently vague; he did say he saw everyone at some point or the other, and yet no one in particular. Stephan on his part, however, staunchly maintains that Eric didn't move from his seat.'

'Hmmm …' she was lost in thought, the gears in her mind grinding, trying to process all the information known to her, and trying to fit the pieces in together.

'Either one of them is lying, or both of them are lying, or maybe one is telling the truth, or they both are,' he surmised.

She nodded lackadaisically. Truly this man was a different type of an idiot.

But at least his heart was in the right place.

Unlike his father's.

'That being said, I find it difficult to believe that Stephan, given his height and build, could climb this wall, knock out Arjun and jump back down.'

'Then it had to be Matheson,' Tej inferred. 'But Stephan vouches for him, thereby implicating himself … hmmm … I still think it's the work of the Revolutionaries' spy, if not the Zamindar's ghost.'

Sharvani grinned. 'And pray tell, if there even is a spy, how would Arjun's death benefit the Revolutionaries?'

'They're anarchists, these Indian Revolutionaries.'

Sharvani rolled her eyes. 'You're from Assam, Tej. It is still Hindustan. We're not Britishers.'

He ignored her. 'The spy was sent by the Revolutionaries to sow discord amongst the order established by the British.'

'Their method of being overlords you mean?'

He glared at her. 'They never stopped sending spies. In fact, there was one planted during my father's time as well. It was because of the spy that the Zamindar killed himself.'

'Nonsense,' she exclaimed.

'Yes …' he nodded. 'The Zamindar would help the Revolutionaries time and again.'

'I never heard of that happening, Tej …' she protested.

'What did I tell you about my gut feeling always being right?'

Sharvani stared at him, 'Literally, nothing.'

Tej rolled his eyes. 'Well, my gut feeling has always proved right till now … so that's that.'

Sharvani nodded condescendingly. 'And do you have anything, anything at all, on which you base this gut feeling?'

'Well … I have. Being Rai Bahadur's son comes with certain advantages … and opportunities to eavesdrop.' From his expression and demeanour, Sharvani guessed he didn't seem to be particularly proud of the fact. 'Take my word for it, the Zamindar was a true patriot; he supported the Revolutionaries and provided food, water and guns.'

'And yet they were defeated every single time.'

Tej sighed, nodding his head. 'Maybe the Britishers were better equipped?'

'Maybe,' she said, looking towards the manor. In the hazy, grey light of the morning, it donned a foreboding appearance, discouraging visitors from entering, like a cave dwelling of some unholy beast that had unpleasant surprises lurking inside.

Truly, the manor itself had its fair share of secrets.

'Hello …' another voice came out from the fog. 'What are you doing here?'

The duo's blood froze.

'I can explain …' Tej began, as he turned around.

'Well, it's a good thing I met you here. Saves me a trip.'

Sharvani looked visibly confused, but a smile appeared on her visage, as the friendly face of Ramesh Katwal came into the picture.

The town's postman had a grin plastered on his face. His old, weathered face was covered with a monkey cap, he donned three layers of clothing, had two shawls wrapped tightly around his neck, and a satchel slung across his shoulders.

The familiar ringing of the bells tied around the handlebar of his cycle cut through the air, as he wheeled it along at a snail's pace.

'Ramesh bhai …' Tej cried, visibly relieved. 'What are you doing here?'

'Tej,' he mumbled, his teeth chattering because of the chill in the air. His crooked nose was red due to the cold. He adjusted his glasses, which had fogged over.

'I'm the postman, Tej. I'm supposed to be here. Question is, what are you doing here?' he said with a knowing grin.

Tej smiled back sheepishly.

'Never mind ... I have a letter for you,' he said, as he handed Tej an envelope. It looked regal from the outside, and was sealed with J.D. Mistry's stamp.

'Mistry,' Tej groaned. 'I wonder what's in this now?'

'One way to find out,' Sharvani smiled.

'Miss Mehra ... I have one for you too,' he said, as he handed her a letter that looked exactly like the one Tej held.

'Thank you,' she smiled politely, although she seemed to be as confused as the hapless Tej.

'The postman always delivers ... achoo ...' he cleared his nose again, 'no matter what the weather ... now if you'll excuse me, I have several more like these,' he said, eyeing the envelopes in their hand.

'I'd appreciate it if you leave out the part about seeing us here,' Sharvani requested softly.

Ramesh Katwal smiled warmly. 'My memory isn't what it once was; I just ensure what needs to be delivered gets delivered. And saw who, my dear?' he said, as he got onto his cycle and rode off.

Tej had already ripped open the envelope and read through its contents. 'If the manor has a habit of attracting ghosts ...' he said listlessly, 'one of them has placed me in Arjun Rana's will.'

Sharvani's hands trembled as she opened her envelope. It was an invitation to the hearing of the last will and testament of Arjun Rana, and Sharvani Mehra had been listed as one of the beneficiaries.

sixteen

There were rows and rows of bookcases, each one dustier than the next. Even the cobwebs had cobwebs.

Sharvani instinctively placed a handkerchief over her mouth as she walked closer to the nearest, empty chair in the room.

She was late.

There was a sea of recognizable faces, their bodies already plopped onto the available chairs. She was greeted with generic salutations, which she returned in kind.

Only the staff of Azad Manor were present, all of them indifferent to the hearing. Tej Bahadur sat distant, visibly out of place in the proceedings. Only Anshul Baghri looked forlorn, with his eyes downcast. Sharvani could sense he was genuinely upset about his master Arjun's unexpected demise.

Archana Rana, however, had fire burning in her eyes. She sat there aloof, a little distant from everybody, anxiously awaiting the contents of the will.

She was dressed in simple garb, sans any make-up and, for the first time, Sharvani noticed how tired she looked. Archana had seemingly aged a decade in the span of two days; her unkempt hair and the no make-up look gave her a haggard appearance.

Sharvani's heart sank to witness the fate that befell Archana.

She had been such a good child.

There were empty chairs adjoining hers, but Sharvani chose to avoid sitting there, for the same reasons as the others.

A foulness of mood was literally radiating off Archana Rana like a cyclone threatening to swallow anyone who came within its vicinity.

'Miss Mehra,' Ishita cried excitedly, as Sharvani plopped herself on the chair adjacent to hers.

'How delightful to see you here.'

'The feeling is mutual, child,' she smiled back.

'I wonder why I've been summoned,' Ishita confided, with a tinge of apprehension.

'Well you're not the only one,' Sharvani whispered back with a slight chuckle. 'Have they started reading the will yet?'

In response, Ishita pointed at the desk—a massive, mahogany piece of furniture, almost big enough to cover the entire breadth of the room.

The wooden table was old but polished to the point where it literally gleamed, and it was kept immaculately clean. There was nothing on the table except a plaque, and a single file that was tied together by a thin string.

The plaque read J.D. MISTRY in bold letters and Solicitor at Law beneath it in a smaller font. Sharvani had to adjust her glasses to read it better. Behind the desk, J.D. Mistry sat tapping his long, bony fingers, waiting impatiently for Sharvani to settle down.

'Are you quite finished?' the old man said with a nasal twang. His voice had a sinister ring, giving Sharvani goosebumps.

JAMSHEDJI DARCI MISTRY.

The man was old.

Like an antique piece.

The pair of Norwood reading glasses balanced precariously on his large, crooked nose was completely disproportionate to his rather small, sickly looking face. Tufts of hair were growing out of his head, nose and ears.

A row of misshapen, rotting teeth, many missing in places, could be seen as he smiled when he untied the strings of a file on his desk. Sharvani could have sworn she heard a cackle even though his weathered face, littered with age spots, did not change.

For the first time, Sharvani felt intimidated.

No, she felt scared.

'Has he said anything yet?' she whispered to Ishita.

'No, he's been quiet ever since I got here. For a second, I felt he was ...'

'... dead?' Sharvani completed her thought. 'You aren't the only one,' she chuckled.

'I mean look at him ... one foot's already in the grave ...'

'And the other on a banana peel!'

'SILENCE,' Mistry screeched, the veins on his neck bulging out.

Sharvani was stunned for a moment.

'You have been summoned because you are all beneficiaries according to the last will and testament of the recently deceased Arjun Rana.'

'All?' questioned Sharvani.

There was a murmur across the room; all the servants started talking among themselves, stunned by the revelation. Only Archana sat deathly still, almost like a statue.

'SILENCE,' he yelled again.

Sharvani complied, for if it went on like this, someone would be needed to read Mistry's will soon.

Satisfied that he had the undivided attention of those present, he cleared his throat of some residual phlegm and began.

For Sharvani, the beginning went in a blur: the usual formalities and disclaimers, cookie-cutter stuff for which she could shut her mind off.

'The total fortune excluding unmovable assets come to a total of twenty lakh rupees, out of which seven lakhs will be disbursed to certain recipients as described in the will.'

There was a collective gasp in the crowd. Everybody knew the Ranas were wealthy, but this amount would have easily propelled them into the top one percent.

'The Rana family and its estate has no debts as to this date. First order of business ...' he said as he cleared his throat. 'A sum of rupees five lakhs will be given to the Digvijay Rana School and Orphanage for the much-required maintenance, fixings and additional facilities such as heating, clothing for the children, etcetera, etcetera. The disbursal of the said amount will be in parts and can only be used for the benefit of the orphans. Safeguards have been put in place to ensure that no misappropriation and embezzlement of funds take place,' he said this while looking at Sharvani from under the rim of his glasses.

But Sharvani's attention was all on Ishita. The girl had tears of joy streaming down her cheeks, and her broad smile radiated happiness.

'Bless him ... bless him,' she cried out, fighting back tears.

'Thank you ... thank you, kind sir,' she said to Mistry, who grunted apathetically.

'I'm just reading the will.'

'Arjun Rana was a saint,' she said smilingly.

'I knew him personally, madam ...' Mistry grumbled, 'and the man was anything but a saint, but now is not the time or place to discuss this.'

Sharvani smiled and embraced Ishita. 'Thank you, Arjun,' Sharvani whispered under her breath. 'You are truly a better man than your father was. Rest in peace.'

'Ahem ...' coughed Mistry. 'Moving on ...'

'Each of the servants excluding Mr Anshul Baghri, for their loyal servitude, are awarded a sum of rupees five thousand.'

There was an outcry of joy, and howls of happiness, as the servants jumped up, embracing each other, unable to believe their ears.

Sharvani grinned. The amount of positivity in the room was impossibly infectious, touching even J.D. Mistry, who allowed them to have their momentary outburst of celebration, as he put the papers in order. Arjun's generosity seemed to have touched everyone's hearts.

Maybe money could truly buy happiness.

Everybody was happy. All except one. Archana Rana. She sat there motionless, a grim expression on her face. There was an anger bubbling underneath, Sharvani surmised. But it would be quelled. This was just the monetary part, after all. The real fortune of the Ranas lay in the estate.

'Are we done with this nonsensical little farce?' she snarled. 'Then carry on, Mr Mistry.'

Sharvani did the calculations in her head; ten servants getting five thousand each meant there was still one and a half lakh rupees left.

'Rai Bahadur loyally served me and my father before. He ensured that no ill will or calamity befell my family, and it would only be fitting that I extend the same courtesy to his family. To that extent, I award the sum of rupees fifty thousand to his only known remaining family, Tej Bahadur.'

Archana shot Mistry a glance that would have melted an ice block in an instant.

He kept reading unperturbed. 'And the remainder amount ...'

'Finally,' grunted Archana with a sigh.

'For all the years of loyalty, love, support and for being a pillar of strength with unconditional love, I award the amount of rupees one lakh to Anshul Baghri.'

Anshul Baghri was stunned. He didn't say a word, but merely bowed his head, cradled his face in his hands and began weeping. Whether they were tears of joy or sorrow was anybody's guess.

'PREPOSTOROUS,' Archana roared, as she shot up from her chair. 'THIS IS A LIE ... THIS WILL HAS BEEN DOCTORED.'

'SIT DOWN, MISS RANA,' Mistry shouted, equally fierce. 'This is the last will and testament of my client Mr Arjun Digvijay Rana and while you're in my office, you will respect its rules. Now please calm yourself. The part relating to you is just about to come in.'

'Hhmph ... don't think I'll let you get away with this,' she grumbled, as she made herself comfortable on the chair once again.

'Oh ... I wouldn't dream of it,' Mistry replied with a sly grin.

'If we are all ready, I will finish off the part relating to the liquid assets. Rupees five thousand will be awarded to Mr J.D.Mistry for his diligent advice and as an additional token of appreciation on top of his regular fees to ensure that the execution of the contents of this will are implemented smoothly, and with immediate effect.'

'Wait ...' Ishita cried, raising her hand. She quickly lowered it when she realized she wasn't in her classroom and how foolish she looked.

All eyes were on her now.

There was pin-drop silence.

'The five thousand ...' she gulped. 'The additional appreciation?'

'Yes?' Mistry asked, raising his eyebrows and adjusting his glasses.

'It doesn't add up ... with the amount given to the servants, Anshul Kaka ... sorry Anshul Baghri, Tej Bahadur and the orphanage.'

'Oh,' he said, visibly perplexed. 'All servants are to be awarded ... da ... da ... da ... ah,' he said. 'Ah! Here it is ... all servants are to be awarded with the exception of the gardener,' he said with a sly grin, as he looked at Archana. 'The other servants are also given their amount without any obligation. They are free to decide whether or not they wish to continue their servitude to the mistress of Azad Manor.'

'That is a choice these miserable wretches won't have,' Archana grunted through gritted teeth.

'From now on, for all practical purposes, they are free to make their own decisions. So yes, does that sufficiently answer your question, Miss Dhiman?'

'Yes … yes … The numbers add up now,' she said hastily, silently cursing herself for opening her mouth in the first place.

'Well, since that's that, we can move to the division of the Rana family estate,' he said, clearing his throat once again, '… and the part concerning Archana Rana.'

'Get on with it,' Archana growled. His voice was beginning to grate on the ears.

'As you wish. With the financial holdings of the Rana estate successfully dispersed as outlined in the will, I now move forward to the real estate holdings.'

'Finally …' Archana grunted for the umpteenth time. 'I will begin with Miss Sharvani Mehra …'

Sharvani could feel her heart pounding. She wasn't even supposed to be there in the first place, let alone be entitled to anything.

Digvijay Rana would be rolling in his grave.

'To my former teacher, mentor and friend, I leave the outhouse, the greenhouse and all of the plants and flora. With the exception of one, the rest are henceforth hers. I can think of nobody better to take care of the property, and I can earnestly hope that she takes good care of the seedlings and nurtures them into plants of pride and joy, just as she had done with her students.'

'What nonsense is this ...' Archana screamed. 'Did Arjun really go off his rocker since his return? I have serious concerns regarding the legitimacy of this will.'

'Miss Rana,' Mistry said calmly this time, 'I can assure you that this is the last revised will and testament of your late husband, Mr Arjun Rana. He requested to make the changes and signed the documents in front of me and two external witnesses. There is documented proof of the same, which you can verify at your leisure. I will make these available to you if you so wish, but all that, AFTER the reading of the will,' he said sternly. 'Do I make myself clear?'

Archana stayed silent, fuming and stewing in her own anger.

'The rest of the property ...' he said, adjusting his glasses and ruffling through the papers of his will. 'The three other buildings, the garage and all of the vehicles stored within, the tea plantations, Azad Manor and the remainder of the fortune in its entirety, I leave to Miss Ishita Dhiman, my lifelong friend and confidant. It is my little way of saying thank you for the countless years of support, and selfless friendship.'

There was a stunned silence in the room. Ishita sat there, her mouth agape. 'This cannot be ... there's been some mistake,' she said, slinking into her chair.

Sharvani was next to her, patting her back, but all her senses were focused on Archana.

She was calm, unusually so, like the proverbial lull before the storm.

And just like that, in the blink of an eye, Archana's fury was unleashed.

She rose off her chair breathing fire, slamming the plaque off the lawyer's desk.

J.D. Mistry sat there unperturbed, his fingers crossed, amused by Archana's antics.

'This is a bloody fucking farce,' she roared.

She was screaming hysterically.

'I'll have you destroyed. You don't know who I am …' she screeched.

'I know you very well, Miss Rana; I have been your husband's family's solicitor for the past forty years. Now, if you will calm down, I will get to the part concerning you. It is but a few lines away.'

'This is a fucking joke: giving all the property to this bitch … this glorified babysitter. He must have been mad or incredibly stupid. She's done black magic,' she blabbered, '… brought back Digvijay Rana's ghost from the grave.'

'Miss Rana …' Mistry growled, growing irritated, 'I must insist that you withhold such commentary, for my office is not the place and neither are you in any position to debate on the deceased's will or talk about supernatural phenomenon. Regarding the will, one must hear it and accept it before voicing one's joy or discontent elsewhere. Now, do you want me to read out the part concerning you or should I have you escorted out of the premises before that?'

Sharvani hoped that better sense would prevail.

Or maybe her greed.

Whatever it was, Archana plopped back down onto her chair.

'Ahem …' Mistry coughed. 'To my "ahem" … in inverted commas, my loving wife, I bequeath the one plant that I doubt even Miss Mehra can adequately take care of. I leave her the *Mirabilis jalapa*, the only one of its kind in the region. I do this keeping in mind her affection for the blooming flower, and how she in, "congress", with the gardener made a regular affair of its care,' Mistry said and adjusted his glasses, looking straight at Archana. 'Mr Arjun Rana also insisted that the word congress be kept in quotes, so each can personally consider the nature of that detail and I, for the death of me, cannot figure out what he meant by that,' Mistry said with a sly smile.

Archana grunted at him. Her past two outbreaks seemingly sapped her of any remaining strength.

'This is a disgrace, Mr Mistry,' she began, as she got up, readying herself to walk out. 'You will hear from my lawyer.'

'I am your lawyer, Miss Rana,' he replied calmly, 'or rather was, since I am now the lawyer to the mistress of the Rana estate, who, for all practical purposes, is Ishita Dhiman.'

'I will rip you and this farcical will to shreds in court. I will not leave Azad Manor. I will not let go of what is mine, without a fight,' she growled, spite dripping off her every word.

'You cannot afford a lawyer that can rip me to shreds, Miss Rana,' he remarked unfazed. 'I have been the solicitor of the Zamindar's family for the last forty years and hitherto yours, until ten minutes ago,' he chuckled, 'but I can assure you in all sincerity that the document, the last will of Arjun Rana, is both legal and authentic. You may feel free to engage anybody in India on the subject of the British common law, and it would bring me no end of delight to watch them hit the proverbial brick wall. As a parting piece of advice though, I'd ask you not to,' he said with a smile. 'The legatees may now leave ...' he continued, addressing the others and Archana.

The ex-mistress of Azad Manor stormed out of the office in a huff, not waiting to hear the rest of Mistry's words, slamming the door on her way out.

J.D. Mistry remained unfazed, continuing to speak as if nothing had happened. 'The details of the aforementioned monetary transfers will be communicated in due course, with the exception of the property transfer, which will be undertaken with immediate effect. Tej ...' he said, '... I trust you will do the needful.'

Tej nodded. With Archana's departure, the tension in the room had dissipated, and the legatees were all smiles now as they took leave of the lawyer's office.

All except Ishita.

She sat there on her chair, unmoving. 'I don't know what Arjun was thinking,' she said, still unable to digest the fact about her inheritance.

'Breathe, dear child, just breathe,' Sharvani offered.

'I don't know what to think of it. I don't know what to do with all this,' she said, visibly perplexed.

Sharvani gave her a warm smile, and placed a comforting hand over her shoulder.

'Well then, darling … join the club.'

seventeen

It wasn't the flies that bothered Tej Bahadur.

Not half as much as the knife handle jutting out of Manohar Mishra's chest.

There were multiple stab wounds and Mishra lay there, his tongue lolling out, and his eyes housing an expression that denoted sheer terror.

'Did he die of fear as well?' Tej thought out loud. 'Was it the Zamindar's ghost ... no,' he shook his head and massaged his forehead as he pushed such thoughts out of his head.

Even though he didn't completely buy into the idea of Digvijay Rana committing murders from beyond the grave, the knife that was buried to the hilt in the caretaker's stomach was an answer to this conundrum.

The knife answered the what, how and where.

The only questions that remained now were who, why and when.

'At this rate, nobody will be left alive in this town,' groaned Tej, slapping his forehead. It hadn't been twenty-four hours since he had left J.D. Mistry's office, fifty thousand rupees richer, and in that span of time, another person was murdered.

'What do we know?' came a voice from behind him.

It was Sharvani.

Tej Bahadur merely grunted, acknowledging her presence. As much as he hated it, Sharvani had proved to be invaluable in this investigation so far, shedding light and finding an opening whenever Tej had reached a dead end.

He wasn't equipped for this kind of thing.

The two murders he was investigating were two more than what he had ever faced in his entire fifteen-year career.

'This is a crime scene. No civilians are allowed,' he barked with disdain. Not even a day after he promised himself there would be no more murders, for this to happen, filled the head constable with dread and frustration.

'Of course they're not allowed,' Sharvani said disconcertedly, as she walked past him and stopped near the cadaver.

An overenthusiastic constable stepped forward in an attempt to pull her back, but was quickly dissuaded by Tej, because Sharvani Mehra was proficient in looking for the overlooked. For doing exactly what was needed to be done at a particular moment.

And he hated her for it.

He hated her for stealing those years where his father chose to warm her bed rather than their family's stove, leaving him and his mother starving. He pushed those grim thoughts away from his head.

Lest there be a fourth murder. This one committed by his hand.

'Ishita was the first intended victim,' Sharvani commented offhandedly, as she carefully examined the exit wound. 'The reasoning is simple …'

'... it's because the killer already knew of Arjun Rana's changed will,' interjected Tej with a grunt. 'Tell us something we don't know, for, as far as I'm concerned, these are two separate cases, and while I thank you for your help, I'm afraid I must ...'

'Hush, Tej ...' she said sternly, as he got up. 'There are no accidents in this universe, and these back-to-back murders in a span of as many days when none occurred for the past forty years would be a little more than a mere coincidence, wouldn't you say?'

Tej looked at her red-faced.

She ignored him. 'The weapon used is the knife ... it's the same type used against Ishita ...' she commented, 'and Mishra was potentially the last person to see Rai Bahadur alive.'

Tej's blood boiled as he heard his father's name escape her lips.

His rising tone wasn't something that escaped Sharvani's attention, but she ignored that nonetheless.

There was a time to be sentimental and a time to be practical.

'In Rai's ...' she stopped as abruptly as she began. 'The Zamindar's aide-de-camp's murder, Mishra was one of the witnesses.'

'He claimed to have seen nothing,' Tej retorted. 'If you remember, his wife found him passed out over the counter.'

'He could have been lying for all we know ...' she surmised. 'Maybe that's what got him killed?'

'You can't be suggesting ...'

'I'm thinking out loud ...' she concluded. 'Maybe that's what got him killed.'

'You can't be suggesting ...' he repeated.

'I'm just thinking out loud ...' she cut him off again. Sharvani was silent for a moment, replaying all the facts, the timeline of events, the suspect's motives and alibis in her head.

This was all connected, that much was certain.

And the Rana family was in the middle of it.

It could have been Digvijay's ghost, she thought, and as much as it pained her, she couldn't completely cross the possibility of a supernatural element off her list. Everything was possible unless absolutely proven otherwise, but until the existence of this ghost was proven, she would treat the killer as one more sinister than a ghost.

One made of flesh and blood.

What had she missed? She racked her brain with all the possible permutations and combinations, replaying all the events from Arjun Rana's comeback, right till the discovery of Mishra's corpse.

Then it hit her.

'I bumped into Arjun ...' she thought out aloud, with a sparkle in her eyes, the one her students would have after figuring out how to solve a particularly sticky arithmetic problem.

'Excuse me?'

'On the night Ishita was attacked ... I bumped into him, as he was leaving this ... establishment.'

'Arjun Rana!' said Tej incredulously. 'In this establishment ... IMPOSSIBLE!'

'That's what I first thought as well; he told me he was here to check on room vacancies for his reception guests, but I wasn't entirely convinced. Although I didn't give it much thought then ...'

'That means Mishra could have seen something ...' he exclaimed, slapping his forehead again. 'Maybe Arjun had come to meet my fat— Rai Bahadur.'

Sharvani rolled her eyes, silently thanking her stars that these were the only murders committed in forty years. The constabulary was obviously not equipped enough to deal with this kind of threat. Unfortunately, Tej hadn't inherited the cunning that made his father the Zamindar's right hand.

'Eric ... that bastard ...' Tej roared, spewing venom.

'... was in custody when this murder was committed,' she reminded him quickly.

He nodded.

'As a matter of fact, he still is … isn't he?'

Tej Bahadur shuffled his feet, trying and failing to conceal his utter frustration.

Sharvani understood immediately. 'Who provided the bail?'

'Guess!'

She sighed.

Deeply.

'How could I have gone so wrong with you, Archana?' she lamented under her breath.

Even at high noon, dark clouds covered the sky, enveloping it in a shade of dark grey.

When Sharvani would look up at the sky, she used to find hope, but now, all she saw was despair and darkness.

'Archana has been readying her possessions,' Tej commented as they left Aneri Plume.

'Oh?'

'The will states that all of its clauses be taken into immediate effect.'

Sharvani stayed silent as she stepped out into the dull, grey rain. The icy raindrops made the drop in temperature even more apparent, and Sharvani could feel an uneasy chill in the air.

In the fifty years she had been in Ooty, never had she felt the cold unwelcoming.

Maybe it was her imagination.

But somehow, the sky seemed darker; the tranquil and sleepy little town of Ooty now seemed infected with gloom. There was a thick fog that blanketed the town. It was so thick that it could almost be cut with a knife.

She shuddered at the thought of a knife, as she instinctively turned her attention towards Azad Manor. The mansion's outline could still be seen amidst the fog, as it stood there menacingly, exuding its old master's evil influence over the town.

She felt a sense of dread on looking at it.

'The gardener is helping her pack ...' Tej said, yanking her out of her thoughts.

'Huh?'

'Eric,' he repeated, 'he's helping her pack. They are going to leave ... Ishita is supposed to move in today.'

She nodded, lost in thought.

Tej decided not to trouble her anymore.

The sound of a horse clopping cut the silence, growing louder with every passing second.

Clip clop.

Clip clop.

It rang from a distance, very faint and distant at first, then more distinct as it kept growing louder and louder.

CLIP CLOP.

CLIP CLOP.

The sounds of the horse's hooves were soon joined by the sound of coarse wheels turning over the craggy road, until a carriage rode into view.

'Good thinking,' Sharvani said to herself. 'Only an idiot would choose to walk through this thick fog.'

'Miss Mehra!'

The buoyancy in the familiar voice was hard to miss.

Sharvani looked up. Ishita was travelling in a simple tanga, even though she now legally had the fleet of the Rana family's cars at her disposal.

A small striped tweed suitcase lay beside her, a collection of all her worldly belongings, and they would fit in less than a fraction of the spacious Azad Manor. The light drizzle touched Ishita's face as she gave a bittersweet smile of acknowledgment to her old teacher.

Sharvani smiled back, noting that the rain did a good job of hiding her student's tears.

'Won't you join me?'

Sharvani looked at her with a single raised eyebrow.

'As you can see, I packed light,' Ishita said with a slight chuckle, trying to make the situation easier, and then her voice broke. 'It's just ... it's just that ...' she said, barely able to contain her sobs. There was a strange melancholy in her voice. 'I'd appreciate the company ... I'm not used to living in such ... I mean, I'm just still so very out of place with the whole situation.'

Sharvani opened her mouth to begin with what seemed like a protest, but Tej Bahadur jumped at the idea.

'Very well, Miss,' he said assertively, as he clambered on the side step, and pulled himself into the carriage.

'I'd also like to make sure that that ruffian Eric doesn't make a scene,' he said loudly. 'And besides, I've forgotten to get my bicycle,' he grunted under his breath.

'I'm more worried about Archana to be honest ...' Ishita confessed sheepishly.

Sharvani stood there for a minute, unsure of whether to join the duo. The slight drizzle was beginning to quickly increase into a drenching rain.

But Sharvani didn't mind the rain, even though it had begun to permeate through her clothing and chill her to the bone.

Sharvani didn't mind walking, but one look at the sorrow on Ishita's face, and Sharvani stepped into the carriage.

The ride to Azad Manor was quiet.

There was pin-drop silence with each of the occupants in the carriage lost in their own thoughts. Only the pitter-patter of the raindrops against the carriage, and the clip-clopping of the horse's hooves, broke the silence.

Sharvani looked at Ishita. The young girl was lost in thought; the emotional burden of inheriting the infamous Azad Manor with all its ghosts, both literal and metaphorical, seemed too heavy a burden on her young shoulders.

'Are you alright?' Sharvani asked.

'I'm fine ...' Tej began.

Sharvani frowned at him.

'Oh,' he exclaimed as he realized his folly.

Ishita chuckled. 'It's funny ...'

'What is?'

'That Arjun decided to change his will and that too so suddenly, and without telling anyone.'

Sharvani shook her head. 'I'm sure Arjun must have told somebody. When you were first attacked, it was difficult, if not impossible, to gauge why somebody would do that.'

'But Miss Mehra ... I told you, it was the Zamindar's ghost ...' she protested.

Tej gasped, his eyes nearly popping out of their sockets. 'Why didn't you tell me this before?' he roared.

'I ... I told Miss Mehra ...' Ishita said sheepishly.

Tej looked at Sharvani Mehra, fire burning in his eyes.

'And why didn't you tell me?' he shouted.

'It slipped my mind ...' she replied calmly. 'And I didn't think it was pertinent to the case.'

'And what is pertinent, do tell ...' he growled through gritted teeth.

'That maybe Ishita's mind played tricks on her that night… are you sure you saw the Zamindar's ghost?'

Ishita gulped. 'Now that you mention it, it was dark … raining … I cannot be completely sure, but his voice was unmistakable … also the boots …' her voice trailed off.

'There you go …' Sharvani nodded triumphantly, while Tej shook his head in frustration.

'Whoever attacked Ishita knew of the changed will, so at that time, there seemed to be no motive for the attack, but now, it seems that the killer was trying to redress Arjun's changed decision permanently.'

'Go on …' Tej said, twirling his fingers together.

'In all likelihood, Arjun must have confided his decision to the one person closest to him, the one person closest to his father: Rai Bahadur,' Sharvani said. 'Rai Bahadur must have let it slip and maybe that is why he too was murdered.'

'My father was killed by the Zamindar's ghost. He died out of fright and Dr Khuranna's report proves as much.'

Sharvani rolled her eyes.

'But all of this is so unfair to Archana,' Ishita reasoned.

'Sometimes, when it rains …' Sharvani said, as she put her hand out of the tanga, feeling the drops of rain moisten her palm, 'one mustn't always look to beat the rain, but accept the fact that one may get wet.'

'That philandering whore deserves no less; ruining families' lives for her own selfish wants,' Tej replied, staring right at Sharvani and not breaking his gaze.

It was clear whom he was referring to when he said those words, but Sharvani remained unfazed.

There was a time for sentimentality and a time for practicality, she quietly reminded herself again.

But with Tej, it was increasingly becoming harder to restrain her anger.

Ishita looked at Sharvani, then at Tej. She was visibly confused.

'But, like I said, I have a professional interest in coming along with you as well ...' he commented assertively, albeit out of the blue. 'I'm curious to see how the wife and the gardener will react when it's time to leave. They may get violent,' he said with a smirk.

'Besides, you forgot your bicycle ...' Sharvani remarked offhandedly.

'I still believe that the house is haunted by the Zamindar's ghost,' he said, ignoring her comment. 'I have seen the apparition with my own two eyes.'

'Oh really?' exclaimed Sharvani, with raised eyebrows. 'Pray tell, when?'

'When I was doing my rounds one night.'

'Oh,' she said with thinly veiled disgust.

Tej glared at her with contempt.

'Besides, Miss Mehra's theories however intriguing and interesting they may sound, are ultimately baseless. My father ...' Tej said, acknowledging Rai Bahadur as his father in longer than he could remember, '... my father died from fright. He was a brave man and believe me you, nothing short of his late employer's ghost would have been enough to faze him. Miss Mehra's theories, though entertaining to listen to, require too many suppositions, because if we look at it, she is trying to make a jigsaw puzzle with no picture to go on and multiple overlapping pieces,' he said with a grin.

Sharvani smiled back. 'For once I agree with you.'

'You do?' he asked incredulously.

'Of course, my dear sir ... for once I can say that with these deaths, both the police and myself have not much to go on, and we practically know nothing. In fact, the head constable's prime suspect is the spirit of a dead man.'

Ishita chuckled.

Tej glared at Sharvani.

Again.

The elderly teacher sighed as the carriage pulled closer towards Azad Manor. The dark clouds circling overhead appeared even more ominous as the carriage brought them closer to the manor.

The manor that stood before them looked bare, ugly even. Stripped of the beautification bestowed upon it a few nights ago, all its unsightly cracks and imperfections were now glaring out at the trio. The house seemed to reek of sadness. And death.

The lively exterior of the manor seen a couple days back was a façade, a facelift given to make guests believe that the Rana family's fortunes would turn at the arrival of its prodigal son, Sharvani presumed.

But it was not to be.

The bleak manor seemed unwelcoming to them, backed by a dark, grey sky. The sight of the once magnificent estate that had now fallen into such terrible ruin saddened Sharvani. Anshul Baghri stood there with an umbrella in hand, and a permanent grin plastered on his face. Whether it was genuine or a habit developed through years of under-recognized service, Sharvani didn't know.

'Welcome … welcome, Memsaab,' he grinned, as he pulled open the rusty old arch that was supported by short columns.

Ishita smiled out of courtesy.

He offered to take her bag, but she politely declined, as she stepped out of the carriage.

'Where … where are the … um … other bags?' he hesitantly asked after a moment, afraid of displeasing his new mistress.

Ishita smiled at him. 'This is all I have, Anshul Kaka,' she smiled warmly. 'And don't worry, my entrance does not merit any degree of ceremony.'

'Oh!'

He wasn't used to the previous maalkin travelling so light, even on her weekend 'botanical' sightseeing tours with the gardener.

The clouds had let way without warning. The rain was light, barely a drizzle, but Anshul walked behind Ishita, an umbrella held safely over her head, ensuring not a drop of rain fell on her.

'Where are the others, Anshul?' Sharvani asked, noticing the conspicuous absence of the other staff.

'Memsaab ...'

'Yes?' Ishita asked, concerned.

'No ... no ... the other Memsaab ...' he said, referring to Archana. 'She let them go ... this morning ... after Arjun Saab's demise and their subsequent ... reward for services rendered, not many chose to stay.'

'Not to mention, Archana's behaviour,' Tej grunted under his breath. 'And you ... why did you stay back? You were the most well rewarded of them all,' he asked, more out of curiosity than concern.

'I've given my life to the Rana family,' he replied. 'Nothing short of my death will make me retire from the service of Azad Manor.'

Sharvani noticed the glint in his eyes when he spoke. There was genuineness, a warmth and more importantly, pride in his voice. Like serving the Rana family was his purpose.

One that he would fulfil above and beyond the call of duty.

'Has Archana Memsaab left?' Tej asked, his procedural instincts coming to the fore.

'No, sir ...' explained Anshul as they reached the main door.

'And Eric?' Sharvani asked quickly.

All three of them looked at her, stunned for a moment.

'Eric ... um ...' stammered Anshul.

'Out with it ...' Tej roared.

'The Memsaab asked him to leave with the rest of the servants,' he said quickly as he pressed the door handle.

It didn't budge.

Anshul had a befuddled expression on his face. 'I swear I left it unlocked,' he mumbled as he pulled out a keyring holding a stack of keys from his pocket. He expertly flipped through them until he found one, completely undistinguishable from the rest.

He placed it within the lock and cursed under his breath when it didn't give.

'That's funny.' He tried flicking it in the lock again, but it still didn't budge.

'Are you sure you're using the right key?' Tej questioned grumpily.

'Sir …' Anshul retorted, visibly cross, 'with all due respect, I have been serving Azad Manor and the Rana family for over forty years, so I'm pretty sure it is absolutely the right key.'

Tej looked at Sharvani for a moment.

Her eyes said it all.

He moved Anshul out of the way, and slammed his shoulder against the thick door.

Once.

Twice.

'Sir …' Anshul protested, 'I must ask you to cease doing that … these doors are made from imported Kashmir willow. Master Digvijay Rana hired the best sculptors to …'

'Oh … I'm sure that the new Memsaab doesn't mind.'

Ishita nodded her approval to Baghri, worry lines beginning to contort her otherwise pleasant face.

Thrice.

The door was beginning to budge, with Tej's strength, and the dampness in the weather played havoc with the wood, loosening it just enough.

Four times.

'One more solid push,' Tej thought.

But it gave way before that.

Tej stumbled through on to the floor.

'See ... I told you ...' he said with a chuckle as he began to pick himself up and turned around.

There was silence for a moment, their jaws agape as all four of them stood there, taking in the gruesome sight.

And then, Ishita screamed.

Archana Rana's lifeless body lay on the stairs. Her wrists were slit and blood was oozing from her veins and flowing down the stairs. A bloody knife lay beside her, appearing to have dropped from her cold, clammy hands. Her kajal was smeared, presumably from her tears when she committed the heinous deed. Her tongue was dangling out of her mouth lifelessly. Her once pristine white gown was now smeared with patches of red. There was a note clutched tightly in her hand—the words on it were bold, emblazoned in red.

Sharvani was the first to step closer to the corpse. She stooped down and picked up the paper.

Tej came up behind her as she uncrumpled the note.

'What do you think?'

YOU WILL NEVER GET RID OF ME, the note screamed, its words littered in blood.

'Well ...' Sharvani said calmly, 'if there wasn't a ghost in Azad Manor earlier ...' she commented, as she looked at Archana's lifeless body, and then at the note, 'there certainly is one now.'

eighteen

Sharvani dreaded having to be in the manor.

It seemed to be cursed.

She looked around at its palatial interiors, regal furniture and expensive paintings and the taxidermized animal heads that adorned its walls. All of it was so familiar to her, and yet today, it looked completely unknown.

It looked sinister.

Anshul Baghri had scrubbed the remnants of Archana Rana's blood off the carpet, till his fingers were chafed.

There were still some blotches, reasoned Sharvani, but she wasn't sure if they were actually there or if it was her imagination. They were too well camouflaged by the velvety blood red carpet.

'Goodness …' Ishita exclaimed, feeling as if the room were expanding all around her. It was the first time that she actually noticed the enormity of the manor.

Her words actually echoed off the walls.

'It is a little big for one person…' Sharvani commented dryly.

'Well … that's why I invited you … and Tuffy.' As if on cue, the little Shih Tzu came rushing in towards her, licking her hand with the unconditional love that only animals could give.

'And …' she said with an extended flourish and a broad grin, ' tea…' she exclaimed, as Anshul Baghri, having cleaned up, stood behind a small perfectly decorated round table, with a pot and immaculately placed cutlery.

'I promise I'll have sherry the next time around,' Ishita commented. Sharvani chuckled.

'You'd better,' she said with a smile as they walked over to the table. Baghri politely pulled the chairs for the both of them, as Tuffy circled around in excitement.

'Will there by anything else, maalkin?'

Ishita was at a loss for words. She looked at Sharvani with her version of the 'help me' expression.

'Maybe some scones or might I suggest a delightful bread pudding?' Anshul said in his soft, buttery tone.

'Some pakoras if you please, Anshul,' Sharvani interrupted. 'You will find that your new maalkin's tastes are rooted closer to home.'

Anshul smiled warmly at them. 'Excellent choice, madam,' he said, then he walked off.

'Oh and Anshul …' Ishita cried.

'Yes, maalkin.'

'Go easy on the chillies, if you please. Tuffy doesn't like too much spice in the food.'

'Oh,' he exclaimed and left.

'There was genuine surprise on his face.'

'Of course.'

The women smiled at each other once Baghri was out of earshot.

'Well, MISS MEHRA, HOW'D YU LIKE YAH FIRST CANDLELIGHT SUPPA ...' Ishita said mockingly, in a heavy English accent.

There was a delicate, intricately carved candleholder placed in the middle of the table.

Two sturdy candles were balanced on both ends, which Ishita proceeded to light.

'Will you manage here?' Sharvani asked with genuine concern.

There was a frown on Ishita's demure face. 'Truth be told ... I don't know? It's been two days since that awful incident with Archana ... and I can't help but feel responsible for her taking such a step.'

'Don't be ...' Sharvani consoled her. 'Archana was beyond help ...' she said with a tinge of sadness. 'A lifetime of bad decisions had culminated into this. It wasn't anybody's fault. Thank you for choosing to listen to me and deciding to stay here ...'

'Honestly ...' Ishita said, 'I was much happier in that tiny little shack I called home. But like you said, when it rains, one mustn't always look to escape the rain, but accept the fact that one might get wet.' She poured Sharvani and herself two cups of the hearty, hot liquid and couldn't help but pour Tuffy a little in a saucer, when she saw him showing her puppy-eyes.

No sooner was the saucer placed in front of him did his tail start wagging in wanton excitement, and he began to lap up the warm beverage.

Ishita smiled. It did her heart good to see the love and excitement this little bundle of joy held within him.

He was so simple in his nature, only giving love and asking for love in return. 'Why couldn't humans be more like animals?' she wondered out loud, looking at Sharvani for her opinion on the matter, but the elderly matron's attention was diverted elsewhere.

'This smells a bit ... odd,' Sharvani remarked. 'A little bit like bitter almonds ...'

'Does it? I wouldn't know. The tea leaves, Anshul said, were picked fresh from the plantation,' she said, taking in a deep whiff of the warm aroma.

'Maybe the taste will give us better insight,' Ishita commented as she picked up the cup and brought it to her lips.

'Ishita ... don't,' screamed the older lady.

And then, without warning, the lights went out.

There was a shrill scream and the sound of china crashing that pierced the air, followed by Tuffy's stifled yelp and the distant pitter-patter of paws running further down into the darkness.

'I'm sorry ... I'm sorry ...' Ishita gasped.

She was out of breath. Her heart was pounding. 'The lights ... the lights ... just going off like this ... I was startled.'

'Tuffy,' Sharvani yelled, but there was no response.

She couldn't help but feel her heartbeat quicken, as her mind began to expect the worst. She swiftly pulled a candle out of the holder and handed it to Ishita.

'The tea?' she asked. 'Did you have any of it?'

'Huh?' Ishita was dumbfounded.

'The tea ...' she yelled again, snapping Ishita out of her trance.

'No ... no ...' she replied breathlessly.

'Take this,' she said, handing her the candle. 'Find Tuffy and then go to Anshul ... don't let that man out of your sight.'

'Where is the fuse box?' she asked Ishita, although the question was redundant, for Sharvani knew the layout of the house as well as any of its previous inhabitants.

'I ... I don't know.'

'It's okay,' Sharvani said calmly. 'Find Tuffy, I'll get the lights.'

Sharvani could see her pupil nod in the dim light afforded by the candle. The older lady didn't hesitate as she rushed up the stairs, towards the fuse box.

She took a couple of turns, zigzagging her way through the corridors.

The fuse box was there in front of her, but the sight she saw, the entity that stood between her and the fuse box froze the blood in her veins.

Digvijay Rana.

Sharvani stood there motionless, her body petrified.

She tried to move, but her body wouldn't listen, although her mind was wishing she could take back every word she had said to Tej about the non-existence of the supernatural.

She had said several times that she wouldn't believe anything of the sort till she saw proof with her own two eyes.

And now, Sharvani Mehra was a believer.

The body of her deceased lover was floating in front of her.

Digvijay Singh, the Zamindar, stood in front of her, his feet several feet above the ground.

'Digvijay,' Sharvani stammered.

He didn't respond, but stood there as still as a corpse, his eyes wide and white as marble.

'Sharvani,' he whispered.

Her blood froze. She felt an uneasy chill seep inside her. The Zamindar's words came out as white steam in the cold, darkened manor.

Sharvani stood there silently, an uncomfortable feeling rising up from the pit of her stomach; it was one that she hadn't felt in a long time.

She felt fear.

She looked at him again. The Zamindar was only a husk of his former self, stringy hair and a gaping mouth with two sets of bony arms. The skin hanging from his body seemed deathly grey. His clothes were weathered, a dampness emanating off them, as if they were just pulled out from a dirty river. There were several dark blue marks around his neck, no doubt the remnants of the gashes of the knife wounds on his neck.

'You killed me,' he moaned.

'You killed yourself ...' she mumbled defiantly, drawing on courage from some obscure part of her heart.

'You must help me ...' he groaned again. As he opened his mouth, his jaw dropped.

Literally.

His flesh began to rot, and his eyes began to turn a polluted white, and shrivelled back into his skull.

His bluish skin began to crack, emanating an odd glow amidst the darkness. The fear Sharvani felt was now replaced by panic, which quickly began to rise in the pit of her gut.

Her eyes darted across the phantom, desperately searching for something logical and tangible to bring her mind back to reality. He was clad in the same clothing that his body was found in: mud was dripping from his thick gardener's boots.

Was he really the killer?

Had his ghost come back to exact revenge on those who had wronged him?

And now, was it Sharvani's turn?

'You must protect my legacy,' he whispered again. His jaw lay squirming on the floor, but his mouth still moved, bringing out an eerie sound, which was bloodcurdling.

'Arjun is dead,' she replied calmly.

'SILENCE,' he roared. 'My legacy still endures.'

'Digvijay.'

He grabbed her hand mid-sentence, sending dark daggers of ice into her bones.

Sharvani's legs weakened and a ball of nausea rose in her gullet.

'I made several mistakes in life,' he said, as he drew a strained, rattling breath, 'but this mistake is not letting me rest. The Rana family endures. My heir exists ... PROTECT my legacy Sharvani, lest you end up like me.'

'Like you?'

'Many more will die if you do not act ... and then it will be you, Sharvani Mehra. Death will come for you, as it had for me,' he warned. 'Protect my legacy.' His breath was putrid, and Sharvani recoiled.

'Aren't you killing the others? You are responsible for their deaths.'

The phantom snarled. 'I may be responsible, but I'm not the cause of their demise. The ones who were killed had their own reasons to be killed; they were not pure of heart. They were men of evil, like I was. Like you are ...' he chuckled eerily.

Sharvani gulped. Her mind was reeling, refusing to accept the evidence of her other senses.

'Remember my words, Sharvani. Protect my legacy; it will be your only salvation, the only way you will be saved. And remember that I chose you, and think ... think long and hard upon why ... and the consequences of being blind towards what you know to be right.'

She struggled to control her breathing, to focus on something logical, but she could find nothing.

She was, in fact, staring at the ghost of Digvijay Rana, her erstwhile lover.

The Zamindar's ghost.

His once-thick hair turned stringy and soon even that began to wither and fall, revealing a cracking skull beneath it.

'Protect my legacy. Only then will I find peace, only then will I be released from the shackles of this mortal coil,' he croaked. 'But trust me you, as long as my ghost roams these hallowed halls, no one is safe.' The modality and tone of his voice was the same, but to Sharvani, it sounded different.

The voice now sounded evil.

The words a threat.

'Wait,' Sharvani yelled, 'Digvijay.'

His body began to wither to dust right in front of her eyes. She looked on, as a gust of icy wind sent the dust swirling around into the air, away even, though there was no sign of wind merely seconds prior.

The feeling of dread grew and began to push down on her like a physical force, until her legs finally buckled and she sank to her knees, horror gripping her very soul.

The hall was illuminated suddenly, the lights coming back on in quick succession, bathing the manor in a grandeur that it was once accustomed to.

Sharvani knelt there, still as a corpse, trying to piece together the events of the last few minutes.

What had he meant?

Her heart was still racing when she felt an icy hand grip her shoulder.

'AAAAAAAAYYYEEEEEEGGGHHHH!' She screamed in fright, as her heart nearly jumped out of her skin.

She turned around—the startled figure of Ishita Dhiman stood there, with a candlestick in her hand.

Even she was visibly taken aback by Sharvani's reaction.

'I'm ... I'm sorry to have startled you,' she apologized, still trying to comprehend Sharvani's reaction.

Sharvani was breathing heavily, taking in long gulps of air. 'Did you unpack?' she asked breathlessly.

'Huh?'

'Did ... you ... unpack ...' she asked again, slower and louder this time.

'No ... no ...' Ishita stammered.

'Good ... we're leaving.'

'Why? You were the one who convinced me to stay.'

'We are leaving,' she said as she brushed past Ishita and rushed down the stairs.

Ishita knew that tone. It meant that there was no room for debate. She had heard it hundreds of times while growing up in Sharvani's care. It was the same then and it was the same now.

It was assertive, totalitarian even. For when Sharvani Mehra spoke in that tone, all and sundry were expected to listen.

The only thing that troubled Ishita was that for the first time since she could remember, the assertiveness of the tone was tinged with fear.

Sharvani turned around.

Ishita was still rooted in place.

'Are you deaf?' she scolded. 'I told you we have to leave. Did you find Tuffy ... and Anshul? I need to speak to him.'

Ishita remained silent, her eyes welling up with tears.

'Tuffy ...' she whispered, her voice beginning to crack, a portent of the sobs to come.

'Tuffy ...' she cried, '... Tuffy's dead.'

nineteen

To whomsoever it may concern,

        This is to be treated as a signed confession of myself, Mr Alexander Spencer Stephan. I am writing this because I have recently come to hear of the death of Mrs Archana Rana.

Everything is lost; everything I have worked for, plotted for, is all for naught, and now … now my conscience cannot bear the burden. I am tired of these lies. All I wanted to do was become a successful entrepreneur in my own right, but the price I had to pay for that is far too high for my already damaged morals.

The testimony I gave to the police about the events that transpired on the night of Arjun Rana's murder was a lie.

Eric Matheson climbed the wall at the purported time of Arjun Rana's death. He climbed over onto the carriage and from there, he jumped onto the terrace to access another window and made the footprints in the wrong direction, to mislead the police.

I lied on the behest of Archana Rana. I was still around after the time of the accident, when the police decided to round up the guests at the party. Archana took me aside then and asked me to lie about Eric's presence near the carriage, and also about other small things too trivial to mention here.

I hesitated at first, but she seemed to be a lot more predisposed to my offer of buying out Azad Manor and after Arjun's death, she was obviously the next in line to inherit the entire Rana fortune, including the manor. At the time, it seemed prudent to finally get my hands on the coveted property for a mere pittance. After all the years of begging and grovelling at the feet of the insufferable Digvijay Rana and his equally self-entitled son, the idea of turning Azad Manor into the Alexander Stephan Resort for the privileged was too great to pass up.

And all it cost was one little white lie.

I asked Archana at the time who killed Arjun Rana, and she simply replied it was the Zamindar's ghost.

I remember her perfect teeth when she smiled at me, before quickly turning her business deal into a veiled threat. She insisted on full cooperation, lest the Zamindar's ghost come for me too, like he had for Rai Bahadur. The smile remained the same, but it seemed twisted somehow, coupled with the evil in her eyes.

What a fool I was.

To have bought into her fake allusions of grandeur. I was soon to find out after the reading of Arjun Rana's will that naught had been passed onto Archana.

I should have known. I should have been smarter.

The warnings were in the air. The whole staff knew of Archana's affair with Eric, and the servants have a habit of gossiping.

If you ask me, the butler did it.

Anshul Baghri must have told his master about Archana's infidelity. And it is only as I type this confession does the thought strike me, it may entirely be possible that after this revelation, Arjun may have consulted with the one man closest to him, with the most experience in these matters.

His father's aide-de-camp.

Rai Bahadur.

He would have told him about his intention to change his will.

And maybe, just maybe, Rai Bahadur leaked this information to Archana. He was rather fond of her … in spite of his infamous expulsion from Azad Manor.

I know this because several times, I have seen the good Mrs Rana leave Aneri Plume in a manner which can best be described as only half-decent, after what could presumably have been hours of strenuous activity.

Aneri Plume is a forward-thinking establishment and offers rooms to guests as per their needs, which typically only extends to a couple of hours. Only one guest had been staying there over an extended period of time.

Rai Bahadur.

The shocking revelation during the reading of Arjun's will only adds to my theory. However implausible it may seem, there can be only one explanation.

Arjun Rana was supposed to put in the changes in the will after the reception, but unbeknownst to others, he secretly went to J.D. Mistry and changed the will before time.

Archana's plan was foolproof and, if not for the unexpected little quirks of fate, things would have gone on splendidly. She had got Arjun killed to retain the property; as well as Rai Bahadur who had quickly become an obstacle, turning from a confidant to a liability.

What I don't understand is why she insisted that the Zamindar's ghost was behind these killings. I trusted her because her greed resonated with mine. She wanted to sell the property, pack up her fortunes and disappear with Eric, her lover, leaving this life behind as a very, very wealthy woman.

I have, to the best of my capabilities, tried to put down the events as clearly as my memory serves me.

I realize that I can and will be tried as an accomplice to a murder, and for misleading the police, both crimes for which I take full responsibility.

I do not hope for, nor do I ask for, any leniency or mercy, but only pray that with this act, I can absolve some of the wicked deeds I have committed, and the police can apprehend the other criminals in this sordid little affair, and finally end the curse of the Zamindar's ghost.

'Ghost,' recalled Alexander, as he downed the glass of whiskey, the ice clanking in his empty cup. He was safe in his little manor.

He felt a sense of inner peace on seeing his collection of expensive antique furniture, his bookcase filled with first editions, and countless paintings by renowned masters.

He didn't care much for actually reading the books, using the furniture or enjoying the paintings. He just wanted to own them, to hoard them.

The good things in life were free he heard, but he wanted the best things in life, and they were bloody expensive. Case in point, he poured himself another glass of exorbitantly priced whiskey.

The night was still, with a clear full moon after days of dampening rain.

'The worst is over,' he said to himself. Come morning, and Tej would get the letter, bring him to custody and arrest Matheson.

'The Zamindar's ghost,' he snickered, as he took in another lingering sip of the warm, gold liquid. The gall of Archana Rana, referring to her lover as the Zamindar's ghost.

Alexander Stephan didn't believe in ghosts. He was a businessman after all. No religion was truer than business, and no God more powerful than money.

He recalled the letter he typed once again, every letter of every word pounded in his head like the ribbon of the typewriter hitting against paper.

He couldn't get it out of his mind, no matter how hard he tried. Even though it had been an hour since he posted the letter to Tej Bahadur, time wasn't passing fast enough. The words still circled around his eyes, every word in it seemingly learned by-heart.

He could only trust Tej, not even Sharvani. Something was off about that woman, but he couldn't quite put his finger on it. Ideally, Alexander would have chosen to meet the head constable and tell him everything face to face, but trust Alexander's rotten luck to betray him at the last moment, as Tej was called out of town to complete the legal formalities regarding the Rana estate.

But Alexander Stephan was nothing, if not resourceful. He immediately rushed home and banged out his confession on the typewriter, describing the events to the best his memory allowed him. He hastily rushed off and posted the letter. The postman would have already collected it, he surmised, but Alexander Stephan could not help but feel a sense of dread creeping up on him.

He double-checked the locks on his door. The trusty tala, padlock, the chain were all in place. Multiple lights lit up the room to a point where it was almost mimicking daylight. There was nothing to be afraid of.

But in his heart, he knew, maybe Archana wasn't lying about the Zamindar's ghost.

No, he debated with himself in his mind. He was letting his imagination get the better of him. He smiled as he chuckled to himself, finishing his drink in a single gulp. 'Not even a ghost can get in ...' he grinned.

He felt a false sense of bravado until there was a slight buzzing sound, and the lights went off, bathing the entire room in darkness. There was an eerie whistling sound, and Stephan shuddered.

He had goosebumps.

The wind was moving up against the curtain of an open window and creating the howling sound. He smiled, wiping the sweat off his brow, as he slammed the window shut.

'Not even a ghost can get in,' he snickered, until a terrible thought came to the forefront of his mind.

All the windows were closed when he had entered the room.

'Nor can a ghost get out,' he heard a hoarse voice cackle. Stephan couldn't make out where the voice was coming from. Was it truly Digvijay Rana's ghost back from the grave?

'Eric … you bastard … You don't scare me. You won't get away with this.'

'Eric?' the eerie voice croaked. 'Nobody has ever confused me with Eric!' There was a sardonic chuckle in the air that seemed to originate from nowhere and everywhere at the same time.

Stephan couldn't hear anything over the clattering of his teeth, the wildly pounding heart in his chest.

'Who … who are you …' he stammered.

'The Zamindar …' the voice croaked evilly. 'The Zamindar's ghost.'

The darkness of the room was cut for a second with the gleaming shine of a knife, and the silence ran in ebbs and flows, broken only by the repeated muffled sounds of cold, sharp steel thrusting into soft, flabby flesh along with Stephan's subdued screams of terror.

And then, the night was still again.

twenty

The rain didn't show any signs of stopping.

Ishita looked at the weather outside, from the porch of Sharvani's plebeian home. For now, the humble little abode seemed to be infinitely more comfortable and homely to the unassuming schoolteacher and caretaker, than the palatial and spacious Azad Manor. She spent whatever was left of the night gathering her belongings and came away with Sharvani to stay in the latter's house first thing in the morning.

There was sadness in the air. The rain didn't bring with it a sense of tranquility, only sorrow.

It was as if the heavens were weeping for the fate that had befallen the town.

Sharvani came and stood beside her, offering a cup of piping hot tea, but her student declined.

'Maybe a glass of sherry perhaps?'

Ishita chuckled, but her laugh was hollow. 'The joke didn't work,' she said.

'What makes you think I was joking?' her teacher said with raised eyebrows.

'This is all my fault,' Ishita said, teary eyed.

'You mustn't blame yourself, child,' Sharvani added, but her words went unnoticed.

'I'm responsible for Archana's death,' Ishita said, sounding like she was in some sort of trance.

Sharvani wanted to console her, and say something, but she held her tongue; it was better for Ishita to take the weight off her chest first.

'Can't you see …' Ishita said, almost sobbing, 'I took away everything from her … all of what she thought she deserved was snatched away. Can you imagine what that feels like …' her voice trailed off.

'And Anshul,' she exclaimed. 'I knew him since I was a child. Why … why would he do such a thing?'

Sharvani had the beverage in the pot of tea tested. It was poisoned. Cyanide.

In a lethal enough dose, to kill a full-grown adult. Poor Tuffy didn't stand a chance.

Sharvani's keen olfactory senses picked up the bitter smell seconds before Ishita had almost taken a sip.

Otherwise, along with Tuffy, there would have been another cremation today.

It hadn't taken long after that. Tej had been summoned, and Anshul Baghri was taken away in chains. Sharvani vividly remembered seeing the fear in his eyes, as he screamed his throat sore, proclaiming his innocence.

But all to no avail.

Even when he was being taken away, the last thing he told Sharvani was that he was innocent.

And something about Anshul's words hit the mark.

She felt he was telling the truth.

'Ishita … you don't …' Sharvani began to speak, but was interrupted by a vigorous knock on her gate.

Sanjeev stood there with an umbrella nestled between his arms. 'Good day, ma'am,' he said, shuddering from the cold.

The constable was drenched to the bone, his cotton uniform sticking to his scrawny frame like it was a second skin.

'Sanjeev,' Sharvani yelled. 'What are you doing, you'll catch your death of a cold.'

'Tej sir has requested your presence,' he mumbled through chattered teeth.

'I'll come by when the rain stops …' she said worriedly. 'Use the umbrella … go back.'

'He insists on you coming now, ma'am. He says it's terribly urgent.'

Sharvani looked cross. 'I told you …'

'Go …' Ishita said calmly.

'Are you sure?' she asked with a hint of worry in her voice.

'I'll be fine; you raised a tough little nut, Miss Mehra.'

'I'll be back soon,' Sharvani said, almost apologetically.

'Take your time.'

Sharvani motioned to Sanjeev to come in closer and open the umbrella. If she were going to go through this deluge, she would try and make sure that she remained as dry as possible.

Ishita looked on with a bittersweet smile, as her teacher and the constable moved in unison, the teacher chiding the policeman like one scolds a particularly difficult child.

She turned around and went into the house. Maybe she would have that glass of sherry Sharvani had suggested after all.

If she had stayed out a minute longer, she would have seen the fearsome figure bounding in closer towards Sharvani Mehra's house.

Drenched to the bone, there was only an unfettered rage in his eyes, a sharp knife clutched tightly within his fist, and his feet were draped in thick, rugged boots, leading a trail of murky footprints that Sharvani had seen a little too often for her liking in the past few days.

* * *

'What was so important, Tej?' Sharvani chastised him as she entered the police station. 'God himself is out there urinating over us. What was so important that it couldn't wait?' she scolded.

'This,' he said quietly, as he pushed a piece of paper towards her.

'What's this?'

'It arrived this morning ...'

She wanted for him to elaborate. He stayed silent.

Apparently, he wanted her to find out for herself.

She looked at him again before going through the note.

Her mind raced as she processed what was put down in the written word.

It took her less than thirty seconds.

She stared at him. She was at a loss for words.

'We found Stephan's body after breaking down his door, or at least whatever was left of it. He was stabbed mercilessly, too many times to count. We left for his place immediately after receiving the letter. We shouldn't have let Eric go,' Tej lamented, 'but his plans failed ...' Tej added, giving out a hollow laugh. 'He may have gotten off scot-free, but he didn't leave with a single paisa.'

Sharvani grunted in acknowledgement, but she didn't necessarily agree with what Tej thought. She knew men like Matheson.

They were brutes, incapable of complex thoughts and had a very low tolerance towards failure. She knew what his knee-jerk reaction would be.

Revenge.

And then, an ominous thought hit her.

'Tej...' she yelled out.

'You don't have to shout, I'm right here.'

'How do you know Matheson left?'

'Anshul said so ... Anshul Baghri ... you were there.'

'We have to go, Tej ... NOW,' she said hurriedly, not bothering to explain. There was fear in her eyes, and an urgency in her step, which worried Tej.

In all his life he had never seen Sharvani lose her calm demeanour, and to see her like this worried him to no end. He followed her wordlessly as they rushed out of the police chowk, into the unrelenting rain.

The sprint to Sharvani Mehra's house was a quiet one, with the only sound being that of their footsteps in puddles, and the heavy panting of the duo. Sharvani didn't care about getting drenched in the rain anymore, not when one of her student's lives was at stake.

She failed to save two of them; she would not fail a third time.

Tej didn't want to know why they were in such a hurry, nor did he ask, until she stopped abruptly outside her house.

'What ... huff ... happened?' he panted. She pointed towards the ground. Her breathing was much more controlled than the out-of-breath Tej's.

He looked at the ground and his eyes widened in shock. There were deep, thick footprints embedded in the mud leading to Sharvani's porch. The gate was ajar, and so was the door.

'We must exercise caution ...' warned Tej, but Sharvani was already past the gate and entering through the front door.

Tej sighed and rushed in after her. The time for temperance had apparently come to pass.

The elderly matron didn't bat an eyelid at the sight in front of her. It was as though she was expecting it all along.

Eric Matheson stood there with an untempered madness in his eyes: the look of a man so far down the path of anger that no humanity remained within him; there only was the feral instincts of a beast.

Ishita was held in place in front of him like a human shield, struggling to get out of the vice-like grip of the monster behind her. He had a knife dangling precariously close to her neck; the edge of the blade had already drawn a thin, almost imperceptible line of blood.

'You ... you ... bitch,' he roared with a malicious grin. 'You've ruined everything.'

Sharvani looked at him unfazed. 'Let Ishita go and we can discuss this,' her voice was cold as ice, yet it had a serene composure in it.

'I'll cut her up ... and then it's your turn, bitch,' he said, pointing the knife at Sharvani.

Tej barged in and assessed the situation within seconds. All of his previous sepoy training kicked in, and he looked around for a makeshift weapon, his eyes narrowing in on the rusty rifle that hung harmlessly over the wall.

Without thinking, he rushed towards the rifle and placed it against his shoulder, aiming it at Matheson. His movements were as swift as lightning, with each thought processed and executed by his body in a series of movements that seemed as natural as breathing.

'Put the weapon down,' he warned Matheson. Even the words came out as an extension of his reflexive movements.

Matheson grinned evilly. 'Two for the price of one ...' he snarled. 'Dont'cha worry copper, I'll get to you as soon as I'm done with these two lovely ladies.'

'Put the weapon down, SIR ...' Tej roared again, the assertiveness clear in his voice.

'This isn't going to change anything … you are all right where I wanted you …' he gave an oily smile. 'Do your worst.'

Sharvani was confused. Matheson was clearly outnumbered, and backup would be arriving shortly. Matheson had no way out.

He was cornered like a rat. He didn't know that the gun wasn't loaded, yet he stood there staring down death, which could come at him from the end of the barrel, with a defiance that Sharvani knew only came from madmen or those who knew they had already won.

Why on earth was Matheson feeling triumphant?

'Can't do it, can you? Pfft …' he spat. 'Fucking worthless fool, just like your father.'

The words had an unexpected effect, awakening some long forgotten memory in Tej Bahadur.

He didn't flinch as he pulled the trigger.

twenty-one

The sun had come out of its unwarranted sabbatical after several days, bathing the town in a glow that made it look no less than heaven on earth.

Pristine, untouched woodland all around, clear dew-kissed meadows, sparkling streams of water in the distance and the fresh, invigorating air of the clear open sky.

It had only been a few days since Matheson's death at the hands of Tej Bahadur. He was elevated to the status of a hero literally overnight: an alcoholic cop turned protector of the town. Thank God that Ishita had loaded the rusty rifle with live ammunition as a precaution.

But all of that only constituted minor details.

Sharvani breathed a sigh of relief; the reign of terror that had gripped Ooty had finally come to an end. She could see it all around her—there was an undeniable feeling of relief like the one that came after a terrible fever had broken.

'Morning, Miss Mehra!' Tej Bahadur was at her door. Even he had warmed up a little more towards her, but she knew the seeds of animosity were planted deep.

'Morning, Tej ...' she said with a smile.

'Is Ishita around?'

She shook her head, 'She's moving back into her old house.'

'AZAD MANOR?' he exclaimed.

'No, that place has too many ... unpleasant memories,' she said with a frown.

'Well, as long as everything bad is put behind her ...'

'I'll miss her. Even in the few days she has been with me, she has been invaluable ... doing all the small chores of the house. It's been like a vacation for me.'

Tej chuckled.

'Even now, she's stepped out to pick up a few things; I needed some strawberries to bake a cake ...'

'Hmmm ...' he said. 'No wonder her wards are running lax,' he pointed behind Sharvani.

The elderly lady turned around, looking visibly cross.

Young Vijay was digging a hole right in the middle of her flower patch, with the other children egging him on.

'I'll leave you to it then,' he said with a slight snicker as he walked off.

'Yes,' she said, 'I'd appreciate that.'

She rolled up her sleeves as she made a beeline towards the children. Vijay had his back towards her, but the rest of the children saw the advancing matron and scampered away.

All of the children were out of the garden within seconds.

All except Vijay, who was too engrossed in digging.

She stood behind him, her arms crossed, her huge shadow falling over the diminutive boy.

'Where are all you cowards running off to?' Vijay sneered. 'She doesn't even have her stupid dog anymore, and it's not like that old hog's anywhere close … gawwrk …' he was unable to complete the sentence, as he yelped like a puppy when Sharvani caught him by the collar.

'Didn't I give you a fair warning?' she said sternly, as she sat and held him tightly over her lap.

Sometimes, the old punishments worked best, she thought, as she pulled down his pyjamas, much to the amusement of the other children who were viewing the spectacle from safe vantage points out of the old lady's grasp.

Vijay turned red in the face because of the embarrassment, as he heard the hushed giggles and snickers from the rest of his group, especially the girls.

He tried to squirm and wiggle out of her grasp, but to no avail. Sharvani had enough experience in keeping children locked in place with her grip.

She raised her hand over his bare bottom, and he closed his eyes tight and clenched his fists, awaiting the stinging burn of her palm on his backside, one that never came.

He opened one eye; the children were all still staring at him. Many awaited the corporal punishment with bated breath; it was no doubt going to be a source of extended amusement to many of them.

He moved his eye to the furthest it would stretch, and from the corner of his eye, he could see Sharvani, and her raised hand, all set to deliver the painful blow, but her hand was frozen in place, and her eyes fixed onto the boy's bare bottom.

She sat there wide-eyed in shock.

'Put your pants back on,' she said quickly, 'and don't let me catch you here again … the next time, I might not be so forgiving.'

But Vijay, even in his youthful innocence, could feel the shift in her tone. The wind had been knocked out of her sails, and the anger she felt, dissipated instantaneously.

But he wasn't one to look a gift horse in the mouth, and he quickly pulled up his pyjamas, and rushed towards the rest of his gang. He remembered the faces of those who laughed at him.

They would have a lot to answer for.

Sharvani watched dumbstruck as the young boy raced towards his friends.

The boy was smart for his age, enterprising too. She took a look at the hole he was digging, there were seeds strewn about. He wanted to plant sunflowers, she guessed by a quick glance, identifying the seeds.

He just needed some love, care and understanding.

Her mind was reeling now. She stepped inside the house slowly. It was still morning, but she needed a glass of sherry to calm her nerves.

It could be a while before Ishita would show up with the strawberries. Maybe she would bake an orange and almond cake instead.

Yes, Sharvani thought.

A light, fluffy orange cake with crunchy almonds would be perfect.

twenty-two

Ishita entered through the front gate like a beam of warm sunshine. There was a happiness glistening on her face, and a small basket of freshly picked strawberries hanging idly over her forearm.

Her face beamed when she saw her teacher at the table at the porch. The table was already laid out.

Two cups of piping hot tea, a bottle of sherry, some empty glasses and a wonderful, summery orange cake embedded with almonds, with two slices cut out, rested on the table.

One slice, untouched, was kept on Sharvani's side, who was busy sipping on her cup of tea.

'This looks heavenly,' Ishita commented as she took a deep whiff of the wonderful, zesty, freshly baked cake, wafting through the air.

Her face was positively beaming as she took a bite of the moist, fluffy goodness. 'Miss Mehra ... I can't believe that this tastes even better than it smells.'

Sharvani gave a polite nod in appreciation.

She studied her student's face. She looked positively radiant.

Her bandages had come off and the wounds had healed up nicely.

Sharvani smiled warmly as her younger counterpart hungrily tucked into the slice, and began helping herself to another rather generous portion.

'Please don't mind ...' she said with a childish grin, and mouthful of crumbs, 'either this cake is overly delicious, or I'm unusually hungry.'

'Don't worry, my dear ...' Sharvani smiled warmly, 'I've baked it especially for you.'

'I thought you wanted to bake a strawberry one?'

'Well ...' she said, finishing the last of her tea, 'I thought orange would complement the return of the summer.'

Ishita grinned at her. 'You haven't even touched your slice,' she commented.

Sharvani shrugged, 'I'm not feeling particularly hungry. Have you thought of what you're going to do now?'

Ishita shrugged, taking in another mouthful. 'I don't know ... maybe travel a little. I still have some responsibility towards the orphanage; I will support it financially, of course, but maybe it's time to look for a replacement ...' she said in a tone that sounded almost like an advance apology for her next statement. 'I don't know if I would want to stay a matron to them now. You do understand, don't you?'

'Of course, my dear ...' she smiled warmly. 'Travel is a good way to broaden one's perspective and clear one's mind, but tell me one thing ...' she said in a sympathetic tone.

'Sure, Miss Mehra ... anything,' Ishita said with a smile that could have rivalled the brightest rays of the sun.

'Are you planning on taking your son with you?'

Ishita Dhiman glared at her for a moment. A sardonic smile appeared on her face. While her previous smile radiated sunshine, her current one seemed to reflect weather of a darker nature.

'Oops …' she whispered coyly. 'Before I answer that … do you mind if I get a little more comfortable?'

'Please,' Sharvani insisted, as she poured herself another cup of tea.

Ishita unbuttoned the first few buttons of her simple, drab dress, revealing the uncomfortable swathe of a corset wrapped around her body.

Sharvani looked at her, emotionless, as her student reached around and untied the binding hooks of the corset, revealing her ample bosom.

A chest that rivalled Sharvani's own, one that would undoubtedly make men look twice, and with this one movement, Ishita's figure turned from cylindrical to voluptuous.

Sharvani looked at her with growing contempt, an unwarranted envy stemmed from the pit of her stomach.

Ishita had the face of an angel and the body of a devil, one that could make men go weak in the knees.

She looked on as her student made herself more 'comfortable'. She pulled out the pin that held her hair in a bun, and long, lustrous locks fell carelessly over her shoulders.

Her hair shone in the light, perfectly accentuating her soft features.

She looked like a goddess.

An evil goddess.

She dropped her corset clumsily, and rebuttoned her blouse, allowing for her ample cleavage to be shown.

'There …' Ishita sighed. 'Much better.'

The old lady winced as she took in another sip of tea.

'Oh come on now, Miss Mehra, won't you offer me some sherry today?'

Sharvani looked at her, her eyes narrowed with anger, and then she smiled politely, 'Sure. I think I need something a little bit stronger as well.'

She nonchalantly poured two glasses and handed her one.

'Salut,' Ishita smiled as she downed her drink in one gulp.

Sharvani refilled it wordlessly.

'It must have been painful … hiding your charms for so many years, and that corset didn't look particularly comfortable.'

Ishita fiddled with her glass, taking in a long, lingering sip.

'I suppose not,' she began, choosing to relish her drink this time around, 'the corset wasn't to hide my assets, at least not the first time around. I only used it to relieve the pain in my spine. I was too young when I gave birth,' she said as she pulled out a pack of Maspero Gold, and offered her mentor one.

'My favorite brand,' Sharvani commented as she helped herself to one.

Ishita smiled. 'As is mine. I picked it up from you: similar tastes,' she grinned.

'It was your cigarette we found at Azad Manor, when Stephan crashed into Baghri?'

She nodded. 'I told Archana, and she educated Stephan enough for him to play along. I couldn't let the sweet little matron's nasty little habit come out into the open,' she said as she lit Sharvani's and her cigarettes with a pair of matches she retrieved from her pocket.

'I always advised you against it,' Sharvani said, taking a deep drag. She hated to admit it, but the sweet burn of tobacco filling her lungs gave her an almost therapeutic relief.

'A child follows a parent's example more than their advice,' Ishita retorted. 'And like I said, the corset and the suffering accompanying it are vestiges from another life,' she said as she blew out a puff of smoke.

'Can I ask you a question now?' Ishita said.

'You already did,' Sharvani replied dryly.

Ishita chuckled. 'How did you know?'

'That Vijay was your son?'

Ishita nodded.

'By chance, if I'm to be completely honest.'

Ishita raised her eyebrows, confused. She needed more details, and Sharvani was happy to oblige.

'He was up to his usual mischief in the garden, and if a gun couldn't discourage him …' she smiled at the thought, 'I felt the older form of punishment would work better.'

This time Ishita couldn't control her laughter. 'Don't tell me …' she said good-naturedly, 'bare-bottom spanking?'

Sharvani smiled, but then her expression turned bittersweet. It was reminiscent of a fleeting moment of camaraderie she had once shared with her student, one that would never come again. Whatever they had between them was now shattered.

'His condition gave it away, didn't it?'

Sharvani nodded, taking another sip. 'Vitiligo. It's hereditary. If one parent is afflicted, there is a 90 per cent chance that the offspring will have it as well.'

'Well, I'd be lying if I said I'm not glad. I was almost disappointed you didn't figure it out early on. Back in the orphanage, you always caught my lies early on.'

'I always felt you couldn't keep a secret … I was wrong,' Sharvani admitted. 'Maybe, somewhere deep down, I always suspected something, but you were so close to my heart, I didn't want to consider it,' she said glumly, a frown appearing on her otherwise beautiful visage.

Ishita smiled warmly. 'I knew I picked the right role model. I'm so glad you figured it out,' she said as she dug into another slice of cake. 'So tell me, Miss Mehra, tell me what the others have missed,' she said, with a mischievous glint in her eye. 'Tell me about my life,' she said between the noiseless mastication of the cake.

'Only if you fill in the blanks wherever they are incomplete or missing.'

Ishita nodded happily.

'You left my care when you were but sixteen. An old aunt who lived in Bombay traced you down, your father's sister I believe ...' she said, looking at Ishita for approval.

Her ward didn't say anything at first, but kept listening with rapt attention.

'Go on ...' she encouraged.

'She offered to be your guardian. I protested, despite the Zamindar's pressure to let you leave. It was only upon your insistence that I reluctantly let you go. You left the orphanage, went to Bombay, spent eight years there completing your education, and returned to your roots, replacing me as the head matron at the orphanage.'

'At your behest,' she added.

'At my behest,' Sharvani repeated with regret.

'And how much of that do you think is true?'

Sharvani shrugged and said dryly, 'That you replaced me ... that's about it.'

'And what do you think is true?' she asked coyly.

Sharvani grinned. 'Now that, my dear, is a question. Let's see ...' she folded her hands together and moved in closer. 'In the September of 1925, you realized you were pregnant, carrying the illegitimate child of your secret lover, Arjun Digvijay Rana. When you told him you were expecting his child, he did what he was conditioned to do since childhood: he went to his father for advice.'

'He was much nobler than his father then ...' Ishita spat out. 'He was a better man than his father. He proposed marriage, and went to get his father's blessings.'

'Well, I guess that went about as well as you expected.'

Ishita stayed silent, a tsunami of rage over the past events enveloping her. Sharvani felt it prudent to merely continue.

'The anger was to be expected. The Zamindar's son fathering a child out of wedlock that would leave the Rana's reputation in tatters, and you know how particular they are with reputation.'

'The Rana family's name is only as good as its reputation,' Ishita droned on mirthlessly.

'Besides, a Rana marrying a commoner would have been out of the question, especially when Digvijay had his eyes set on the Sharma plantation. So, even marriage, with or without his blessing, was unacceptable, and the timid Arjun going against his father's wishes was out of question.'

'The Zamindar would have done anything to get rid of you,' Sharvani thought out loud. 'I wonder why Digvijay didn't? Was it because he was worried that his overly emotional son might have committed some untoward step?'

She looked at Ishita for clarification.

'He didn't do it because of you,' Ishita sighed. 'He knew how close I was to you, and that my sudden disappearance without any correspondence would be looked upon with suspicion. He did consider killing me though, but whether it was the fear of you finding out or the reasoning by Rai Bahadur that tipped the scale, I know not.'

'Why did you accept?'

'Rai Bahadur lied to me, I'm guessing on his master's behest. I was told that Arjun and I could be together provided I gave birth away from him.'

'I'm guessing that encouraged your stubbornness to leave the orphanage?'

She nodded.

'Digvijay, you bastard,' Sharvani thought. He played his cards right, entrapped the impressionable young girl with false promises, and took her out of the picture, both satisfying Sharvani's curiosity and playing upon Ishita's feelings towards his son, leaving the family reputation intact. 'May you rot in hell,' she prayed silently, as she continued. 'They set you off to Bombay with a promise that you would be united with Arjun. I'm guessing, at least that must have been the initial offer.

Enough to keep your mouth shut.' Sharvani cringed as she spoke those words.

Ishita was the brightest of her students.

How could she have been so foolish?

Maybe love truly made one blind.

'Digvijay, with the help of Rai Bahadur, then invented an old, long-lost aunt, and a home for you, which in actuality, would have been an inordinate sum of money. The Ranas have their shortcomings no doubt, but stinginess is not one of them,' Sharvani smiled as she finished her drink.

'You should know … you inherited an outhouse for merely lending a sympathetic ear.'

Sharvani ignored the tasteless comment.

'The rest, my dear, would require too many suppositions, ones I'm not willing to make at the moment. If you could be so kind as to fill in the blanks …'

'Only if I could have a refill,' Ishita said, raising her empty glass.

Sharvani obliged and filled it to the rim. Ishita began after taking a small sip, 'I was left alone in Bombay, in a rundown boarding lodge near Churchgate. The city scared me, and I chose to live in seclusion for months on end, until one day, by chance, I came across the news of the Ranas acquiring the Sharma plantation. It was then I learnt, much to my horror, about Archana and Arjun's engagement. It was then that I decided to return. I wrote a letter to Arjun outlining his promises to me, and about his son. I waited for a response, and got one in the form of Rai Bahadur,' her voice had cracked, the inevitable sobs of a painful time gone by coming to the forefront.

Sharvani frowned. Even though Rai Bahadur had been her lover, that man had a heart as black as coal.

'The Zamindar had got wind of the letter, and delegated Rai Bahadur to take care of the matter discreetly. He found me before I could've left for Ooty, and told me that Arjun wanted nothing to do with me. I was heartbroken,' she said, teary eyed.

Sharvani felt her heart ache. The girl was like a daughter to her, and to learn about all that she had gone through pained the elderly matron to no end.

Fate dealt her an unfair hand, and it was all because she made the error of falling in love with the wrong boy.

'The date of the wedding was set,' she continued. Her sobs were now replaced with an eerie, steely resolve. 'I was offered more money to stay away, but that wasn't enough for me. I decided I wouldn't stay quiet. I wrote a letter to the Zamindar, threatening to expose my affair with his son and his legacy that was growing in my womb. I wanted to lash out at them, and what better way to punish them than to hit them where it would hurt the most?'

'Their reputation.'

'I waited for a few weeks. My condition changed dramatically, making travel an almost unbearable exercise. I didn't receive a reply from them. The marriage took place anyway, but a few weeks later, I learnt that the Zamindar took his own life. I couldn't help but gloat, I'm sure that my letter and the mounting guilt would have made him take such a drastic step.'

Sharvani kept silent. She pitied the girl more for her naivety than her foolishness.

'The matter was buried by Rai Bahadur, and whether or not Arjun wanted to have anything to do with you, will remain a mystery that he has taken with him to the grave,' Sharvani interjected.

'The birth was premature. I wanted to get rid of him before he was born, but the early delivery ensured that option was off the table. I gave birth by paying a local midwife to pull the baby out. I named him Vijay, because the Zamindar had, through his actions, inadvertently chosen the child's destiny. When I held him for the first time in my hands, I felt opposing emotions; love for he was my son, and hatred because of the bloodline he shared. I couldn't bear to see him then, and I couldn't afford to raise him. Thoughts of his pitiful future flashed before my eyes. I envisioned the life of poverty and destitution he would have to endure, when he had the birthright to all that the Zamindar owned. I decided then and there, my son would get what was rightfully his.'

Sharvani could see the bitterness and anger in her eyes when she said those words. The Ishita Dhiman she knew and loved died the day her son was born. The model student and Arjun Rana's sweet lover gave way to this demonic seductress who sat in her place.

'I needed someone to care for my child, while I planned my revenge. I came back to Tamil Nadu and dropped him off at the Venkatesh Orphanage and Care Home, the nearest one to Ooty. To be honest, I didn't even care much for him then—at the time only one thing motivated me.'

'Vengeance,' Sharvani sighed. ' I ... I don't think I want to hear any more,' she whispered.

'But Miss Mehra,' Ishita exclaimed animatedly, 'this is where it gets good.' Her voice had a little more enthusiasm than was necessary. 'I went back to Bombay. That city, even with all its flaws, had its charms. I spent the next two years planning my revenge, "arming" myself so to speak, giving free rein to all my desires and demons. Men, women, drugs, alcohol ... I denied myself nothing,' she said with a sardonic smile. 'I learned how to turn on the charm, something which was characteristic of you; to bend others to my will, and completely bring alive the fantasy of their pathetic existence. I had them all under my spell. All of them learnt the intimate secrets of my body, and worshipped me like I was the goddess of love. I won't lie to you, it was fun while it lasted.'

'I'm sure.'

'You would know now, wouldn't you?' she said with a sly smile. 'But it wasn't just fun and games. I learnt a lot in the seedy underbelly of Bombay. The right people taught me a lot of valuable skills like how to dose cyanide, wield the dagger with skill, how to dispose a body ...'

'Colourful crowd you hung out with.'

'Oh,' she exclaimed. 'You don't know the half of it.'

'I don't think I want to know.'

'I threw myself completely into bringing down the Ranas, and had fun while doing it. You should be proud, Miss Mehra ... I truly blossomed from the shy young girl to an assertive young woman.'

'That's what hurts the most, Ishita,' Sharvani replied solemnly.

'I'm sure you can resume the rest of the deduction,' Ishita requested as she helped herself to another slice of cake.

'If you insist,' Sharvani said and sighed.

'Please.'

'Eric Matheson was a thug for hire, judging from his appearance. I'm guessing you must have met him during one of your wanton visits to places unmentionable. He seemed to have been a crook turned killer, or perhaps the opposite? Whatever it was, he suited your needs.'

Ishita nodded, chewing on the cake noiselessly. 'I knew he was mine to command after I asked him to break a man's neck because he eyed me the wrong way. He was handsome, strong, violent, well-endowed and, most importantly, interested in money. It was everything I was looking for.'

'Even then, your plan rested on a lot of presuppositions. You returned to Ooty, confident in the fact that you would take my place. The letter I sent you stating that I needed a replacement was all you needed. All you needed to be the next matron, was my recommendation ...'

'And how could you deny your favourite student anything?'

Sharvani didn't say anything. Ishita was right and, for the first time, she hated her student for being right.

'Eric was meant to only find work and learn about the town and its inhabitants. When he did find work however, it completely exceeded my expectations. After the Zamindar's death, they needed a gardener, and Eric secured the job, more so because he caught the lovely Archana's eye, than for his gardening abilities.'

'To catch her eye is a mild understatement,' Sharvani said, her tone brimming with sarcasm, 'and I get he tended more to Archana than the plants.'

Ishita giggled. 'Haven't we discussed this enough already?'

'I understand that maybe luck was kind towards you; after dealing you a particularly unfair hand, the success of your plan worked on luck and blackmail.'

She nodded.

'Blackmail that could only have worked, everything in fact could only have worked on one small detail: the presence of Vijay in Ooty. How did that happen?' Sharvani questioned.

'Why, Miss Mehra ...' Ishita said with a particularly malicious grin, 'you already know the answer to that one.'

'I forbade myself to consider that possibility,' she replied glumly.

'I forbade myself nothing,' came the ominous response.

'He was the only thing that survived the Venkatesh Orphanage fire. Authorities had no choice but to transfer him to the closest orphanage.'

'Digvijay Rana Orphanage in Ooty.'

Mehra looked at her student with disgust. 'You set fire to an orphanage to make sure that he would land up here?'

'I had to make sure it seemed like chance. I couldn't risk having him connected to me. Like you said, the success of my plan depended on blackmail, and blackmail as a tool is quite useless if everyone knows the secret,' she said with a beatific smile.

'How could you?'

Ishita grinned at her as she took another cigarette and lit it up. 'Like this,' she said, 'with a match.'

'Children died in those flames,' Sharvani said through gritted teeth, her voice and demeanour resisting the rage growing within her.

'Children die all the time, Miss Mehra,' she said, blowing out a ring of smoke. 'But not all of them serve my purpose. Besides, who would weep for them?' she chuckled. 'Their parents?'

Sharvani could feel the frustration grow like a weed inside her. She felt shame and guilt overcome her completely.

She felt like a failure.

First with Arjun.

Next with Archana.

And now with Ishita.

What she wouldn't do to turn back the clock, to do things differently, a second time around.

'Why did you stay back?' Sharvani questioned, massaging her forehead. Her head felt like it was about to explode from the revelation, and the guilt that came with it. 'Arjun was presumed dead, Archana was the heiress, and I don't think she even knew of your affair with Arjun.'

'But Rai Bahadur did,' she said, her words laced with poison. 'And after all I went through, I wanted to make sure that my son, the rightful heir, got what was due to him. Plus, there was another reason that I stayed back.'

'Oh!' Sharvani exclaimed, curiosity getting the better of her, 'And what was that?'

'You, Miss Mehra,' Ishita grinned. 'I never got tired of being by you side, constantly learning and improving myself. Truth be told, you're the only family I have.'

There was earnestness in her voice, and a childlike innocence, when she said those words.

Sharvani wanted to believe her, but she couldn't. The girl she loved, raised and cared for like her own child, disappeared, leaving a monster in her stead. She couldn't trust a word Ishita said; she was a snake, poisoning anyone foolish enough to cross her.

'Meeting Alexander was a stroke of luck as well. Eric told me of his obsession with buying Azad Manor. He was narcissistic and conceited. He was an opportunity not to be missed. I manipulated Archana through Eric, and subsequently, indirectly guided Stephan's actions as well.'

'I can't imagine Archana being that easy to influence … especially not by someone like Eric,' Sharvani pointed out.

'Oh,' Ishita clarified. 'It wasn't Eric all the time; he just helped with the final push. You see, Archana and I were close … very close. Like you said yourself, Archana used to defy her parents to spend nights with me,' she said with a suggestive smile.

Sharvani didn't say anything, as the implications of Ishita's words began to dawn on her.

'Arjun was the first man in my life,' Ishita admitted, 'but Archana preceded him in my bed. Being a few years older, she taught me tricks I wouldn't have ordinarily dreamt of. She was better than most men I was with, so naturally …' she shrugged with a wink. 'After returning, we got involved again. I was single and her husband was missing, and we shared our lover Eric as we indulged in a regular ménage à trois in the inn … at least that's what I think it's called. I was introduced to the term and the activity by a Frenchman I met in Bombay.'

Sharvani listened with equal parts interest and disgust.

Was there no end to this girl's depravity?

And then Ishita's words rang in her ears. 'A child follows a parent's example, not their advice.' She felt remorse, and a terrible weight of guilt burden her. She instantly regretted her actions and pitied those of her proclaimed children.

She was jolted out from her sad thoughts, as Ishita continued, unmindful of her mentor's changed demeanour. 'Manohar Mishra also got to join once or twice a month, when we were bored, or feeling particularly charitable. It was a payment in kind for his silence.'

'Go on ...'

Ishita looked at her with a mischievous glint. 'Oh, come on Miss Mehra ... I've spoken enough, and you're smart enough to have already figured out the rest. Tell me ...'

'I'd rather hear it from you.'

'Humour me ...' Ishita insisted.

'If you insist ... the haunting of Azad Manor by the Zamindar's ghost was a legend that the town was already talking about in hushed whispers, due to his mysterious death. You merely exaggerated the legend ...'

'We did partake in activities of a carnal nature in Azad Manor every now and then. It was particularly empowering, especially in the Zamindar's bedroom. There were always nosy people trying to catch an eyeful of Archana's charms; even the head constable wasn't immune to their effects. But he, like several others, dismissed the other set of eyes in the house to being that of the Zamindar's ghost.'

The ghost is real, Sharvani thought. She had seen it with her own two eyes and finally understood what Digvijay's ghost wanted to tell her.

But she didn't say anything to Ishita; she wouldn't understand and by now, Sharvani didn't care.

'And this was after Rai Bahadur left the manor ...'

'I made him leave the manor,' she said with a hint of pride. 'A few well-timed lies into the impressionable Archana's ears was all the push she needed to evict him. My heart sang as I engineered his fall from grace. I wanted him to suffer in poverty like I did.'

'Well done ...' Sharvani clapped slowly, visibly disgusted.

'Bravo, Miss Mehra. You made me reveal more than I wanted to, but it would be better now if you tell me. I want to know if you're as smart as I think you are.'

'The morning of Arjun's return was when I had seen you genuinely happy after a long, long time. It wasn't because you got back your lost love or a childhood friend, but only because after all these years of patiently waiting, you could finally have the revenge that you wanted so badly.'

'I was happy that day, wasn't I?' she grinned. 'Go on.'

'The next day, I bumped into Arjun as he was exiting the Aneri Plume, but you already knew that, didn't you? Because he had just left your company,' Sharvani said without waiting for her pupil to answer. 'The Aneri Plume was the safest place, Mishra would keep his mouth shut, and no self-respecting citizen would want to be caught dead near that establishment. The windows were open and you eavesdropped on our entire conversation.'

Sharvani's face cracked a slight smile. 'I hate to admit it, but I am a little impressed.'

'About what?'

'It is the ability to improvise that distinguishes truly great minds ... and criminals,' she added as an afterthought. 'You knew from eavesdropping that Arjun's excuse was not at all convincing ... thinking on his feet was never the boy's forte, as it was yours. You knew I would wonder about the identity of the person that he had come to visit. Granted, it could have been Rai Bahadur, but you knew of my "association" with him, and couldn't risk my outright asking him. In the end, it wouldn't matter who Arjun met that night: it could be anyone in Ooty for that matter, as long as you didn't feature on the list. So, you did what you had to. You dressed up quickly, and dashed home while Arjun and I strolled along merrily, catching up on each other's lives. It didn't matter to him that we passed the alternative hotel I was going to take him to, as that was never his intention anyway.'

'You are as smart as I give you credit for,' Ishita commented incredulously, a grin plastered on her face.

'You knew exactly how far we were when you let out your first scream. The gash on your forehead wasn't because of an attack, but because in your haste and due to the slick ground, you slipped and accidently hit your head against the gate. What was meant to be a clue against the attacker and his hasty departure was actually a clue of your clumsy arrival.'

Ishita smiled, 'That injury inspired the rest. I saw the gash on my forehead and invented the fake assault. Nothing much really: I just threw around some furniture and pushed off a mirror.'

'And your arm?'

'I slammed it against the door on my way in.'

Sharvani smiled. 'But that wasn't all, was it? How could you be both the attacker and the victim? So, you put on a pair of boots belonging to your lover and faked the footprints.'

'I remembered the legend of the Zamindar, and how he walked out in the middle of the night in his gardener's boots and slit his throat. I thought why the hell, if not while he was alive, maybe I could ruin his reputation after his death. The people of Ooty are a superstitious lot; it didn't take much to get their tongues wagging, not after my whisper campaign,' she said and winked.

'But it could have all gone for naught now, wouldn't it? Arjun's slip up and your game would have been up. I didn't think much of it then, but I did notice his surprise on seeing you at the house. A surprise which was indeed warranted, seeing how he had left you hale, hearty and happy at the Aneri Plume, not a quarter of an hour back.'

'Not happy,' Ishita said, 'but I faked it convincingly enough.'

'His one blunder nearly undid all your efforts,' Sharvani said, ignoring Ishita's last comment.

'But you cut him off, asked him to find the attacker, and then fetch Khuranna. I never thanked you for pulling my fat out of the fire then.'

'Well, even you slipped up, didn't you?'

'Excuse me?'

'You said the Zamindar's ghost attacked you!'

'So?'

'So, since when do ghosts bleed, Ishita?' she asked, as she finished her drink.

There was an uncomfortable silence between them.

'I don't know whether to feel sorry or marvel at the depth of your rage.'

'Hell hath no fury like a woman scorned.'

'So Archana was telling the truth: Matheson was actually with her every time they asked him to verify his alibi?'

'I guess so … she was insatiable …' Ishita admitted, half thinking of the happier times involving pleasures of a more carnal nature.

'It was you who went to Rai Bahadur at the Aneri Plume, not as the shy matron of the orphanage, but as the wily seductress. Aided by Mishra's silence, it was easy for you to gain access, even whilst wearing the muddy gardener's boots.'

'I thought it wise to pin the murders on an entity beyond the reach of the long arm of the law.'

'Rai Bahadur had been Rana's right hand, and the one who kept you out of Arjun's life. You hated him and laid out your implacable plan. You did the one thing you were now proficient at: you shook him with a proposition of a very … personal nature, something you seemed to enjoy. Whatever it was, you showed him your true nature, and the sight stopped his heart.'

'Like they say: too much of good thing can be bad for you ...' she giggled without remorse.

'That brings us to Arjun's homecoming reception. A minor detail actually undid everything again: you dropped a cigarette when you helped Stephan up. You couldn't risk your image of the sweet teacher being tarnished by your guilty pleasure, and you knew such a detail wouldn't have escaped my notice, and it would likely be something that I would question Stephan about.'

'So?'

'So, between Arjun's death and Stephan's late interrogation, you had enough time to educate Archana on what to tell Stephan. With Azad Manor being dangled like a carrot, he would have admitted to anything you asked him to, but he never knew that you were involved, did he? Even in his letter, he ratted out everybody but not you, because although he had an idea of someone else's involvement, he didn't know who it was.'

'Oh, he did come to know, right before I stabbed him multiple times in his obese gut ...' her eyes were bloodshot, clearly showing the rage that lurked within. 'I enjoyed watching him bleed to death, but you're right. He didn't know it was me ... that's why he had surprise in his eyes before he breathed his last,' Ishita said, and the full meaning of the Zamindar's ghost's words dawned on Sharvani.

'I may be responsible, but I'm not the cause of their demise,' Digvijay Rana had told her.

Sharvani realized how true his words were, as she said with a deep sigh, 'Stephan was right in a way though; his letter stated that Archana told him that the murders were being committed by the Zamindar's ghost. In a way, she was right. You were created as a result of Digvijay Rana's actions, however heartless or cruel they might have been. His cruelty and wickedness were what turned an innocent, lovable girl into this succubus sitting in front of me. In a way, he was responsible... For the murder of Ishita Dhiman, and for giving birth to the Zamindar's ghost, the restless spirit that is hell-bent on punishing everyone for their sins and depravity ... but we're digressing again. We should get back to the topic at hand.'

'Please ...' Ishita said, 'by all means ...'

'When Arjun and you left me at the party on the pretext of bringing Archana from her room, you had no inclination to go and get her; you both merely wanted a quick tryst in his study, and I handed you the opportunity on a platter.'

'That much is true ...' Ishita said, her glass now empty. She didn't bother Sharvani, choosing to fill the glass up herself.

'Once you were alone upstairs with him, you slipped into the study, promising him, no doubt, a brief moment of intimacy, and knocked him senseless. You then proceeded to fabricate the footprints of the Zamindar's ghost with the muddy boots that Matheson had already hidden there earlier.'

'And after that ...'

'And after that, all that remained was for you to bring Archana down the stairs and play the victim card. Irrespective of how she was with you, it was evident that Archana harboured feelings of animosity against you. Ones that only came to the forefront after she had had a drop too much. Her behaviour towards you warranted my sympathy, and you were out of the suspicion range. The rest of it ...' she said, 'we learnt from Stephan's letter. Eric climbed onto the carriage and entered the office, broke the son's neck, like you had seen him do in the past. You shut off the lights while being away on the pretext of looking after the children. Eric then proceeded to fling the body off the railing, before making a similar exit, with enough time for you to quickly lock the window and come back to join the guests in the darkness.'

Ishita applauded slowly again.

'It was well thought out, I will give you that. Your alibi was water-tight. After inheriting the manor, you couldn't act like you wanted it all along. After Matheson's unceremonious deposition from Rana's servitude, he lay low and returned to Azad Manor on the day you moved in. He coordinated with you and switched off the lights, thereby creating sufficient ambiguity on whether it was the Zamindar's ghost or an actual killer hell-bent on your death. The ruse was unnecessary though, since you already poisoned the tea in the kitchen … skills you picked up in Bombay, no doubt.'

'You're smarter than I imagined.'

'Lifting the cup was a masterstroke; you completely averted suspicion from your name. You never intended to taste it, but you wanted to point my thinking in another direction. Tej began to believe in the Zamindar's ghost and so had I, to a little extent, but Matheson was quickly becoming a liability, so you needed me to keep my investigations pointed towards a killer of flesh and blood.'

'He was getting greedy …' Ishita mumbled with disdain, 'and I'm truly sorry … sorry about Tuffy.'

Sharvani felt her heart skip a beat. She loved that dog to the moon and back. He wasn't just a pet, but he was family and now, even he had been snatched away from her unfairly. Her heart wept, but she didn't let it show.

'The other liability was Archana. After she lost everything, she couldn't accuse you without lifting the veil off her own numerous demons. She realized she was manipulated, hurt and eventually ruined. Left with no other option, she chose to take the easy way out, and ended her life, writing a farewell letter addressed to no one else except to you, Miss Ishita Dhiman.'

Ishita gave out an evil grin, applauding slowly.

'I'm not done yet,' Sharvani continued with a strange, stoic determination, 'though I must admit, your plan really turned to genius when it came to finally getting rid of your accomplices. You stabbed Mishra in the chest after luring him with a promise of some intimacy like you had, by your own admission, done numerous times in the past. You invited Matheson into my house to set a trap, ostensibly for me, but you did not count on Tej's presence. You loaded the gun thinking that you would use it on Eric after he had taken care of me. Nobody except you and I knew that I kept the gun loaded with blanks.'

'You were getting too close to the truth,' admitted Ishita. 'Stephan told me of the letter he sent, but the stubborn old bastard didn't tell me what was in it. I made his death slow and painful, but he still didn't talk. I respect that kind of determination.'

'So you made Eric the back-up plan: kill two birds with one stone, thereby absolving yourself of everything, and having a free rein over your new-found wealth?'

'You could say that,' Ishita said and shrugged mirthlessly.

'You told Eric that I would reach for the gun most likely, and assured him that it was empty. Only in this case, neither did I take the gun, nor was it empty. That is why he was calm even though Bahadur had aimed the rifle right at him.'

The pieces had begun to connect. Matheson's words rang in her ears. 'This changes nothing ... nothing at all.'

No matter who held the gun, the result in Matheson's mind was the same: a harmless click, a look of shock, followed by his vicious attack.

'Well done ... well done,' Ishita chimed as she raised her glass in a toast, and downed the drink. Sharvani followed suit.

'You figured out the whole thing perfectly, except for one tiny error ...'

'And what is that?'

'It wasn't Eric. I broke Arjun's neck,' she said sardonically.

Sharvani shuddered. She knew what her pupil was going to say, but once again, her emotions trumped logic. She couldn't get herself to believe Ishita would do something so diabolical.

To her lover, and the father of her child.

'I learnt it from Eric. It's not that difficult,' Ishita said nonchalantly. 'Once you figure out where to apply pressure, and at what point …' she admitted calmly. 'And besides, the timid Arjun didn't offer any resistance. On the contrary, I think he soiled himself,' she chuckled menacingly. 'Nobody could rob me of that moment, Miss Mehra. No one. The day Arjun returned was the day I believed in God. It was the day heaven answered my prayers: Arjun Rana returned from the dead, only to die at my hands.'

With her glass refilled, Sharvani asked her nonchalantly, 'How did you manage to get Arjun to change his will?'

'The night you bumped into him at the Aneri Plume, I had asked to meet him there on the pretext of discussing something. He was already there when I arrived. He was a snivelling, grovelling mess of a man, begging for forgiveness, and assuring me that he had nothing to do with the decision to marry Archana. Seeing him like that, crying and grovelling, made me sick to my stomach. I wondered what I saw in him: the spineless toad, who called himself a man. He said he was forced into the marriage by the Zamindar, that the marriage was done only so that he could maintain the Rana name and stature. Can you believe it?'

Sharvani shrugged in response.

'He claimed he tried to find me, and then and there, he proclaimed his undying love for me. That lying bastard,' she said, making no attempt to hide the rage that she felt.

'He told me we could still be together, if it weren't for his family's reputation and Archana. He went on about how she was true to him all these years, so I enlightened him. I was surprised that the shock didn't kill him then and there.'

'What did you say?' Sharvani asked. The levels Ishita would stoop to, Sharvani hadn't imagined, even in her worst nightmares.

'I told him that she and Eric were at it like rabbits, and that the only reason there hadn't been a sign of their affair was because Archana was sterile. If he continued with her, the Rana lineage would come to an end with him. But it didn't have to be that way. I told him of his son as I undid my dress, told him that Vijay was the only true heir to the Rana lineage. He was flabbergasted,' she chuckled at the memory. 'At hearing about his son, or by the sight of my tender breasts, I cannot exactly say. It didn't take long for him to be reminded of our previous torrid trysts, but after my numerous experiences, I couldn't even feel him. I just went through the motions to stroke his ego.'

Sharvani tried blotting out her words, to selectively hear what she was saying. She cringed when she heard the words coming out of her student's mouth, and the images forming in her mind's eye.

She felt disgusted.

'I told Arjun of his son's condition, the one keepsake he inherited from his father. He was at a loss for words, asking me what I wanted. He told me that this would be a scandal, and he didn't want to ruin the family name. Such a wimp,' she said with disgust.

'But I promised him I wouldn't drag the Rana name through the mud, and in exchange for my silence, I whispered in his ear, as I licked the lobe, all that I wanted for my son, and nothing for myself. That if he ever were to disappear again, I wanted him to prove to me that I was his one true love, that's all. Repeating his trite family motto helped a lot,' she chuckled. 'That, and my mouth on his …'

'Stop …' yelled Sharvani. 'Stop,' she said, calming herself down again.

'Besides, your pep talk to him definitely helped. He was always so impressionable. Do the right thing ...' she said, imitating Sharvani, 'reclaim your life,' Ishita laughed. 'Why does this talk bother you so, Miss Mehra? What I did with him, you did exactly the same with others ... I had seen the obsession men had over you, and the power that it gave you over them. I had seen many people come down to the orphanage: Rai Bahadur, Digvijay Singh, and so many Britishers, that I lost count ... I've observed you for years, Miss Mehra, always admiring you, imitating and learning, because you were always my role model and I was always your best student. But now, I'm afraid, it's the end of the road. You've lived a good, long life, haven't you?' she said, as she pulled a gun out from within her dress. 'After all, after a certain point, the student does become the master,' she said, pointing the gun at her erstwhile teacher.

Sharvani remained unfazed; a hint of a smile cracked at the side of her face. 'All that is left for you to do is sell Azad Manor ...'

Ishita frowned. 'A part of me wishes it didn't have to be this way, but everything said and done, one must consider the end.'

'Yes, one must, mustn't one?'

Ishita suddenly felt lightheaded; her muscles refused to listen to the commands given by her brain. Her arms felt like rubber, and she was unable to hold the gun steady. She could feel her heartbeat quicken, beads of sweat forming on her brow.

'Do you know why I chose to bake an orange and almond cake?'

Her words sounded like bongo drums to Ishita: distorted and deep. The words seemed slow, as the world went hazy around her. Her head was spinning, or was it the rest of the world, she couldn't be sure.

'Because almonds easily disguise the taste and oranges the smell of cyanide,' she answered her own question with a sly smile.

Ishita Dhiman tried to stand up, but her legs didn't listen. She persevered anyway, only to fall on her side.

'You wouldn't dare.'

'Wouldn't I?' she grinned.

The young matron struggled to hold on to consciousness, and her motor functions were beginning to shut down, each of them in quick succession. She could see black spots in front of her eyes as her vision slowly faded.

Her last, clear sight was the body of Miss Mehra standing over her. 'Maybe it's just the one glass that'll kill you this time …' Sharvani said with a wicked smile. 'Don't breathe, my dear, don't breathe,' were the last words she heard as hollow, distorted echoes, before falling off the edge of consciousness.

twenty-three

The prison stank.

Sharvani held her breath. Whenever she needed to, she took breaths from her mouth, for every time she inhaled through her nose, her olfactory senses were attacked by the stench of a cocktail of rancid faeces, urine, blood, sweat and tears.

There was a dank wetness in the walls. The whole place reeked of despair, of a hope that was silently destroyed like a cancer had eaten through it, till it was quashed completely.

She had watched her step ever since she felt a rat scamper in between her legs. Atleast, that's what she thought it was: it was difficult to make out in the erratic lighting of the prison.

The jailer walking ahead of her looked incredibly intimidating. Strong, thick forearms, scanty blonde hair, a day-old stubble, and rotten teeth ruined by years of tobacco abuse.

If it wasn't for the skirt, Sharvani could have sworn she was a man. There was a bandage on her misshapen nose, indicating a recent wound. Apparently even the jailers weren't safe here.

She followed the jailer wordlessly, as the latter led her through multiple passageways, illuminated only by the rickety lantern the jailer held, and guided by the desperate pleas of mercy from the prisoners.

Sharvani felt sick, as if this visit would coat her with layers of filth that no number of showers could ever get rid of, but she tightened her grip around the papers rolled up in her hand.

She had to endure this.

She knew she was the only one who could do it.

Her and no one else.

'She's in there,' croaked the jailer, her cockney accent dripping off her every word.

From her demeanour, Sharvani guessed the jailer must have been a criminal back home in England, and had fled to their colonies in India to escape prosecution.

'Life's little ironies!' Sharvani couldn't help but smile this time.

She eyed the door that the jailer was pointing at. With the minimal illumination that the lantern provided, she had to squint to see through the darkness. A sturdy door lay in front of her, the only one in the narrow corridor.

'Yuz, sure you want to go through with this d'ya?'

Sharvani nodded.

The jailer shrugged. 'FIVE MINUTES. NO MORE,' the jailer said as she unlocked the door.

Sharvani nodded again as she entered the dark cell. 'Why have you kept her in solitary? To protect her from the other prisoners?'

The jailer shook her head. 'To protect them from her,' she croaked, as the door slammed shut behind Sharvani.

Ishita sat there unmoved. The only source of light were the thin rays of weak sunshine coming in from a grilled window placed impossibly high.

'You look good,' Sharvani began, as she sat on the granite slab that served as a bed. Her posterior could feel the discomfort, as jagged edges and the rough serrated surface ate into her backside. How Ishita was managing to sit on this 'bed', let alone sleep, was beyond her.

But she didn't bother with such questions.

The clock was ticking, and she had work to do.

'The jailer tells me you have been behaving well.'

There was a slight crack of a smile on Ishita's face.

'Funny she would say that.'

'Why?'

'I broke her nose last week.'

Sharvani ignored that, choosing to talk about other topics. She only had five minutes after all.

'How have you been?'

There was an awkwardness, both real and palpable. Sharvani cursed the grim turn of events; a student and a teacher who were so close to each other, who could talk about anything and everything under the sun, now suddenly had nothing to talk about.

Sharvani looked at Ishita, the distance between them was lesser than they had at her table during tea, yet they were now further apart than ever.

'I've been doing okay,' she replied mirthlessly, seemingly uninterested in the conversation.

There was a silence again, both of them at a loss for words. Like they were both trying to fix a shattered mirror, but the cracks seemed to remain, no matter how hard they tried.

'I've been doing some thinking,' Ishita said woefully.

'Oh?'

'The cake: it had extracts of passiflora and hawthorn, with a hint of valerian, most likely procured from Dr Khuranna, I suppose?'

Sharvani smiled at her. Not much could get past Ishita.

She had taught her well.

Perhaps a little too well for her own good.

Sharvani's smile turned into a frown.

'Well done. While the recipe takes time to act, it is very effective …
you were still snoring when the constable put you in cuffs.'

'Well, I wouldn't have shot you …' she said softly.

Sharvani smiled.

'No, my dear, you definitely would have.'

Ishita's face broke out into a twisted, sardonic grin.

'Of course, I would have,' she replied. 'Not shooting you was the
second biggest mistake I made.'

'What was the first?'

'I underestimated you,' she said dejectedly. 'Me …' she cried,
placing her hand on her bosom, '… your greatest admirer. Am I that
stupid?' she asked, hitting her forehead from the side.

'No,' Sharvani said warmly. 'You are merely young, angry, reckless
and … and …' Sharvani looked away, a sorrow in her eyes, 'and
heartbroken.'

'Why did you come to meet me?' Ishita asked Sharvani, while
putting on a wide smile. It was her turn to change the topic.

'Just wanted to see how my favourite pupil was doing!' she smiled
back.

'Oh,' Ishita grinned, 'and those papers in your hand, those are
today's newspapers, I presume?' she chuckled.

'I didn't know you could see in here …' Sharvani said, visibly
surprised.

'My eyes have gotten used to the darkness. It pales in comparison
with the darkness in my heart.'

Sharvani unfolded the papers wordlessly and handed them to
Ishita.

Ishita's pupils shrank, as her eyes and fingers raced through the written word in the dim light, afforded by the cell.

'Pen,' she asked after a second.

Sharvani complied with her request.

Other than the scribbling of a signature on the paper, there was pin-drop silence.

Until a knock came on the door.

'Well,' Sharvani sighed, 'that's my cue.'

'Will you come visit again?'

'Of course, my dear,' she cried reassuringly as she took back the papers from Ishita.

Ishita grinned, 'You were a better liar back in the day, not any more.'

'Takes one to know one,' Sharvani smiled back, more out of courtesy than sincerity.

Her work here was done.

She turned and walked towards the door.

'Sharvani?'

She turned around and raised her eyebrows, a smile crept at the side of her lips. 'Whatever happened to calling me Miss Mehra?'

'Don't think I'll be seeing you again, so I thought I'd listen to you one last time.'

'Pity ... I like the sound of Sharvani.'

Ishita smiled for a moment, and then her face turned grim all of a sudden, as if shouldering some unseen burden.

'All my life, I've always looked up to you, wanted to be like you and make you proud. You were everything to me and now ... now ... I'm afraid to ask ... but are you ... have I disappointed you?' she asked, her eyes welling up with tears.

Sharvani's heart sank.

She looked at the signed document in her hand.

She smiled warmly, 'No … no, my dear, you haven't.'

'Take care of Vijay for me, will you?'

Sharvani looked at her.

Her heart wept, but she didn't show it. After a second, she nodded.

'He just needs some love, and understanding … just some care…' Ishita began.

The door clanged shut as Sharvani walked out.

'Just some love and understanding,' Ishita sighed, as she was engulfed in darkness once again. Her face had a bittersweet smile, a single teardrop rolled down her cheek. She was tired after the entire ordeal. Ten whole years of her life were spent on one single purpose: to bring down the Zamindar and his family.

For betraying her and her love for them.

For cheating her and her son of what was rightfully theirs.

She had succeeded, to an extent, but it didn't bring her peace. Only contrition.

It only drained her, physically, mentally and emotionally.

And now, all she wanted was a little rest.

twenty-four

Anshul Baghri was a happy man.

He had a smile on his face.

He was being called Anshul Kaka after a long while, and was still getting used to the fact.

Azad Manor was lit up, not for show from the outside, but from within. Sounds of laughter, real genuine laughter, filled up its hollow halls. Silhouettes of children playing could be seen through each of the windows.

'How are the rascals doing?' grinned Sharvani. Anshul's hair was ruffled, his normally pristine appearance completely dishevelled, but his face held a look of joy, and his eyes sparkled with a contentment that was lost through all these years.

He was a good man, Sharvani concluded. He could have taken his fortune and started a new life somewhere, free from the shackles of servitude. Instead, he chose to donate it all to charity.

All of it.

Maybe servitude was in his blood, but he didn't do it for the money. He did it out of genuine concern, and Sharvani could think of nobody better to oversee the care and upbringing of the new occupants of Azad Manor.

Save for herself maybe.

'What about the new caretakers?' Sharvani asked the attentive Anshul.

None of the old staff had chosen to stay on, understandably so. Sharvani had handpicked an entirely new team of caretakers, keeping in mind the specific demands of the new occupants. Each of the new staff, from the cook to the gardener, loved the children as much as she did.

She settled for no less than the absolute best, and with the considerable resources at her disposal, it wasn't a particularly difficult task.

'The young masters and mistresses are indomitable, but their caretakers are quickly adjusting to their new duties,' he replied.

'That's good,' nodded Sharvani, giving her distinct acknowledgement.

'And bedtime?'

'Nine o'clock on the dot.'

Sharvani looked at her pocket watch; there was only a minute left to nine.

'On the dot?'

He smiled, and as if on cue, the lights in the house started switching off in sequence, as a wave of darkness ate over Azad Manor.

'On the dot,' he replied with pride.

'Not all of them,' Sharvani smirked. In the corner of the house, one solitary light still burned bright, indomitably holding out against the wave of darkness scheduled at exactly 9 p.m.

Anshul frowned, 'It's Master Vijay.'

Sharvani nodded. She didn't need any further explanation.

'If only his mother had taken the proper care, and disciplined him correctly,' he muttered.

Sharvani felt her heart sink. Ishita's words rang in her ears.

'You were the closest thing to a mother to me.'

Anshul's words could be held as true about Sharvani, even they were about Ishita. Those children were her responsibility, and she had faltered.

She looked at Anshul, 'Whatever people say or think, they will always be in part wrong about her. She had her reasons, Anshul, and it'd be best if we all accept that ... and it would be good for us to remember that she generously decided to grant her entire inheritance to the orphans.'

Anshul nodded. He had known Sharvani long enough to know the tone she adopted when the matter at hand warranted no further discussion.

'Ishita is where she belongs,' cried a hoarse voice from behind her.

'Tej ...' she cried. 'I hope you aren't here to maintain "vigil" again,' she said with a soft smile.

Tej blushed, his cheeks turning red with embarrassment. This lady always managed to bring out the worst in him.

'I just came to check on the new mistress of Azad Manor.'

She looked at him, visibly cross. 'We don't call it that any more. Besides, it doesn't belong to me. It belongs to the children.'

'Miss Mehra,' the squeaky voice of a young boy cut through the night air. She turned around with a warm smile.

'Vijay,' she said warmly, as she motioned the boy to come over to her.

'Evening, sir,' he said to Tej, as he trotted over.

'What's the matter?'

'I can't sleep.'

'Now come here, young master,' cried Anshul, as he rushed in to intervene, but Sharvani motioned him to stay.

He complied. Anshul was nothing if not subservient.

'They are asking me to switch off the lights, and I want to know what happens after Ravan kidnaps Sita,' he said, almost pleading with her.

She smiled at him, ruffling his hair. Ishita was right about one thing: he wasn't a mischievous child. He merely needed some love and understanding.

Sharvani smiled as she looked into his innocent hazel eyes, another trait passed on from his father and his grandfather before him. She understood the real meaning of the words of the Zamindar's ghost, and the task he entrusted her with.

'PROTECT MY LEGACY,' he warned her, and she understood the meaning a little too late. The Zamindar's ghost had returned from beyond the grave not to exact revenge, but to atone for his sins, and fix the mistakes he made whilst he was alive.

With Sharvani's actions however, she hoped it would finally find peace.

'So, will you tell me?' Vijay asked her again.

Sharvani smiled and nodded. 'Run along now … I'll be with you shortly. In fact, I'll tell you what happens after Sita is taken to Lanka, and Ram meets with Hanuman.'

Vijay looked at her, his eyes widening. He was literally unable to hold his excitement. 'You promise?'

'I promise,' she grinned back, ruffling his hair.

'Good night, Tej Uncle,' he chimed, as he rushed back into his room.

'Good night,' Tej replied with a smile, even though the boy was out of earshot by then. Vijay's innocence managed to thaw even Tej's icy heart to an extent.

'I say, madam …' Anshul said, good-naturedly, 'I was the butler for the Rana family since the time Master Arjun was his age,' he said referring to Vijay, 'and in all my years, I have never seen you treat the children with such …' he paused for the moment, taking the time to pick out the most appropriate word, 'leniency.'

'I made a mistake, Anshul,' she admitted reluctantly, 'with Arjun, Archana, Ishita and the rest. I was too much of a disciplinarian, and not too long ago, I wished for a chance to make it right, to do it all over again, and this time around …' she said, looking at Tej, 'I won't falter.'

'Of course, madam,' he said, clinking his feet together. 'And might I add that I am speaking for the entire staff when I say we are with you on this?'

'Thank you,' she smiled. 'Tell Vijay I should be along shortly.'

He nodded.

'And take up a serving of kheer when you go.'

'Certainly, madam,' he smiled.

She turned her attention towards Tej.

'Beautiful night, isn't it?'

'Ah … yes,' he remarked, looking up to stare at the firmament after longer than he could remember. The night was clear, the air was crisp and the stars were sparkling. It had been a while since he had admired the sky and its beauty.

She placed her arm in his and began walking towards the gate.

'You did a good job with him, the boy. He was quite a troublemaker, that one,' he commented.

'It's amazing what can be achieved if there is a little love and understanding instead of hate and misguidance. The world would be a better place if we all just decided to talk a little more, and listen with a little more concern, to try and understand each other.'

He nodded.

She looked at him; her heart was pounding in her chest.

'I'm sorry for what happened to your family.'

Tej grunted, and his eyebrows tensed into a scowl.

'I didn't think I would ever tell you this, but I can't go on without ...' she took a deep breath.

Tej remained silent.

'Rai Bahadur was a spy,' she said, with a deep sigh.

'Preposterous ...' he roared.

Sharvani smiled. Irrespective of his hatred towards his father, he could still not bear to hear an outsider fling mud on his father's name and reputation.

So typical of sons.

'My father could never have been a spy for the Indian Revolutionaries.'

Sharvani listened to him.

'He wasn't a spy for the Revolutionaries,' she sighed. 'He was a spy for the British. He used to tell them of any person of interest, revolts, of uprisings ...'

Tej looked at her incredulously, and for the first time, he was at a loss for words.

'But the East India Company, they have said through reliable sources that there is a spy ... one who is selling their secrets to the Revolutionaries, causing anarchy and unrest in the country.'

'Hmm ...' she said. 'Giving out secrets, Tej ... not selling,' she corrected him.

Tej was silent. The weight of her words revealed what she wanted to say.

'I was the spy for the Revolutionaries,' she confessed after a moment's hesitation.

'You ... a spy?'

'I can tell you what I did, and why I did it, but you may not like what I say … it will be bitter, but it will be the truth.'

'The truth always is.'

Sharvani treated his response as a go-ahead. She wouldn't be getting any more from him.

'Digvijay Rana and Rai Bahadur were working for the British government. With his power and influence, Digvijay Rana put up a front of respectability, and his aide-de-camp helped him cover up his awful deeds. You're crying about the time he didn't spend with your family, but his actions uprooted hundreds, leaving only grieving widows and crying orphans in their wake,' she said, as she left his arm and lit up a cigarette.

'You're lying,' he let out through gritted teeth. The vein in his forehead had become prominent, almost bursting out.

'Digvijay Rana supported the rebels,' he growled.

'On the behest of the Britishers,' she added.

'Digvijay Rana provided guns to the Revolutionaries' cause,' he argued.

'They were faulty …' she said, blowing out a ring of smoke.

'The food?'

'Infected with maggots.'

'Water?'

'Muddy sewer water. You know, Tej, sometimes I think the Britishers won these battles only due to the lost morale of the Revolutionaries from using faulty guns and the illnesses caused by eating tainted food.'

'And how do you know this?'

She blew out a ring of smoke. 'One of the British officers who led the charge against one of the mutinies told me right after a strenuous night of stress release. I pretended to be impressed. They were so easy to manipulate.'

'Even the Britishers?' he gasped.

She smiled. 'Espionage makes for strange bedfellows,' she said without remorse. '…literally.'

'And my father?'

'He used to have his way with me after the Zamindar was done … I used to tell him how much bigger and better he was. I lied. Each of them was worse than the other.'

Tej could feel the rage and disgust fill up inside of him with equal measure.

'The Rana family's name is only as good as its reputation… Nothing could tarnish the Rana name except its reputation,' she said nonchalantly. 'Ishita thought the Zamindar committed suicide because of her letter detailing her condition and her tryst with his son,' she began, 'but the letter was never addressed to Digvijay, rather to his wife. Ishita foolishly thought that only a woman could understand the plight of another woman. The wife brought it to Digvijay's notice, but he couldn't care less. He sent Rai Bahadur to take care of the problem and, tired of her husband's atrocities, she put the barrel of a gun to her temple that very night. It was bad enough that her husband was busy with other women, but for her son to commit such a travesty to the family name and impregnate a minor, was too much for her to bear.'

'How do you know all this?' Tej stammered, almost afraid to ask her any more. He knew he shouldn't ask questions he didn't want the answers to, but he couldn't resist.

'Your father used to tell me sometimes, when it got too much for his conscience to bear.'

'And the Zamindar?'

'He didn't care much about the death of his wife and even less about what some orphaned girl babbled without proof; it was an easy task to tear an unmarried pregnant girl's reputation to shreds through slander. Her letter didn't matter to him in the least, but for someone to accuse him of siding with the British and sabotaging his countrymen's efforts, and that too with proof,' she grinned, 'now that ... is an altogether different story.'

'You ... you ... you killed him?'

She smiled, exhaling into the chilly winter night once again. 'I wish. The Zamindar was becoming a little too powerful, for his own good. He amassed enough resources and made a network strong enough to quell the revolutions, and nip them in the bud, so to speak, but he always held on to the foolhardy notions of values such as reputation and respect in the community above anything else, and I had the proof to rip his reputation to shreds.'

'And?' he asked, even though he was talking about the obvious.

Sharvani shrugged. 'If he continued breaking bread with the Britishers, the proof would go out. His reputation would be in tatters and, more importantly, people would be out for his blood. He was too deeply involved with the Britishers to back out, so the smart bastard took the easy way out.'

'And my father.'

'He was a good man,' she lied. 'He always expressed how much he loved you and wanted to be near you, but his duty and loyalty to the Rana family dragged him elsewhere,' she said calmly.

'Thank you,' Tej said softly.

Sharvani shook her head.

Men—always believing what they wanted to hear.

Generations would pass, but that would never change.

'Let it go, Tej ... you are a better man than your father was. He would have been proud of you.'

He nodded, wiping a tear off his sleeve. 'And you ...'

'I'll be coming out of retirement.'

'Back to support the Revolutionaries?'

'I did that for the country, nothing else.'

'And now?'

'I made a mistake myself. The future of the country, and its independence, will not be earned by a bloody coup, or at the hands of bloodthirsty militants or overzealous Revolutionaries, but by non-violence and understanding. War isn't the answer, peace is. Future generations must be taught that all the problems and prejudices in this world can be fought with only one weapon: education. And that is what I wish to impart to these children.'

They reached the edge of Azad Manor. The rickety old gate was supported by metal arches. A banner went on the top of the metal portcullis.

ARJUN RANA'S ORPHANAGE & SCHOOL FOR THE UNDERPRIVILEGED

'With Ishita gone, we'll need to look for a replacement,' he gasped, as he was taken aback by the bold, metal stencil lettering.

It was only now that he could fully admire and appreciate its beauty.

'We don't need to. Like I told you, I'm coming out of retirement.'

'Oh,' he said with raised eyebrows.

'India needs these children. Each will grow up to be successful in his or her own right. They deserve to have the love, kindness and education that any child in any part of the so-called developed world is enjoying, and Arjun Rana's Orphanage School for the Underprivileged will do just that.'

Tej smiled, 'And what of the country now?'

She gave him a smirk. 'I now side with the Mahatma in his approach in the fight for independence.'

'And what's that?'

'He aims to fight the British not with war, but with peace.'

Tej chuckled. 'No disrespect meant to him or to you, Miss Mehra, but this seems to be the most far-fetched, to think one can change the world through peace and non-violence?'

She smiled. 'Mohandas Gandhi,I have a feeling, will succeed.'

'Why do you think that?'

'Woman's intuition.'

'Don't make me laugh,' he snorted.

'Besides, stranger things have happened, like ghosts coming back to make sure their family and their legacy stay protected.'

Tej snorted. 'Good night, Miss Mehra!'

He pulled out a small metal flask once he was sure he under the cover of darkness, and took a deep swig.

'Non-violence and ghosts coming back,' he chuckled to himself. 'Nonsense.'

He smiled to himself. His gut feeling had been right all along. It was in fact the Revolutionaries' spy, Sharvani Mehra, who invariably planted the seeds for the whole messy affair of the Zamindar's ghost.

He allowed himself another quick swig from his flask.

He believed the whole affair to be sorted.

He believed that peace had once again come down on the sleepy little town of Ooty.

What Tej Bahadur didn't believe in were ghosts.

He had seen his mother's ghost at the age of ten.

She never appeared again.

About the Author

Khayaal Patel is a bestselling author. His book *Tarikshir: The Awakening* featured consistently at #1 on the Amazon bestseller charts in the Indian Writing and Fantasy categories.

He has an unhealthy addiction to chocolate and, on occasion, eats cake for breakfast. Sometimes he wants to give up his writing career, train hard and fight crime dressed like a flying rodent. Until that happens, he plans to keep writing books in various genres.

You can connect with him on IG: kyakhayaalhaiaapka

30 Years *of*

 HarperCollins *Publishers* India

At HarperCollins, we believe in telling the best stories and finding the widest possible readership for our books in every format possible. We started publishing 30 years ago; a great deal has changed since then, but what has remained constant is the passion with which our authors write their books, the love with which readers receive them, and the sheer joy and excitement that we as publishers feel in being a part of the publishing process.

Over the years, we've had the pleasure of publishing some of the finest writing from the subcontinent and around the world, and some of the biggest bestsellers in India's publishing history. Our books and authors have won a phenomenal range of awards, and we ourselves have been named Publisher of the Year the greatest number of times. But nothing has meant more to us than the fact that millions of people have read the books we published, and somewhere, a book of ours might have made a difference.

As we step into our fourth decade, we go back to that one word – a word which has been a driving force for us all these years.

Read.

Harper
Collins

HARPER
PERENNIAL

HARPER
BUSINESS

HARPER
BLACK

हार्पर
हिन्दी

HarperCollins
Children'sBooks

HARPER
DESIGN

HARPER
VANTAGE

Harper
Sport